Follow me on

Or J. Steven Butler on Facebook

Taking Boston

J. Steven Butler

Published by J. Steven Butler, 2023.

This is a work of fiction. Similarities to real people, places, or events are entirely coincidental.

TAKING BOSTON

First edition. November 2, 2023.

Copyright © 2023 J. Steven Butler.

ISBN: 979-8223795780

Written by J. Steven Butler.

CHAPTER 1

Boston Evans, nine years old and small enough to pass for seven, extended her arm out the window of her mom's Range Rover. Or as Boston called it, the Ranger. She curled her compact fingers in the wind. She found that if she held her arm the wrong way, the wind shoved it backward, too powerful for her to resist. But if she held her fingers tight enough and turned her palm facedown, the whipping winds whooshed around her hand, and it felt like she was flying. She did this for several minutes, experimenting with different angles, but eventually tired of the game.

Pulling her arm in, she leaned her head back against the seat, letting the wind blow her hair in every direction. She imagined she looked like a lion with a fuzzy mane, and when Daddy turned his head and smiled at her, she made claws of her fingers and growled.

Daddy was driving and Boston's eyes ran over his face. He was pretty. No, the word for boys was handsome. That's what Mommy told her. Boston thought she had the handsomest daddy in the world and the prettiest mommy, too. Mommy reclined in the seat in front of Boston. Mommy's hair was dark, like the night sky, and curly. Nothing like Boston's hair. Boston's hair was blonde like Daddy's. Except for the patch on the back of Daddy's head where his hair was going away. She hoped that never happened to her.

She reached a timid hand to the back of her head and felt the thickness of her hair. It didn't feel like any was missing. That was good.

She looked back out the window, the wind stinging her eyes. Far below the road, the ocean waves made foamy bubbles on the beach of the Pacific Ocean. Like God's bubble bath. But between them and the water was a huge cliff covered in trees. It must have been five hundred and twenty-two feet. Yep, it had to be. Exactly five hundred and twenty-two.

She sniffed at the air. Mommy had said she could smell the salt from the water. Boston couldn't smell anything, but maybe grown-ups had better smellers than kids. Either way, it was a nice thought.

An idea popped into her head and out of her lips as she rolled her window up to block out the wind and noise. "I wanna make You Tube videos."

"Oh, really?" Mommy turned in her seat and crinkled her nose at Boston the way she did when she got tickled about something. Her smile was wide. "And what are you going to make videos about?"

Boston kicked her feet and rolled her eyes. "Anything, Mommy. Maybe Barbies, or puppies, or math."

Behind the wheel, Daddy chuckled. "I hate to break it to you, kid, but I don't think you're going to have much of an audience if you do math videos."

"Okay, not math, but Christa's brother, Turk..."

"Tuck," Mom cut her off. "His name is Tuck, honey."

Boston ignored the correction. "He does stuff about video games."

"You don't like video games," Dad peered at her in the rearview mirror.

"Daaaadd." She made the word long and slow, like when Mrs. Watts wanted to really make a point about something at school. "Turk..."

"Tuck," Mommy repeated.

"...said you get a dollar every time somebody watches it."

"I think he was pulling your leg, honey."

"What?" Boston said.

"You don't get that much money for a view on You Tube. Maybe he just wanted you to think he did so he could impress you. Maybe he likes you."

"Ewwww. Mommy, that's gross." The chant came unbidden, something she didn't really understand the meaning of, but something all of the girls on the playground recited in a sing-song voice any time they were bothered by the little boys from the class. "Boys are users and losers so use 'em and lose 'em."

In the front, Mike and Ruby Evans both gasped. Boston immediately felt like she had said something wrong. After a moment Daddy said, "I don't think you should say that, Boston."

"Why not?"

Daddy cleared his throat. "Just don't, okay? Where do you get this stuff, anyway? Is your mom letting you watch soaps?"

Mommy made a huffing sound. "Of course not. What have you been letting her watch, Michael Wayne Evans?"

Daddy didn't answer. Mommy had used his long name, like when Boston was in trouble.

"I don't like Daddy's movies. They're all guns and blood and bad words."

Daddy squirmed.

"Uh-huh." Even from behind, Boston knew Mommy was giving Daddy a dirty look.

Daddy looked guilty. "They're not that bad, Ruby."

Boston knew better and she bet Mommy would fuss at Daddy later when Boston wasn't around. Daddy was in trouble, and Boston found it funny. "Yes, they are. Remember that one where the robot shot the guy in the face and his head exploded and there was brains on the ground?"

"Mike Evans," Mommy slapped him on the arm.

Mike took his hands off the wheel long enough to shrug his shoulders while keeping his eyes glued to the road. "I have no idea what she's talking about."

"Don't lie, Daddy. Jesus doesn't want you to lie."

Ruby clapped her hands in approval. "That's exactly right, Boston. At least someone in this family has a conscience."

"People die in war." Daddy made a pinched face. "It's realism."

"Fighting robots?" Boston snickered.

"Fine then. It's realistic for the future. It really wasn't that bad. Jake recommended it."

Mommy gave a sound that was something between a snort and a laugh. "Oh sure, blame someone who isn't here to defend himself. I doubt he recommended it for our child." Mommy shook her head and winked back at Boston who giggled then tried to sit up higher in her booster seat.

After a while, everything got quiet again, and Boston kicked her legs to the beat of a song in her head. The song had no words. Just notes she made up. She sighed, contented.

It was only two weeks since Christmas, and the holidays had been great. She got to play Mary in the manger scene at church, and they had a *real* baby. The baby's name was Charlie. He was Mrs. Gibbon's little boy, and he was a happy little guy. He only cried once during one of the practices, and that was because he had a stinky diaper that made Boston's nose burn. But that was just –

"Mike!"

Boston jerked as Mommy's voice shattered the quiet in the Ranger.

Ahead of them, coming around a long curve, a semi had blown a tire. Boston saw it all like slow motion – the driver of the rig, a man with a beard and a baseball cap, yanked on the steering wheel trying to get control of the truck as it sort-of wobbled from the blowout. He swerved into their lane, coming right for them.

Suddenly, the big truck filled their windshield, and Daddy tried to swerve too. He pulled to the right to miss the truck, but it still hit them on the left side. There was a big crunching sound and they were rammed farther to the edge of the road.

Mommy and Daddy were screaming. She was screaming. The Ranger slid off the road, over the embankment, and began to tumble.

CHAPTER 2

At ten minutes until two, Pastor Jake Wilson pulled into the parking lot of 3254 Westbury Street in Atlanta, GA, found a fortuitous parking place near the building's entrance and swung his Hyundai Santa Fe into it. He killed the engine, exited the car, and grunted as his thirty-five-year-old body protested when he stretched from the two-hour trip up from middle Georgia. He was too young to have such aches and pains. Maybe it was just his current level of stress.

He gazed up at the five-story office complex in front of him. It was impossible to see into the mirrored windows as they reflected the afternoon sun, stinging his eyes. Anyone could be watching him from behind those windows, and despite telling himself he was being paranoid, the feeling ate at him.

He whipped his phone from his pocket and dialed the number for his best friend, Mike Evans. Mike lived in California with his wife and daughter, Jake's goddaughter, and was returning from a trip today. Jake needed to hear his friend's voice again. They'd spoken the day before.

"You're worrying about nothing, Jake. Tyndale loves you. You're like a son to him. You're not in any trouble." Mike's words played over in his mind as the phone rang, but this time all Jake got was Mike's voicemail. He considered trying Ruby's cell but decided against it.

Jake sighed and shoved the phone back in his pocket, ran his hands over the front of his shirt in a futile effort to smooth out the wrinkles caused by his seatbelt, and shut the car door before moving to the entrance twenty paces from his parking spot.

The automatic doors swished open with an accompanying rush of warm air infused with the scent of cleaning solvent. They always kept this place pristine.

Despite the relative stillness of the parking lot, the first floor of the state headquarters of the New Creation in God denomination was a bustle of activity. On either side of the space were glass-walled offices. Behind most, men and women sat at desks typing on computer keyboards or talking on phones. Each office had a stencil on the door denoting the position of the occupant – Director of Evangelism, Georgia Missions Director, State Secretary, and so on. Directly ahead, a young woman sat behind a marble-topped welcoming desk that mirrored the pattern of the marble floor.

He stood for a moment, his eyes taking it all in, everything as he remembered it. So many memories.

Jake willed his feet to move, and as he approached, the young woman behind the desk tilted her head, gazing up at him. "Can I help you, sir?"

Jake pushed himself forward, his lips curling up in what he felt was an obviously forced smile. "Hi. I'm here to see Bishop Tyndale."

"Of course." The girl was appropriately cordial while remaining businesslike. "What's your name?"

"Jake Wilson. I have an appointment."

The young woman pursed her lips and glanced at a ledger – something Jake thought ironically outdated considering the computer sitting to her right – and nodded after a moment of searching. "Sure, Pastor Wilson. Mr. Tyndale's office is on the fifth floor. You'll see his office as soon as you get off the elevator."

Jake nodded. In truth, her instructions were superfluous. He could have made his way blindfolded as many times as he'd followed that exact route. As she returned to whatever task she'd been consumed with before his intrusion, he plodded to his left to the bank of elevators and punched the "UP" button with a quick jab. Once inside, he took a deep breath, the musky-metallic smell of the lift familiar but not comforting.

The doors closed and the elevator climbed, contemporary Christian music playing through the speakers as it rose swiftly to deposit him in front of the office doors of the State Administrative Bishop.

Jake crossed the hall and pushed through.

The waiting area inside was ornately decorated with two leather couches on opposing walls, each facing identical black coffee tables. Directly ahead, sitting behind another desk, was a middle-aged woman with curly brown hair and horn-rimmed glasses. Her disposition on first inspection was considerably sterner than the young woman downstairs. Jake thought he remembered her name was Susan. She was looking at a computer monitor and pecking away at the keys, but stopped as Jake came in and strode across the office to stand in front of the desk.

"Hi. I'm Jake Wilson. I have an appointment at two to see Bishop Tyndale."

"Of course, Pastor Wilson. We've been expecting you. If you'd like to have a seat," she gestured to one of the sofas, "I'll let Bishop Tyndale know you're here."

Jake gave a polite, nervous nod and moved to sit.

State Administrative Bishop William Tyndale was a long-time friend and mentor to Jake. He had been influential in getting Jake his pastorate at Life Church in Warner Robins, a church that some on the board felt was too large to be taken on by such a young, upstart minister. The politics of the denomination often dictated that you didn't get appointed to a large church until you had done your time in the "trenches".

After several minutes, the door behind the secretary opened and Bishop Tyndale emerged. He walked quickly to erase the distance, his pupils large and welcoming, and took Jake's right hand as Jake stood. Tyndale was in his early seventies, his gray and white hair thin and wispy, but his embrace belied strength still in his body. Despite his age, he was full of energy and life, and as such had always been an inspiration to Jake.

Tyndale leaned back from the hug, his hands still on Jake's shoulders. "Jake. It's so good to see you. Sorry to keep you waiting. Please come in."

He led Jake back the way he had come and held the door to the office open.

Tyndale said, "Barbara," – not Susan, Jake noted – "make sure we're not disturbed for the next hour, please." The secretary nodded as Tyndale closed the door behind them, and Jake swallowed hard at the ominous implication of the words.

The office was much the same as Jake remembered. It was a simple setup with Tyndale's desk sitting in front of the left wall so that the older man could turn and look out at the city without having to spin his chair all the way around. Heavy bookcases lined the opposite wall, filled with all manner of religious books and commentaries, some so old and brittle that they looked like they could crumble into dust at any moment. Even from across the room, Jake could smell the rich aroma that only an ancient text could give off.

The lighting of the office was soft, save for the sun blazing through the window that took up the entire outer wall, but even that was stilted by the dark tint on the windows. Tyndale hated fluorescent lighting, and as such, preferred desk and floor lamps as his primary sources of illumination. The effect was normally calmative, reminiscent of the way Jake had set up his own office at Life Church, but not today.

"I've got a fresh pot of coffee, Jake." The old man stepped to a KitchenAid coffee maker resting on a counter next to a small sink and mini fridge. "I also have sodas." He gestured at the fridge. "Care for anything?"

"No thanks. I'm good." Jake tried hard to read the older man, but so far, he only seemed genuinely pleased to see Jake.

Tyndale made a cup of coffee – black – as Jake slid into one of the chairs facing the desk. The familiar surroundings felt cold to him, and he closed his eyes, sighed.

Tyndale made his way back to the chair behind his desk and plopped down in it, his eyes bright. Jake didn't say anything. Only watched as the man drank a sip of his coffee. Tyndale wrapped wrinkled fingers around the cup and took a deep breath of it like it was incense.

"Are you sure you don't want some?" He gave the mug a little tilt in Jake's direction.

Jake forced a laugh and shook his head. "Don't really have a taste for it. The only way I like coffee is if it's a Starbuck's Frappuccino with enough sugar to choke a bull. Not really good for the waistline."

Tyndale guffawed. "Like you need to watch what you eat."

Jake had been blessed with one of those metabolisms that devoured anything he took in regardless of how unhealthy it was. It was a good thing, because he had a voracious sweet tooth and drank sodas like water. Still, he maintained a slim physique, something his staff members often complained about with good-hearted derision. Jake had the sneaking suspicion that one day it would catch up to him, but for now, he was content to take his chances. Besides, his job left him little time for working out.

Tyndale, however, had always struggled with his weight. He had tried more diets and workout gimmicks than most, and he had done well in keeping his weight in check. But it had been difficult for the older man.

Jake felt a sudden wave of nostalgia, remembering the many church conventions with Tyndale. It had been some years now since he and Jake had attended one together. Jake had learned so much during that time. Tyndale had treated him like a son, carefully guiding and instructing him. He'd given Jake a masterclass in pastoring that rivaled any doctorate program in the country. Jake had been unbelievably blessed to have that friendship, something for which he would always be thankful.

"I've been watching your stats." Tyndale paused for another sip of coffee. "You broke thirteen hundred in Sunday morning attendance. That's fabulous."

Jake nodded, but the compliment did little to assuage his frazzled nerves.

"Always remember, though," Tyndale gave Jake a pointed look, "that's not what it's all about. There are thousands of great ministers all over the world that work hard every week to care for the little flocks God's given them."

One of the things Jake loved about Bill Tyndale was his humble spirit and his ability to do his job as State Administrative Bishop without prejudice about church size. He was fond of saying, "Some pastors are called to shepherd big churches while others are called to lead ten or twenty people in places no one's ever heard of. But they're both still called, and equally important in the Kingdom."

Tyndale's mood seemed pleasant, friendly, like old times. Somehow it made things worse. Jake realized he was white knuckling the arms of his chair. He forced his arms to relax and swallowed hard. "Bill. It's good to see you but..." he trailed off.

Tyndale's brows furrowed, his expression growing dark.

Here it comes, thought Jake. *Time for the hammer to fall.*

Old friendships aside, Jake was all too familiar with the stories he'd heard from other ministers all his life. Getting summoned to see the State Administrative Bishop out of nowhere was never a good thing. It usually meant problems. Complaints from the congregation, or maybe a discrepancy in funds. He'd even had a friend who'd been removed from his pastorate for accusations of sexual infidelity. The claims had ultimately been proven false, but the man's ministry had never recovered.

Tyndale sat forward and steepled his fingers on his desk.

"I'd rather just get to it," Jake said, steeling himself for a gut punch.

Tyndale squinted, considering for a moment. Suddenly, his eyes grew wide and his expression took on one of horror. "Jake, are you under the impression I called you here to reprimand you?"

"Well, yes." The words tasted like gravel in his mouth.

"Good heavens my boy. I'm so sorry. This is a happy occasion." He reached into a drawer on the right side of his desk and pulled out a piece of paper. He laid it down on the desk and turned it to face Jake. "This is what I wanted to show you. I wanted to congratulate you in person since you've always been like a son to me. The State Council approved your request for the building project. You've got a green light for your new family life complex."

Jake leaned in close and perused the document, stunned. At the bottom were six signatures, the members of the Georgia State Council. He smiled broadly; a smile that was matched by Tyndale's.

"So soon?" he managed. "I thought that would take months."

Tyndale beamed at him.

The two arose in unison. Jake rounded the desk and wrapped the older man in a gigantic hug.

"Thanks, Bill. Thanks so much. I'm sure your recommendation went a long way in making this happen."

Jake released Bill who pulled back to arm's length. "Nah. They didn't need my recommendation at all. They looked over the church stats, the proposal...had legal verify everything. Now you just need to get financing and you'll be ready to break ground."

Jake bounced on his tiptoes. He'd had a desire to build a family complex for a couple of years now, but the State Council had some concerns. Namely, an upgrade of the sanctuary took place a few years prior, a major undertaking for which Life Church still owed a lot of money. The State Council wanted to be sure the finances of the church were stable, and that attendance didn't wane before Life Church took on another expensive building project.

They asked Jake to draw up a detailed proposal including cost analysis. After that, they would follow the financial statements of the church for an indeterminate period before giving the thumbs up to proceed.

The church was performing well, and Jake knew that it might be approved sometime within the year, but he had no idea it would come just one month from the initial proposal he had submitted. Now he had the go ahead to proceed with financing for the addition he believed would be a huge boon to the church's growth and continued outreach to the city.

As he stood there grinning like a fool, Tyndale squeezed his shoulder.

"Jake, I'm proud of you. I can't wait to see what God has in store."

Jake's phone buzzed in his pocket, and he pulled it out. He glanced at the number. Not one he recognized. He did, however, recognize the area code as the same as Mike's and Ruby's. New number? He swept his finger up the screen to answer it and placed the phone against his ear.

"Hello?"

"Is this Jake Wilson?" An unfamiliar voice.

"It is." He pulled the phone away and looked at the number again. Telemarketer? He got ready to hang up.

"Mr. Wilson, this is Captain Alan Wheeler with the California Highway Patrol."

Jake's stomach lurched with sudden dread. "Okay. How can I help you, Captain Wheeler?"

Bill Tyndale eyed Jake carefully. He must have sensed the change in Jake's mood.

"Mr. Wilson..." there was a pause, and Jake knew. He just knew. The lurch in his stomach became a full-blown pain – a deep ache like his intestines were being twisted into knots. The man on the other end of the line continued. "I'm afraid I have some bad news."

Please God, don't let it be. Please, please, please!

The officer's next words knocked Jake to his knees.

CHAPTER 3

The drive to the airport was a blur. Somehow Jake managed to throw some clothes in a suitcase – he couldn't even remember what he packed and hoped he had everything he needed – called one of his staff to come by and check on his dog, Peaches, while he was away, and made his way from Warner Robins to Hartsfield International Airport in Atlanta.

What he could remember was that the entire drive he had flipped and flopped between moments of agonizing loss and sheer terror at the prospect that lay before him. The conversation with Bishop Tyndale the day before seemed like a year ago, and what had seemed so important to him at the time now seemed like a silly side note to an unspeakable tragedy.

He arrived at the airport and zombied his way to a parking space in the weekly lot. Thankfully, his mental clarity returned briefly enough for him to have the forethought to snap a picture with his phone of the section of the lot he was parked in, otherwise, upon return, he would have been in trouble.

He stumbled through the purchase of his ticket; his eyes concealed behind dark sunglasses. He imagined he looked like an idiot with them on inside, but his eyes were bloodshot from crying and he didn't care what anyone else thought.

Security was the typical Atlanta nightmare. A serpent of people undulated through turn after turn of roped passageways leading to a long line of x-ray scanners. All along the way, TSA officers with drug dogs walked back and forth, the animals sniffing bags – and sometimes people – at random. Then he was at the scanners. Please remove all items from your pockets. Remove your belt, shoes, put them all in a bin. Use a separate bin for electronics, blah, blah, blah. He was so bumfuzzled that the guard had to remind him to remove his shoes when he tried to walk through the scanner with them on.

Dear God, help me. I'm all over the place.

By the time he made it through security, rode the tram to gate B4, stood in line to board the plane, and sat down in the window seat of row H, he was utterly exhausted. He couldn't remember feeling this tired in ages, and he knew the next several days would be more of the same.

His thoughts circled back to Mike Evans for the umpteenth time since he received the news the night before. It had all started eighteen years ago.

For as long as Jake Wilson could remember, he had wanted to attend Lee University. His mom and dad both attended there, met, and fell in love. The stories of their experiences stuck with Jake from an early age. By the time it was his turn to leave home for college, Lee was a magical wonderland waiting just for him.

Established in 1918 as the Church of God Bible Training School, from its humble beginnings it had grown into a thriving, highly respected private University of over five thousand students. Although it drew a diverse group of students from all fifty states and over fifty countries, it had always been a rite-of-passage for children who had grown up in the Church of God denomination. Especially for PK's – preacher's kids – Like Jake – although Jake was not from the Church of God. The New Creation in Christ Denomination had no Bible university.

Jake leaned his head against the windowsill of the airplane, closed his eyes, still hidden behind his glasses, and drifted back to that first day.

THE CAMPUS FLOODED with a mix of new and returning students on that blistering day at the end of August. All over campus, jam-packed cars and vans and U-hauls occupied every possible parking space and created spaces out of many that weren't. Indeed, the entire city of Cleveland, TN pulsed with the influx of thousands of people who had not been there the day before, an infusion that filled the streets and restaurants and markets.

All around him, the atmosphere crackled with expectant energy as kids registered for classes and hefted furniture into dorms while meeting new people and reconnecting with old friends. It was contagious, and eighteen-year-old Jake Wilson was no exception.

He was here. He was finally here. And with this moment, his whole life extended before him with purpose and calling like an endless train track stretching into the unforeseeable future. He was destined to be here. It was about so much more than falling in love with the stories his parents had told. It was about more than all the lessons of ministry his dad had learned here and passed on to him. Now, standing on the campus, everything felt *right*. This was where he was supposed to be, not because his parents had gone here, but because it was what God planned for him. The excitement bubbled out of him like a boiling kettle.

Jake nearly bounced up the front steps of Medlin Hall to the double front doors. They swung open as two other boys came out. The boys nodded politely, and he did the same. His parents came up the steps behind him more slowly, their faces reflecting his own excitement and no small amount of poorly concealed trepidation at leaving their only child on his own. But there was also pride, and Jake couldn't help but think they felt the same sense of purpose for him that he felt about himself being there.

He caught one of the doors before it closed and stood at the landing, holding the door open for his parents who were only about halfway up the external staircase. His dad waved him on, and Jake clambered inside, eager to take it all in.

In front of him was a great lobby – old and worn – but somehow the most beautiful place in the world to Jake. Mischievous students had once managed to carry a Volkswagen Beetle up the steps and deposited it in this very lobby. His dad swore he had not been a member of the offending party. Now, sans automobiles, the smell of old carpet and new paint mingled with the sour-sweet stench of sweat as people milled about like ants. Two large, semi-circular staircases led to the second floor from either side of the room, a mirror set of Jacob's ladders of comers and goers.

Ahead, a cardboard sign written with a Sharpie read "Resident Director" with an arrow pointing to Jake's right. Below that in smaller writing, "Please check in".

Jake made his way around the corner to the RD's small apartment. The door was wedged open and the tiny living room visible beyond was a flurry of activity. The air conditioning system fought like a gladiator to cool the room, but the air was tepid at best. A college student a few years older than Jake met them at the door.

"Checking in?" he said.

Jake nodded.

"Go on in. That's Gary over there," he indicated a skinny man with a Caesar haircut that appeared to be in his mid-twenties, sitting on the edge of a frayed couch with a clipboard and pen in his hand. Another kid stood in front of Gary as he wrote something on the clipboard then dug through a box to his right and pulled out a key. Gary gave the kid some instructions Jake couldn't overhear and the kid smiled, took the key, shook Gary's hand, and bounded past them on his way to check out his dorm room.

Jake glanced at his dad and mom who had only just caught up with him. "Do you think I'll get one of the single rooms?"

His father leaned in close to make way for the other kid to exit through the doorway. Dad chuckled. "Probably not. They're usually reserved for upper classmen."

"A guy can wish." Jake was aware that the fourth floor of Medlin Hall was comprised of single occupant rooms. His dad had known a couple of students that had stayed there in his day. The rooms were exceedingly small but having no roommate might be nice.

Despite his giddiness, one thing concerned Jake, and that was having to live with someone he'd never met before. Jake thought of himself as personable and easy to get along with, but still, you never knew. And he'd be spending at least the first semester with this stranger before he'd have a chance to change rooms if there were personality conflicts.

He took his turn with Gary who checked his name off a list and gave him a key to room 201. It was close, main floor, south wing, and first room on the left. He inserted the key into the lock and turned it, but the room was already open, and he pushed the door in.

Inside it was cramped and sparse, with a sink under a mirror, a couple of desks with one well-worn chair each, a single chest of drawers – that would be challenging – and a set of bunk beds. A lone window looked out the back with a view of a fence and the side of the neighboring house. It was just about what Jake had been led to expect: tiny, Spartan, painted cinder block walls.

It was perfect.

Sitting at one of the desks was a bronzed, tow-headed young man who had to be roughly Jake's age but could have passed for fifteen. He wore flip flops with gray cargo shorts, frazzled at the ends, with a faded Ron Jon t-shirt and a Giants baseball cap. Underneath the cap, his hair was long and curly just shy of ringlets. A plethora of leather bracelets clung loosely to his left wrist. He couldn't have looked more like a surfing afficionado if he'd had help from a magazine crew from a Billabong shoot. He looked up as Jake and his parents entered and gave a shy smile.

Jake wasted no time and crossed the small space. He reached his hand out to the other boy who stood in response.

"Jake Wilson. I guess we're roomies."

The other boy had a firm handshake but spoke with a softness of tone that mimicked the same shy smile still held on his face.

"Hi. I'm Michael Evans." He shrugged. "Mike."

And that was that.

Jake immediately liked Mike Evans. He proved to be every bit the shy and sometimes awkward young man he appeared to be on that first day, but they developed a bond.

Mike Evans was the polar opposite of Jake. Mike was an orphan, raised in foster care until he finally reached age eighteen and moved away to Lee. A bright student, he managed to get a full academic scholarship, and he and Jake spent hours bouncing ideas and dreams off each other.

Mike was not a ministry student like Jake, but the experience of one of his foster homes when he was thirteen changed his life. The Robinsons, Ella and Tim, had three children of their own and were avid churchgoers. They went religiously every Wednesday night, every Sunday, and every special event in between; they made sure all their kids, including Mike for that short time, knew church was a priority.

Mike had loved it. Church gave him the sense of family that was otherwise so fleeting in his life. He found camaraderie and purpose, and most of all, he found out that Jesus loved him enough to die for him. He was forever changed. Mike's life was rough at times, but ever since Jesus found him, he had a hope that overcame every negative circumstance.

His story fascinated Jake, who also had a serious commitment to God. But Mike's faith had been tested in ways Jake's never had. In comparison, Jake had lived a sheltered life, and as a result, he looked up to Mike. Sure, Mike was quiet. Yes, he often needed Jake's help with introductions to others and making friends, but to Jake, Mike was a hero. A person of deep character born of hardship and an insane will to persevere.

They were inseparable. Whatever clubs Jake joined, Mike joined, and vice versa.

During their sophomore year, Mike met Ruby Delisle. A freshman, and a year younger than Mike, they were kindred spirits. Mike sat a few seats down from her during a chapel service one weekend when Jake had gone home to visit. Mike was so smitten with her that for once, he overcame his shyness and approached her on his own. The way Ruby told it later, Mike was trembling from fear, but rather than see it as a weakness, she saw it as sweet.

She gave him her number and he called the next night. That weekend, they went to William Shakespeare's Romeo and Juliet starring Claire Danes and Leonardo DiCaprio at the dollar theater in Chattanooga – neither of them were well off, and neither of them cared for the movie – and a week later, they were inseparable.

Ruby, like Mike, had a rough backstory. She had been raised by a single mom, Danielle, in NOLA – New Orleans, Louisiana. There was never a father in the picture. Her mother didn't even know who the father was. A strung-out drug addict who had fallen to sleeping with men for money or pills, she had gotten pregnant with Ruby at the age of sixteen.

Danielle's family had long since disowned her by then, and it was a miracle Ruby survived her first few years of life. Her mom took her along for "tricks-and-trips" as Ruby would say with a strained smile. Danielle usually wrapped little Ruby in a blanket and placed her in a bathtub while she was doing her "work" and of course they had no home. Danielle, though emaciated and sunken eyed from drugs, was still beautiful, and usually managed to coerce a night's stay in a hotel from her clients as part of her "fee". Other times they slept on the street wherever they could find respite from the weather, usually in a cardboard box or some other makeshift contraption.

It was no life for a baby. It was no life for an animal.

Ruby once asked her mom why she never gave her up for adoption or left her at the nearest hospital. Danielle's answer had surprised her.

"You were my only link to sanity, Ruby. No matter how far I'd fallen, having you depend on me kept me just above the line of ending it all. I can't tell you the number of times I wanted to die, to jump off a bridge or slit my wrists with the top of a tin can. But what always kept me alive was you. You depended on me, no matter how little care I could give. As bad as it got, as terrible a mom as I was, you were the only thing that loved me."

One night when Ruby was a year old, Danielle had found herself cold and tired in Jefferson Parrish. She'd stumbled into a tiny, turn-of-the-century church in a drugged haze. Ruby dangled precariously from one arm, as Danielle could hardly even stand up straight.

The church appeared warm and inviting, and Danielle, seeing the lights on inside and hearing a droning voice, went in. Her intention was to sit in the lobby. She knew once the service was over, they would find her and kick her out, but at least for a while, she would have a comfortable chair to sit in. She might even be able to catch a few winks and Ruby would be warm and dry.

That night a widow, Catalina Hernandez, sat in her regular seat at the Christ Alive Baptist Church on the corner of Wall and LaCroix streets. It was a Wednesday, and the typical paltry attendance they had on Sundays was even smaller. There were twenty at most in the sanctuary as Pastor Dan Davidson – a gentle soul that pastored the church for thirty-six years – spoke from the book of James.

Catalina had a clear view of the lobby from her seat. She preferred the back pew. The less distance she had to walk from her car, the better. In her eighties and arthritic, she had the hunched demeanor of a wizened grandma and that's how everyone regarded her. She saw the scrawny young woman and child the moment they entered the building and moved instantly. She would later say she was drawn to them, but if pressed, she probably would have confessed her concern was that Danielle was going to drop the baby.

She rose from her seat and exited the row with pained steps. A couple of the other patrons glanced at her but gave no mind. *Mrs. Hernandez probably has to go to the restroom again.*

When she exited the sanctuary doors and Danielle caught a glimpse of her, Danielle's immediate response was to turn and leave, but Catalina grabbed Danielle's shirt with a frail arm and gave the girl the warmest smile she could manage. "Hello, dear. Would you like to come and sit for a while?"

It was obvious from the confused look in Danielle's eyes that she was strung out.

"I'm jus' gonna..." Danielle slurred, but Catalina reached out for the baby before Danielle could protest. Danielle found herself relinquishing her child, instinctively trusting the old woman. At the very least, any notion that Catalina meant harm to the child seemed ridiculous.

Ruby cooed up at Catalina, and Danielle thought it would be nice to have someone watch her for a little while. *I just need a little time to get myself together.*

Catalina grabbed Danielle's hand with its dirty, broken fingernails, and gently led her into the sanctuary.

"I don' really wanna go in," Danielle's words were a nearly inaudible whisper.

"Nonsense. I need to sit and so do you. I'll watch your baby for a while, and you can rest. You can even sleep if you want to. No one will mind. Pastor Davidson is a good man, and you might find his voice soothing."

Catalina led Danielle to her usual place and motioned for her to sit next to her. While Danielle drifted in and out of lucidity, Catalina held the baby and snuggled the child in a warm crocheted blanket she had made herself and kept on her pew for use when the air conditioning got a little too enthusiastic for her liking. By the time the service came to a close, Danielle had brightened a bit from her stupor, and when Pastor Davidson gave the invitation, she made her way to the altar, the dear old widow right behind her with baby Ruby.

Danielle had heard precious little of the pastor's sermon, but when he asked if there was anyone that wanted to come forward and become part of Jesus' family, she got up, timidly at first, but with growing boldness as the others in the sanctuary began to applaud and smile at her when she took a step into the aisle. It had been a long time since anyone had treated her with kindness like the old woman had, and even longer since she'd felt safe the way she did here. Maybe that's why she went down to the front. She wasn't sure. But she gave her heart to Christ that night, and the resulting change was nothing short of miraculous.

From that night, Danielle strove to be the best mom that she could be. It wasn't a quick turnaround, but it was steady, and with every passing day she gained more and more traction and determination to leave the streets behind. The church provided housing at a halfway house where she started attending Narcotics Anonymous and got a job during the day at a Waffle House as a waitress. Catalina had become a mentor and a Godsend, watching baby Ruby for her while she worked her way up to being a short order cook.

At the end of six months, Danielle was clean. Her once-diminished beauty had again become vibrant, and her body had filled out. When it came time for her to leave the halfway house, Catalina, who by now had fallen in love with them both, insisted that Danielle and Ruby come and live with her. Danielle was only too thrilled at the prospect, especially with the only other option being public shelters where the pull of the old life would have been an ever-present ghost always beckoning her back to the destructive forces that had nearly ended her.

Catalina had a small, white-concrete bungalow with light-blue shutters and a splash of welcoming rose bushes inset against the eastern exterior. Though never wealthy, Catalina's husband, Enrique, had made a modest living working for the railroad. They never lived beyond their means, and spent wisely, and by the time he passed, the little place was debt free, and Catalina had a respectable pension to live on. The house had two bedrooms, one which Danielle and Ruby shared.

For the next ten years, the unlikely trio spent some of the happiest times of their lives in that little home. Danielle eventually became a Waffle House manager, and Ruby was an excellent student. Ruby had taken to calling Catalina Grams. Catalina, who'd never had children of her own, saw them as her own daughter and granddaughter and dedicated herself to the mission of making sure Danielle and Ruby knew they were loved and wanted.

Around the beginning of year nine, Catalina's health began to decline. Over the next eight months, Danielle and Ruby cared for her and nursed her. When the end finally came, Catalina passed away peacefully under the care of hospice. She left the little home to Danielle, and they carried on for a while. Sadly, as is often the case, life wasn't done delivering misfortune to them yet.

Two and a half years after the passing of Grams, Danielle began to have pain behind her ribs. At first, she figured she pulled a muscle, but then the coughing began, then the wheezing. At Ruby's insistence – "I don't have time for doctors," Danielle protested more than once – she finally scheduled an appointment.

The news came on a cold day in December, two weeks before Christmas. Lung cancer. Stage four. There was little to be done. It had progressed too far, and now Ruby, having lost her surrogate grandmother, was faced with losing the only family she had left. Thirteen days after Ruby's seventeenth birthday, Danielle passed away in the night.

Ruby was alone.

Danielle, carrying the heavy knowledge that her daughter would have no one else should anything ever happen to her, had taken out an insurance policy after Catalina died. The policy ensured Ruby had sufficient money to live off of for a while. Danielle had also passed on the widow's home to Ruby, and Ruby successfully petitioned the state to be considered an adult so that she could live there on her own. After finishing high school, she took what money she had left from the settlement, and at the encouraging of Pastor Davidson, completed the application process to attend Lee University.

When Mike and Ruby finally came together, it was as inevitable as sun and warmth, clouds and rain. It was two forces of nature melding in a coherent bond and no one who knew them doubted for a second that theirs was a relationship that would last a lifetime. They were kindred souls. Two halves, alone in the world, who found their completion in the other, and it was a beautiful thing to behold.

JAKE REACHED UP A HAND and swiped tears from under his glasses, avoiding the awkward glances of boarding passengers who happened to notice the grown man sitting alone crying like a little child.

A love to last a lifetime, he thought again. And it was true, only the lifetime had been like a tree hewn down before it could fully blossom. They were supposed to grow old together, have more children, live a full and happy life, and die peacefully in their sleep. It was all so tragic and unfair. For two people that had been through so much hardship already in their short lives, dying a young death was the ultimate cosmic insult.

No. He stopped the thought short. Realized its origin. Such thinking was of the enemy, not of God. Jake had reconciled that truth long ago.

It was a question that had plagued intelligent men for centuries, and one that he'd encountered a multitude of times as a pastor. If God is good, why does He allow bad things to happen to good people? Does He *cause* bad things to happen to good people? There were many people of faith who would say yes. It was not uncommon to hear well-intentioned ministers saying things like "Everything that happens is part of God's plan" and "God allows us to suffer to build character" or faith, or patience, or any other number of things that might seemingly fit whatever painful circumstances were being addressed.

Of course, God did use bad things to shape and mold and grow his children, but only in the sense that He worked all things together for their good. Jake didn't believe God bestowed tragedy upon those He loved. But in His ever-growing understanding of grace, Jake had come to realize that there was a simple explanation for why bad things happened to good people: they lived in an imperfect world. As Jesus had told the disciples in the Garden of Gethsemane, "In this life you will have persecution, but be of good cheer, for I have overcome the world."

The plane was almost full now, and Jake had that terrible, hopeful expectancy that maybe, just maybe, the seat beside him would remain empty and he would be able to stretch his legs a little and extend his arms during the flight. The flight attendant began making announcements, and passengers scrambled to get their bags stowed and take their seats. Jake held his breath. Surely, God would give him this little blessing on such a horrid day. There were no more passengers boarding now, and Jake breathed a sigh of relief. He glanced at his watch, and they were already past time for departure.

Thank you, Lord, he thought.

The flight attendant paused in her announcements, pulled the microphone away from her mouth, smiled and motioned to someone Jake couldn't see in the direction of the doorway. A lone, heavy-set gentleman carrying a leather bag that was stuffed to its breaking point, squeezed past the flight attendant, and made his way to...

No, God. Please, no.

On he lumbered, his bag striking more than a few of the heads of passengers seated on the aisle. On, and on, and on, and maybe he would pass. Surely there was another open seat on the plane. Maybe there was still hope for an easier ride.

It wasn't meant to be. The man stopped right beside Jake and consulted his ticket, then the aisle and seat number on the underside of the baggage compartment. The man stuffed his bag in the overhead, smiled down at Jake. Pastor Jake Wilson felt in no way Christ like, but somehow, he managed a smile that was certainly more of a grimace. The gentleman sat down, and the resulting loss of space was immediate. In his defense, the man tried to keep as much to his own seat as possible, but there was only so much space to give.

"Sorry," he muttered to Jake. It was obvious he was embarrassed by his size.

All things. All things. And just like that, in an instant, Jake's frustration seeped away, and he felt compassion.

"It's no problem." He extended his hand. "My name's Jake."

The man shook it with a smile that lit his eyes. "I'm Curtis."

CHAPTER 4

Jake sat in a worn plastic chair in a utilitarian office in front of a utilitarian desk behind which sat a utilitarian woman. Her demeanor perfectly matched the décor of the room. The kindest description Jake could manage of both was austere.

As it turned out, sitting next to Curtis on the plane had been a blessing in disguise. True, Jake had considerably less room than he would have otherwise had, but the man had been quite pleasant and intelligent, and he'd managed to distract Jake with worthwhile conversation during the flight, giving Jake's shock-stricken mind a welcome repose from the grief and fear threatening to overwhelm him. Jake wished the man was here now. At least Curtis had seemed to like him. The San Diego Department of Family and Children's Services worker in whose office Jake now sat seemed to find him dreadful.

Her name was Margaret Pierce, her surname an apt description of the way her eyes judged Jake with furtive, periodic glances. She cleared her throat– a habit she performed at least every fifteen seconds, and one which was already infringing upon the stability of Jake's frayed nerves – for the umpteenth time since he'd been ushered in.

Ms. Pierce pecked away mercilessly at her keyboard, every keystroke an attack against the poor, defenseless machine. Clack, clack, clack, clack, clack. Another cough, another appraising glance at Jake. Clack, clack, clack, clack, clack, clackity-clack.

Jake determined not to let it get to him. Normally a patient man, he felt his control slipping and the temptation was strong to give way to irritation. He whispered a silent prayer for the Holy Spirit to help him. He knew stress and grief were exacting upon him no small amount of emotional overload.

He turned his mind to Boston. The daughter of his best friends. The little girl whose own emotions had to be in such a state of agonized turmoil and fear that surely nothing he was feeling could compare. He was about to meet her. A person he had only ever known through video calls and conversations was about to materialize in front of him in flesh and blood, and then...

Jake shivered at the thought. He was taking in a child to raise.

Jake had already spent a couple of hours doing paperwork for transfer of custody while making periodic calls and fielding questions about Mike and Ruby. With no other family members, the responsibility of preparing for the funerals had fallen to Jake, something he took on with honor, but with everything crashing together in such a short period of time, he was feeling the enormous strain and pressure of it all.

"Mr. Wilson, you're a single man, right?"

She'd been quiet for so long – not including the coughing and pecking – that Ms. Pierce's voice startled him.

"Yes ma'am."

She perused something on her computer, then scribbled something on a piece of paper on top of a manila folder.

She set down the pen and returned her hands to the battered keyboard. "And you pastor a church?"

"I do, yes." This earned him another appraising glance. This time there was no doubt about it, there was something akin to venom behind the shrewd, snakelike expression of the social worker. Perhaps Ms. Pierce had no love for pastors, or maybe just God in general.

"And no children of your own?"

Jake cleared his throat nervously. "No."

She frowned. She abused her keyboard a bit more – Jake wondered if the lettering had worn off the keys from the force of her strokes falling upon it daily like little finger-hammers – then turned away from the monitor, leaned forward, scowled in a way reminiscent of a high school principal getting ready to lay out punishment to a wayward student, and fixed him with a stare.

"Mr. Wilson, have you ever been around young children before?"

Jake had the deep sense that he was being interrogated. Bring out the thumbscrews, boys. We've got a no-good single pastor about to take over the care of a little girl that he knows nothing about. He's never raised kids and has no clue what he's gotten into. It's the obligation of the state to press him on every little detail and make absolute sure he knows how unqualified he is.

Jake took a silent breath and smiled with as much good nature as he could manage.

"Um, yes ma'am. There are plenty of children at the church I pastor. It's a pretty large congregation..."

She held up a hand and peeled her eyes from his face long enough to glance down at the paperwork in front of her.

"I understand that Mr. Wilson. But have you ever had any small children in your care for any length of time? Any younger siblings you used to look after?"

Jake shook his head. This was a losing battle.

"A cousin? Babysitting?"

"No ma'am," his voice sounded pitiful in his own ears. "I'm sorry," he added instinctively. Self-defense.

The expression on Ms. Pierce's face softened ever so slightly. A sigh parted her lips.

"All of the paperwork is in order. I'm not out to belittle you..."

Jake distinctly felt otherwise.

"...or make you feel uncomfortable. I'm just concerned about the child. She's been through the most traumatic thing a child can experience, and no offense, but you don't know anything about raising children."

I thought we'd already established that ad nauseum, Jake thought.

Jake shifted in his chair. "I know, but couldn't the same be said of any new parent? Mike and Ruby Evans have been my best friends since college. More than that. They're family." He stopped, his eyes stinging, his throat suddenly thick.

She gave him a moment to collect himself. "I'm sorry. I understand your pain. Really, I do. Normally, children in this situation are given to family members, but Mr. and Mrs. Evans had no other family to speak of. Even if there were, that was not the wish of the decedents. They wanted custody of Boston to go to you."

"Yes." He'd been surprised when Mike had approached him during Ruby's pregnancy about being Boston's godfather and accepting responsibility for her should anything ever happen to them. But as Mike had pointed out, Jake was the closest thing to family they had, and they trusted him to raise their child in a Godly home. All the legal documents had been drawn up and signed, and that was that. Jake had taken the responsibility seriously. He'd just never expected to have to fulfill it.

Ms. Pierce continued. "Like I said before, all the paperwork is in order. Either way, Boston is your responsibility now, yet you've never met her before, correct?"

Jake looked around the room nervously, then caught himself and forced his eyes back to hers. "Not in person. But I've talked to her often on the phone, and we've done video calls."

Ms. Pierce raised unimpressed eyebrows.

"No, I've never *actually* met her," Jake conceded. "We always meant to get together, but we had busy lives and lived on opposite ends of the US. We kept in touch, but visits were few and far between. And yes, the last time I saw my friends was before Boston was born, but that doesn't mean I don't care for her."

Ms. Pierce coughed, and Jake couldn't tell if she was clearing her throat to say something, or if it was one of her habitual clearings. Either way, she did speak.

"I have no doubt of that, Jake." The use of his first name felt out of place and had the effect of making Jake even more uncomfortable – something he wouldn't have thought possible mere moments before. "I just want you to be prepared for what you're about to face in the weeks ahead."

Jake waited for the axe to fall.

"Boston just lost her family. Now, you're moving her to a new city, a new state. That means she also loses all of her friends. She must adapt to a completely new environment. She may have to – will likely – have to deal with PTSD. It's going to be a strain on both of you."

She paused and bit her lip. Jake stared dumbly, processing the information. Of course, these were all things he had given a great deal of thought to, but hearing someone else say it made it all the more daunting.

When Ms. Pierce spoke again, there was something almost akin to tenderness in her voice. Or perhaps pity.

"No one would blame you if you're not up to this."

"I can do this," he forced himself to sound confident. "The Lord can get us through."

Jake realized his error as soon as the words parted his lips. At the word "Lord", Ms. Pierce's expression assumed a pinched look. She sat back in her chair as if physically trying to distance herself from Jake. Anger flashed in her eyes, and she opened her mouth to speak, thought better of it, then went ahead anyway.

"Mr. Wilson, let me tell you something. That little girl in there," she waved a hand towards an adjoining room, "rolled down that mountainside with her parents. She never lost consciousness." A pause for emphasis. "*Never lost consciousness!*

"When the state patrolman arrived on the scene, he said the driver's window had been busted out. At some point, Mr. Evans's head got wedged between the body of the vehicle and the ground or a tree. It was mashed off. Mrs. Evans was impaled by a foot wide limb of the tree that eventually stopped their fall. It took the rescue team over an hour to free Boston from that wreckage. Time she was awake and aware."

Jake couldn't understand what lay in Ms. Pierce's past that could make her tell him these things about his friends with such unfeeling carelessness. Tears flowed freely from his eyes, and he worked hard to stifle the sobs threatening to choke him.

"Now you tell me," she continued. "What kind of a God would let that happen to a child? Would let her see that kind of thing? Huh? I know you're a pastor," there was no mistaking the distaste in her tone, "but if that's the kind of God you serve, I don't want anything to do with Him."

Jake sat dumbfounded. For a long time, there was silence. Finally, something occurred to him.

"If it was as bad as you say it was, then it's a miracle that Boston came out alive, much less uninjured. That's the kind of God I serve. Sure, it was a terrible thing, but at least she has her life ahead of her."

Ms. Pierce regarded him. "Frankly, Mr. Wilson, if it were me, I'd rather be dead than live with those memories."

BOSTON EVANS STOOD beside a large window looking out over a small patch of grass in front of the DFCS building parking lot. In the lot, cars came and went, each on its own errand of life, oblivious to the little girl not thirty yards away whose own life had been turned upside down.

A woman came into view and meandered across the grassy clearing holding the hand of a toddler. The little boy took halting, tentative steps, tottered, and fell to his rump. His mom picked him back up and he started again, placing one tiny foot in front of the other, crossing them, and going down again, all while his mom laughed and encouraged him to get up once more. Although her words were muted through the window, they were soothing and warm, her laughter musical like the tinkling of wind chimes carried on a summer breeze.

The toddler looked up for a moment and noticed Boston behind the window. He raised a pudgy hand and waved. Boston, her face a mask of shock and pain, raised a hand in return. The boy smiled at her, but she did not return the smile. The mom noticed the interaction and waved to Boston as well. This time, she didn't raise her hand. The effort to do so would have been too great.

Boston continued watching them for a long time as they moved on. Her crystalline green eyes tracked their movements, but her mind was elsewhere, struggling to make sense of her new reality. She was exhausted. The last two days had been a nightmarish whirlwind.

The accident happened the afternoon before last, and most of that evening and night she had spent at the emergency room surrounded by doctors and nurses and police officers as they fretted over her and ran all kinds of tests to make sure she was truly as uninjured as she seemed.

The state patrolman who first arrived on the site of the crash had stayed with her the entire time. Eddie was his name. He kept telling everyone that it was a miracle that Boston had survived. It didn't feel like a miracle to her. But Eddie's smile was kind, and he had tended her with exquisite attention. He helped her function, especially during those first few hours.

The other constant had been Ms. Pierce, who arrived not long after Boston had been taken to the hospital. She had worked tirelessly, making phone calls, researching, finding out everything she could about Mike and Ruby Evans and Boston. She had tracked down Jake Wilson after Boston had given her the name, and even went to Boston's home and managed to find the legal custody documents remanding her over to Jake's custody.

She had examined Ruby's cell phone – Mike's was destroyed beyond repair – and located a couple from Boston's church who had been good friends with Boston's parents. Kathy and Brandon Davis gladly came to the hospital to be with Boston and took her into their home for the following two nights.

Boston tried to remember being with them, but somehow, it was all hazy. She remembered snippets of the time, like Kathy trying to get her to eat, and Brandon sitting on the couch holding her as she cried and cried and cried until there were no tears left. But mostly, there was just grief, as if it had swallowed her entire existence and left a consuming blackness.

Yesterday she had talked to Mr. Wilson on the phone. He said he was coming to her as fast as he could. Boston's parents talked about Jake all the time, and sometimes Boston talked with him on the phone. She knew he was a pastor. Knew he had gone to school with her parents. But she didn't really *know* him. Not in the way you know someone who is there every day sharing your life and walking beside you. Now that he was here to get her and she was about to meet him in the flesh, she was terrified. It was an odd sensation, because the terror was just the most recent predatory emotion threatening to devour her, and Boston could feel herself on the verge of shutting down from overload. She was starting to feel like the zombies on that show Dad watched. Her body was moving, but there wasn't much going on inside.

THE ONLY DOOR TO THE room clicked, and Boston turned towards them in a daze. Ms. Pierce, her expression now replaced with one of empathy for the sake of the child, ushered Jake in.

Ms. Pierce turned to go. "I'll give you two some time."

Jake waited as she left, closing the door softly behind her. Boston and Jake looked at each other, neither moving, both filled with uncertainty. Then slowly, hesitantly, Jake came forward. Boston stayed where she was until he reached her, watching him, unspeaking. He stood there trying to think of what to say.

"Hi, little one." It's all he had.

A single tear raced down the right side of Boston's face, navigating her cheekbone, and trailing down to the edge of her chin where it halted, clinging stubbornly, refusing to fall.

"You look just like your pictures," Boston's voice was strained, tiny.

Jake took the statement in. It had been four or five years since the last video call he had with the Evans. Of course, she wouldn't remember his face from anything other than pictures. He'd spoken to her on the phone often, maybe once every few months, but no video calls.

"You look..." Jake choked on the words, stopping them in the nick of time. He was going to say, "like your mom", but he couldn't complete the sentence. It was out of place, the tragedy too fresh. He started again, "You look so grown."

That's when Jake noticed it. Something he would come to know well in the following months and weeks. Something he'd seen in some of his church members who had returned from deployment. The thousand-yard stare. Boston's eyes were on his chest, but whatever they were seeing, it wasn't him. His heart broke afresh for her loss.

"I'm so sorry," he managed.

She moved then, a bird cowering in a storm, her movements timid and wary. Slowly, she put her tiny arms out in desperation.

It was too much, and Jake plopped to his knees and welcomed her into an embrace.

Boston began to wail. "I want my mommy and daddy!"

All Jake could do was cry with her.

CHAPTER 5

That night Jake checked them into the Hilton Garden Inn and Suites near the airport. He didn't ask Boston's opinion, but he didn't think he could rest being in Mike and Ruby's house tonight. He suspected Boston would not be able to either. Tomorrow they would go there – Ms. Pierce had given him the key – and they would begin the arduous task of preparing for Boston's return with him to Georgia.

He took her to McDonald's for dinner and they sat near the playground. Boston watched the other children with melancholy eyes. She ate little of her food, and only because he kept prodding her to do so. She needed nourishment. According to Ms. Pierce, she had refused anything to eat since coming into their custody. Boston only managed to eat half of her cheeseburger and roughly ten fries, but at least it was something.

Neither of them talked much. Not on the car ride, or at the restaurant, or when they got to their room. They were feeling each other out, unsure what to say or how to respond. Guilt was weighing on Jake like an anchor, pulling him under cold waters of despair. He didn't know how to help her.

After they'd been in the room for half an hour, Boston watching Jeopardy on television, he asked if she wanted to get a bath or a shower. According to Ms. Pierce, Boston hadn't had the opportunity to do much in the way of self-care since the accident. Boston reluctantly agreed.

"Do you…uh…need help?"

She looked at him for the first time in probably an hour. "Help with what?"

He nodded at the bathroom. "That. You know, the bath?"

She blanched. "Mr. Wilson, I'm nine. I can get a bath by myself."

Jake wanted to feel embarrassed, but he was relieved. That would have been extremely weird. Welcome to the new world.

She took a long shower while Jake sat in the solitary office chair scribbling out notes and plans for all that needed to be done in the next several days. He had already settled the funeral arrangements. The funeral home was taken care of, and the eulogy would be done by Mike and Ruby's pastor, a Reverend Garrett Alcorn.

Then there was the trip.

There was only so much of Boston's things they could take on the return flight. It had to be relegated to clothes and a few personal items. He made a note to arrange transport of the rest of her stuff. Maybe one of those pod thingies. He couldn't remember the name offhand, but he'd look it up later. The Davises, the young couple that had cared for Boston until Jake arrived, had promised to come over and help with the packing and organizing and whatever else had to be done that probably hadn't even entered Jake's mind yet.

After a while, Boston came out of the bathroom, her hair sopping wet, but in a fresh pair of pajamas she had pulled from the small backpack of clothing and items a DFCS worker had retrieved from her house. She carried a towel with her, dragging it across the carpet, sat on the bed, and began drying her hair.

He watched her out of the corner of his eye, amazed at her precision. She did a thorough job with the towel, then reached into the backpack sitting beside her and pulled out a small brush. With meticulous attention to detail, she brushed her hair out in sections until all the shower-tangles were gone. Jake was oddly impressed. If it had been his parents that had died, that last thing he would have been worried about was taking care of his hair. Heck, he probably wouldn't have even bothered brushing his teeth. But Boston was all business, navigating the essentials, and after ten or fifteen minutes, her nightly routine was over. She sat back against the headboard and pulled the sheet and comforter up around her chin.

From time to time, she looked over at Jake and he would smile, or ask if there was anything she needed. She always declined, but after a while, she turned off the television that had been droning on the whole time and addressed him in a soft voice.

"Mr. Wilson?"

He looked up from his Bible app – he had moved on from the to-do list. "Yes."

"You're taking me to Georgia, right?"

He nodded, treading softly, knowing this was a huge step for her. "Yeah. Does that scare you?"

She shrugged.

"I know it's a lot."

"Is it a nice place?" she said.

Jake smiled. "I really like it. Gets kinda hot in the summers, but it's pretty. A lot different than San Diego, but not in a bad way. The people are nice."

She hesitated. "Will they like me there?"

"Of course. They're going to love you there. You'll see."

She sat for a while thinking it over and Jake went back to his reading. But though he scanned the words, he wasn't registering them. He was too burdened with distraction and weariness.

A few minutes passed in silence.

"Do you..." she made brief eye contact with him, then looked down at her hands... "want me?"

The question caught him off guard. "What? Sure I want you." But as soon as he said it, the doubts assaulted his mind from every direction like a well-coordinated attack.

How could you want a child? What do you know about raising a girl? You've never even married or fallen in love? Now you'll never be free to. You'll always have someone depending on you for as long as you live. This will change you. This will change everything. Your finances, your routine, your ministry…all of it.

The barrage threatened to overwhelm him, but most debilitating was the guilt. Was he lying to Boston? Was he lying to himself?

It's okay, child.

The deep, familiar whisper in his soul was unmistakable, and the mental barrage eased. It was not because the words in themselves drove away the doubt, but because Jake was reminded that he was not alone. He was never alone. And the One that watched over him watched over Boston, and nothing ever took Him by surprise. Whatever may come, He would be there. Yea though I walk through the valley of the shadow of death, I will fear no evil, for Thou art with me. Your rod and Your staff, they comfort me.

He rose from his chair, walked to the bed, and sat cross-legged on the end, facing Boston. And in that moment, he knew. All doubt dissipated. He wanted her. He wanted to love this child, to protect her, to help her heal. He had no idea how to do any of it, but his Father did, and that was all he needed for now.

"Listen. I know we barely know each other. I know you're going through the worst thing a kid can possibly experience. I confess, I don't know a lot about raising a little girl and this is all so sudden. But I can promise you this. I will *always* be here for you. And yes, I may not have known it a couple of days ago, but I want Boston Evans in my life. For the rest of my life. I can never replace your mom and dad, but I'll spend the rest of my days caring for you and making sure you never lack for anything."

Her response was profound in its utter simplicity.

"Okay."

FIVE DAYS LATER, JAKE picked up his backpack and a small suitcase for Boston in the foyer of the home of Mike and Ruby Evans.

The funeral happened the day before. It was the largest crowd Jake had ever seen for one, and he was overwhelmed with how many lives had been impacted by his friends. Pastor Alcorn performed the eulogy with solemn dignity. Jake always kept Boston close to him. He expected her to break down at any moment, but she never did. There was an odd sort of composure that had crept over her. He had seen adults behave similarly during their own times of grief. In the company of so many fellow mourners and the flurry of activity that surrounded a death and funeral, it was easy to be buoyed by the presence of others and a lack of time to process grief as deeply as needed. It was after all of that, when reality began to sink in, that the truest lows were experienced. But for now, Boston's composure held.

"That's it then?" Jake looked down at her.

Boston, standing in the doorway from the living room, nodded at him with quiet acquiescence.

Boston's home was not free and clear of debt. There was still $30,000 left on the mortgage. Jake had decided with the help of Pastor Alcorn and several of the Evans's closest friends, to put the place on the market, fully furnished. All personal items had been packed up for shipment to Georgia, including the family pictures from the walls. It left the house feeling soulless, like an Airbnb full of all the amenities of daily life but lacking anything to make it personal.

Boston turned and walked from the living room to the dining room, then to the kitchen. As she moved, she looked over the bare walls, ran a hand across the kitchen counter, studied the place as if sealing it into her memory for the last time.

She returned after a couple of minutes to the foyer where Jake stood waiting, giving her time to process it all. She stood for a long,

long time before finally turning and walking out the front door. As far as he could tell, she never looked back.

Later that day, Jake and Boston walked down the offloading ramp and emerged into the enormous concourse of the Atlanta airport. Jake had a backpack slung over one shoulder, and Boston pulled her child-sized pink polka-dotted suitcase on rollers. The place teemed with people like a sea of humanity, and Jake instinctively reached for Boston, placing a hand on her shoulder.

"Stay close, okay? This place is a mess."

"Okay, Mr. Wilson."

Jake turned to look down at her as the throng of people streamed by in both directions. "You know, you can call me Jake. You don't have to keep calling me Mr. Wilson." Jake smirked as something occurred to him. "It makes me feel like I'm in a Dennis the Menace cartoon."

Her nose scrunched into tiny wrinkles. "A what?"

"Never mind."

An arduous five-hundred-yard walk down the concourse, a half mile ride on the underground tram that serviced the domestic terminals, an interminable wait at the baggage claim, and another quarter of a mile walk to where Jake's Santa Fe had been parked in the daily lot – Jake mentally thanked his secretary for making sure he got a cheap booster seat from Walmart before he left – and they were on their way. Two hours later, Jake pulled off I75 onto Highway 96 and turned left heading into Warner Robins.

Boston had been quiet, thoughtful the entire ride. Jake made attempts to engage her, pointing out some landmark or place of interest as they traveled. She was kind and respectful as was always her demeanor – there was no mistaking she was the daughter of Mike and Ruby Evans – but her responses were brief, and he was unable to pull more out of her.

More than once, Jake peered into the rearview mirror and saw tears falling from her eyes.

Dear Lord, help this child. Give her Your peace that passes all understanding.

A hair over three miles from the interstate, Jake turned left onto Regency Drive, passed Burger King on the left and Five Star Mazda on the right and entered the Rockbridge subdivision.

Jake fell head over heels for the picturesque subdivision the first time he laid eyes upon it. After moving to Warner Robins as lead pastor of Life Church, he had rented a small apartment monthly while transitioning into his new role and learning the area. When it came time to buy a permanent place, he had found the light-gray two story at 507 Milner Street through a realty website and gone out to see it. He loved the house itself, but it was as much the charm of the neighborhood as the house that convinced him to buy.

Rockbridge was a tight-knit community. They looked out for each other, shared ideas and events through social media, and kept to certain appearance standards via the diligent work of the HOA. Jake's home was at the junction of Rockbridge and Milner with a solitary, flourishing rose bush underneath a triple-globed streetlamp – a requirement of the HOA, all the homes in the subdivision had matching ones in their front yards.

He came to the stop sign at the junction of Regency and Milner.

"There it is." He pointed at his home in front of them.

Boston craned her neck from the back to peer between the driver's and passenger's seats.

The triple lamp formed a dazzling nimbus above the rose bush, the blossoms underneath glowing like rubies. Soft incandescent lights glowed above the porch and double garage doors giving the home's light-gray color a pearlescent quality.

Jake reached up and pressed the garage remote and the left-most door of the double garage whined and began to rise. He pulled across the street, down the driveway, and into the garage.

"It's nothing huge," Jake maneuvered into the garage, "but I like it."

He turned off the car and hit the garage remote again. The door slid down behind them.

"You can go on in if you like." Jake unbuckled his seatbelt and cracked his door. "The kitchen door is unlocked. I'll get the bags."

Boston had already extricated herself from the car and stood on the far side from Jake. She shut the car door and walked to the one that led to the interior of the house while Jake popped the back hatch and started pulling their bags out.

"...so the moving company will have the rest of your stuff here in a few days" Jake was saying. "Once they do, we'll change the guest bedroom into anything you want."

Boston turned the knob and pushed the door open. Unbeknownst to her, Jake's sleek-muscled, liver and white English Pointer named Peaches waited eagerly on the other side. As soon as the door was open, the dog bounded forward, tail wagging, and came nose to nose with Boston.

Boston screamed. Jake screamed. Peaches whimpered, turned tail, and ran around the kitchen bar top into the living room.

Jake scrambled from behind the car, barely escaping a tumble over Boston's suitcase that would surely have sent him sprawling onto the concrete. He swung around the front of the car and nearly collided with Boston who was running in the opposite direction. She grabbed his leg and clung to it like a life preserver in rough seas.

"Oh my gosh, what's wrong?" He was breathless. His heart drove like a turbo-injected piston.

"You didn't tell me you had a dog!" Her voice was a strained squeak.

Jake realized his oversight. He'd been so distracted by everything that he never told the child. Just assumed that Mike must have told her at some point.

"Oh, I didn't even... yes, I have a dog." Another unwelcome thought occurred to him. "Are you allergic to dogs?"

"No!" Her tiny fingers dug painfully into Jake's thigh. "I'm scared of dogs."

Inside the house, Peaches warily poked her head around the corner, uncertain of this pint-sized newcomer that had just screamed in her face.

Jake forced his breathing to slow and gently pried Boston's talons from his leg. *Sheesh, I think that's gonna bruise*, he thought. He kneeled but kept a protective arm around her.

"It jumped at me. It was gonna eat my face!" she said.

Jake suppressed a sudden urge to laugh. Boston was genuinely frightened, but the thought of Peaches attacking anyone was so ridiculous as to be comical.

"I'm sorry. I'm sure she was just excited to see you. She's been kinda lonely. One of my staff has been coming every day to check on her and feed her and let her out to potty, but she's had to spend a lot of time alone."

Peaches plodded slowly back towards them now from the living room, emboldened by Jake's presence.

"Her name is Peaches and I promise she's the sweetest dog you'll ever meet. I swear. She's going to love you and she will *never* hurt you, okay?"

Peaches arrived back in the doorway. Boston watched her dubiously. Peaches offered a wide yawn as if now bored with the whole show.

"C'mere Peaches. This is Boston."

Peaches took a step forward. Jake felt Boston tense, but she didn't run.

"Don't be afraid. You can pet her, just like this."

He reached out and stroked Peaches head, then scratched behind her ears. Peaches panted happily. Beside him, Boston stretched out a tentative hand until she touched Peaches' head as well. At first, she recoiled a little as if she'd been shocked, but quickly settled into a slow stroking motion, mimicking Jake.

A small smile grew on her face. "She's so soft."

As if that were encouragement enough, Peaches took a step forward and gave Boston an enthusiastic lick on the nose.

Boston froze, then giggled as Peaches sniffed at her breath, her whiskers tickling Boston's lips and nose.

LATER, BOSTON SAT ON the couch petting Peaches, her new favorite friend. Mr. Wilson was right. The dog really did seem to like her. Her fur was super soft, and she laid her head in Boston's lap when Boston started rubbing her ears.

Mr. Wilson had shown her around the house. There were three bedrooms upstairs. He said hers was the middle one. It had its own little bathroom and Mr. Wilson promised she could decorate with whatever she wanted, even unicorns like back home. But she wasn't sure she wanted that. Maybe it would be easier if she wasn't reminded of home.

Sometimes it felt like she was on some strange adventure, like a weird kid's camp or something, and for a while, she would forget – well, not really forget, more like get distracted – that she would never go home to her parents again. It was a vicious cycle, and already, she was exhausted from it.

Mr. Wilson bounded down the stairs and came into the room.

"Hey, I want to show you something." He went to the back door that was next to the tiny area he'd called the breakfast nook. "I think you're going to like this."

Boston felt little of anything in the way of enthusiasm, but she got up and followed him dutifully to the door.

For a moment when he looked at her, his expression changed from anticipation to something different, like he was sad again. Maybe he was like her and kept getting distracted from the reality they were both living. Maybe that would be okay. Maybe if they kept distracting themselves, they could both get through this. Boston hoped and prayed so. But Mr. Wilson's sour expression passed quickly, and he put on another smile.

He opened the back door and Peaches immediately sprang down from the couch and took off into the yard. Boston moved a little closer as Jake beckoned for her. The light from inside the house cast a bright rectangle on the deck with a Mr. Wilson shadow in the middle of it, but other than that, it was too dark outside, and she couldn't see anything beyond.

"Watch this," Mr. Wilson's eyes were wide as she came even with him. He reached over and flipped a switch. Instantly, Boston was transported to a wonderland.

The yard was huge, far bigger than hers at home, with a tall, wooden fence running around it. Strings of light bulbs went all the way around the top of the fence, giving the whole place an atmosphere that reminded Boston of outdoor cafés in movies. Most of the yard was filled with towering, bushy trees that whooshed gently in the wind, their leaves whispering in the night. But the best part of all was in the middle. For there, among the tree trunks, was what appeared to Boston to be a fairy castle, but was in actuality a large, open gazebo, also tastefully lit with strung bulbs and imitation torch lamps on each post that flickered burnished red in the night. In the center were two opposing, decorative couches in front of a large rock-hearth fireplace.

Boston looked closer. All around the "castle", the ground shimmered under the lights. It took her a moment to realize what it was. Water. Water surrounded the place. The only access point was a small wooden bridge stretching over the gulf.

Peaches stood expectantly beside the bridge. She gave one sharp bark, encouraging Boston to come and see for herself the wonder up close.

"Go on. Check it out," Jake encouraged her.

Boston stepped out onto the deck, descended the stairs, and made her way to the oasis in front of her. As she got closer, Peaches ran up and walked beside her. When they reached the little bridge, Boston stepped up and peered over the railing into the water below.

The pond was interspersed with water foliage and lily pads. A pump sent up bubbles from one end, putting out ripples over the water's surface. And it was teeming with life. In all directions, bright orange and silver fish the length of Boston's arm from elbow to fingertips darted about like autonomous torpedoes.

Mr. Wilson walked up behind her. He was holding a brown paper bag in his hand. He handed it to Boston. It was heavy and exuded a grainy-sweet smell akin to some cereals, the kind adults with poopy problems ate.

He nodded at the bag. "They're hungry."

She opened it and found it full of fish pellets.

"How much?" she said.

"Well, there's a lot of them in there," he reached out and made a show of examining her free hand, "and you've got little hands so I'm thinking…" he scrunched up his nose in thought. "Maybe ten handfuls."

"Ten?"

"Oh yeah. Watch." He gestured for her to throw some out, and she began ladling handfuls of feed into the pond. The effect was immediate. The fish swarmed from all over the pond, attracted by the familiar sound of the pellets hitting the water, and attacked the food.

She giggled as she counted out ten handfuls. It was no time before the food was nearly gone.

"Told you," he grinned down at her as they watched the final remnants being devoured by the fish.

She smiled back and handed him the bag before turning and bouncing the rest of the way across the bridge and plopping down onto one of the plush seat cushions where Peaches had already taken up residence. Mr. Wilson walked over and sat across from her.

She noticed him watching her as she gazed at the fish, the same lights sparkling in the water sparkling in his eyes, and for the first time since he came to her, she felt something for him. Not love. No, nothing that strong, but certainly like. He was kind, and he'd been there for her through it all.

"Mom would have loved this place. Dad too." She mused.

Jake nodded. "I wish they could have seen it."

"So do I."

They stayed there for a long time, sometimes talking, sometimes just sitting. It was nice.

That night, the nightmares started.

JAKE SLEPT IN HIS BED in a fetal position, Peaches curled into the crook of his legs. She snored like a piglet, the tones of which intertwined with Jake's own snufflings to create a sonorous semi-melody worthy of any barnyard.

A banshee cry ripped through the night jarring them both awake. Jake sat bolt upright in a flash, confused, disoriented. Then..."Boston!"

He leaped out of bed tossing back the covers, covering a still-befuddled Peaches. He launched down the short hallway and rounded into the middle bedroom.

Boston was sitting up in bed crying in ragged sobs, her tiny form silhouetted in stark relief by the moonlight streaming in through the picture window next to the bed. He made it to her in two large steps and wrapped her in an embrace.

"I'm here. I'm here. Just try to take a deep breath, okay." His own pulse hammered in his ears.

He could feel her trying to settle, trying to control her breathing. He feared she was going to hyperventilate, but he kept chanting words of comfort and gradually her breathing slowed. She was no longer sobbing, but the abundance of tears still flowing from her eyes soaked his shirt where her head cradled against his chest.

"It was just a nightmare," he began to rock her without thought. For a long time, he held her, and she clung to him. Her agony was palpable, like a thick, dark claw threatening to strangle them both.

She mumbled something he couldn't understand, and he pulled back, holding her at arm's length. Her eyes met his in the darkness. He couldn't see the irises in the shadows, but the surrounding tissue was puffy and blotched.

"It was so scary." She swiped a hand across her eyes and ran her sleeve under her nose. Peaches, who had managed to extricate herself from the blankets, joined them and leapt up on the bed. She crossed over to Boston and sniffed at her face.

Jake reached over to the nightstand and flipped the lamp switch, then pulled a few tissues from the Kleenex box he'd put there earlier. He handed them to Boston who wiped her nose more thoroughly this time and balled them into a tight wad. Her fingers continued to knead them nervously, and Jake realized she was shaking.

He sat with her until she fell back asleep. It took a while, and despite his efforts to get her to talk, she refused to give the specifics of the dream, though in Jake's opinion, it was pretty easy to figure out. Jake touched her on the head and said a silent prayer for peace and rest, then stood and tucked the blanket up close to her chin. He reached to turn off the lamp, thought better of, and left it on in case she had another episode during the night.

He moved to the door and turned to look at her one last time. She lay there, her face pink, but as beautiful as a tiny angel, her blonde hair trailing across the pillow like golden silk. He saw so much of Mike and Ruby in her features and a deep longing to see them again stabbed him like a dagger.

He trudged back to his room and settled into bed, staring up at the darkened ceiling. Peaches was already there.

"God. I don't know how to do this. You gotta help me. Please."

Suddenly, Peaches popped up and jumped down from the bed. She gave a short sound that was half-bark, half-crooning howl, then ran out of the room.

"Hey. Where you going?"

He got up again and tracked Peaches to Boston's room where she had crawled up on the bed and placed her head on Boston's chest. Peaches cut her mournful brown eyes at Jake.

"Yeah."

He walked out and returned after a moment carrying his pillow and a blanket. He set them both on the floor next to Boston's bed, laid down, pulled the blanket over himself, and went to sleep.

CHAPTER 6

Dewey Thaddeus Knapp didn't like Jake Wilson. Didn't like him at all.

Dewey was a hard man. He knew it. He was even proud of it. By his own reckoning, he had a right to be. After all, he was rich, had owned several successful restaurants for over thirty years, maintained a lucrative apartment complex, and had a stock portfolio that had seen moderate to high growth for most of its existence. On top of all of that, he owned The First National Bank of West Georgia.

People that knew him well – few though they were – could have summed him up simply enough: Treat him good and he'll treat you good; cross him, and you'll rue the day.

He was strict with his employees, but he paid fair wages. Known throughout his businesses as a hard worker, he was willing to hire those less fortunate and considered outcasts. If they lived up to their job duties, he was all about giving a hand up. This was often misconstrued as generosity by those who worked for him. But it wasn't about generosity. Dewey hired people who were in need because it put them in his debt. Indebted people were loyal, and loyalty was important to Dewey. Indebted, loyal people were easier to manipulate.

Dewey Knapp craved control like some men craved food, or women, or whatever vice had befallen them, and perhaps even more than control, he craved respect. He didn't care if it was earned or purchased. He deserved respect, and he demanded it in no uncertain terms. If you respected him, it was quid-pro-quo. Disrespect him, and you would not get a second chance to do it again.

Horace Knapp, Dewey's father, had taught him the importance of respect. A hard man, much harder than Dewey, Horace raised his son alone after the death of Dewey's mother from cancer, and he did it at the end of a belt. Though not a financially prosperous man like Dewey was now, Horace had excelled in his field. Dewey had no doubt it was the lessons Horace had taught him from an early age that had driven him to succeed.

"Son," Horace would say at the dinner table after a hard day working on aircraft at Robins Air Force Base, "the most important thing you can have in this life is respect. I've learned that by watching the officers at the base. Respect makes the world go round far as I see it. Get respect for yourself, son. Be the man that others look to for leadership. Be hard. Be strong. Be harsh if you need to, but whatever you do, don't let anyone disrespect you."

This little speech was often followed by a speech about the second greatest thing a man could have. In Horace's mind, one that was indistinguishable from the first: power. To Horace Knapp, respect and power were more important than anything, even love. Certainly, Dewey had no love for the man. He'd grown up virtually devoid of such meaningless emotional quibble after his mom died. Horace had made him tough. He'd made him unmalleable. Dewey had taken it all to heart and had become a man that would make his father proud. After all, his father gave him no choice.

Growing up, Knapp's father had never been one for religion or churchgoing. His father may have mentioned his mother going to church from time to time before her death, but Horace never went once in all the time Dewey could remember. So, Dewey never felt the need to go to church either. At least, not until he met Mary.

When he started dating Mary thirty-five years ago, he had been somewhat chagrined to find she was a faithful member of her local congregation. But he loved her, the only person other than his mom he ever loved, and out of nothing more than a desire to be close to her, he started attending, expecting nothing, but was surprised and excited about what he learned of church and God.

First, he found out that he liked the God of the Bible. The old part anyway. The church goers called that part the Old Testament. In it, God laid down the rules and you had better follow them buddy or else. If you did good, you got good. If you did bad, watch out friend, God would smack you into next week.

That was the God that pastor Ed Grogan preached week in and week out. Pastor Grogan was a real hellfire and brimstone kind of guy, and it didn't take long for him and Dewey to fall in together.

Pastor Grogan's God reminded Dewey a lot of Horace Knapp. God demanded respect – the ultimate respect, and there was no doubt He had power. That was the kind of God Dewey wanted to serve, because it was the kind of person he wanted to be.

The second thing Dewey discovered about church was more subtle, and he didn't even realize it until he'd been there several months. In church, Dewey had found another sphere where he was respected and powerful.

Churches always needed money, and since Dewey had an endless supply and was willing to part with it for the benefit of the church – assuming it made him look good – he quickly became someone of importance. It further solidified his place with Pastor Grogan and before long, he was on the Pastor's council and making decisions that impacted Life Church.

Dewey found that if there was something going on in the church that he didn't approve of, usually treating Grogan to a nice steak dinner and having a conversation with him was enough to sway things to Dewey's liking. Dewey didn't see this as a bad thing because he was convinced of his own rightness and wisdom when compared to others. His success in business was testament to that. Besides, what he was doing was for the betterment of the church, or so he told himself.

But that influence had come to a screeching halt when Ed Grogan retired, and the new pastor arrived – Jake Wilson.

A few weeks after Jake's appointment as pastor, Dewey called and set up a meeting with him on a Monday afternoon. They met in Jake's office which was in the process of being remodeled. Pastor Grogan's bookshelves had been filled with the books of its new occupant, and where sections of the newly painted walls had dried, pictures hung.

Dewey sat in one of the leather armchairs facing Jake Wilson's desk and admired a large, framed photo of the U.S.S. Alabama that hung by the spacious window that looked out over the adjoining youth building.

Jake followed Dewey's gaze. "Have you ever seen it in person?"

Jake sat behind Pastor Grogan's old desk. It was littered with knickknacks bearing either military logos or Alabama Crimson Tide.

"No," Dewey shook his head. "Not close, anyway. I've passed it on the freeway and seen it from a distance. I know you can tour it, though, right?"

"Yeah. They converted it into a museum."

The USS Alabama was a retired South Dakota-class battleship from World War II in permanent dry dock in Mobile Bay. Jake had grown up in the Mobile suburb of Saraland and several of his sermons from his first couple of weeks as the new pastor of Life Church had included reminiscences from his childhood in that area.

Dewey had never liked the ocean, and Mobile certainly wasn't the best place for beachgoers, but he liked the city itself well enough. They had good seafood, and that was something Dewey did like.

Jake continued. "Did you know that during hurricanes, the museum staff and their families will go down into the hull to ride out the storm? That's always seemed like a spiritual lesson to me. When storms come along, we ride them out in Jesus. He's our ship and we're safe deep inside His protection. Pretty cool, huh?"

Dewey didn't particularly think so. In fact, he thought it sounded a bit corny as far as illustrations went, but he nodded in agreement anyway. This was the first time he'd had a chance to sit down and talk with Jake Wilson one-on-one, and so far, he liked the kid. True, it was a little strange to have a pastor that was thirty years his junior, but as long as the kid could do the job, so be it.

Dewey found Jake to be a pleasant type, and since it was his intention to get in tight with the new preacher, he was glad the guy wasn't a moron.

"So, I'm guessing you like military stuff," Dewey gestured with a gnarled forefinger to the memorabilia on Jake's desk.

"I do. Again, I have the Alabama to thank for that." Jake glanced at the picture again. "My parents used to take me there every summer when I was a kid and it got me interested in all things military, particularly World War II."

"You must be really excited about Warner Robins, then. What with Robins Air Force Base being the cornerstone of the community."

"I am." Jake's voice was suddenly filled with a childlike wonder that amused Dewey. "I can't wait to tour the Museum of Aviation. I've been busy so far, but I'm going to make it out there sooner or later."

"You should. Did you know they have a Blackbird there?"

Jake's eyebrows shot up. "No way. Are you serious?"

"Dead serious. There're all kinds of craft out there to see. My dad used to work on them back in the day."

"Really? I'd love to talk with him sometime. I'm sure he'd have some great stories to tell."

"He did. I'm afraid he passed away many years ago." Dewey feigned more regret than he felt.

Jake winced a little. "I'm sorry, Mr. Knapp."

"It's okay. Like I said, it was a long time ago. But he did love it – working on the planes."

"Was he military or civilian?"

"Both," Dewey lifted his chin at the memory. "He got his training in the Air Force. Served in Korea. Once he got out, he stayed here and got a job as a civilian contractor. Worked all the way up until the day he passed."

"So, you were raised here, then?"

Dewey leaned a bit farther back in his chair, pulling in a deep breath. "Born and bred. Me and my little sister, Debbie."

"And does she live here as well?"

Dewey laughed, a short, barking sound. "No. Debbie went to college at UCLA and never came home except to visit. She loves the West Coast. LA gal. She's married with two girls of her own."

"What about you? Are you married?"

"Not me. I'm too mean." That was the last thing Mary had told him eighteen years ago when she walked out on him. He decided to leave that part out of the current conversation.

Jake laughed. "So, you're a restaurant owner, right?"

"Among other things. I own a few chain restaurants. Some private endeavors. I also own some apartment complexes and other businesses."

"Wow. Sounds like you're doing pretty well for yourself."

Dewey's chest rose. "I don't want to brag, but I'm doing alright. I've worked hard to get where I am."

"That's really great, Mr. Knapp."

"Dewey, please."

"Dewey," Jake repeated.

Jake rested his elbows on his desk. "So, if I may ask, is this just a social visit, or was there something you needed from me?"

This was his chance, and Dewey knew he must tread carefully. Too assertive, and you scared the prey. Not assertive enough, and you came off weak.

Dewey pursed his lips. "In honesty, I came to offer my help."

Jake waited for him to continue.

"I know you're a young, single minister with a lot of responsibility. I just wanted to let you know I'd be happy to do anything I can for you. Like I said before, I've done well, and if there's ever anything you need, you can come to me."

Jake's face remained passive; a smile locked in place.

Dewey continued. "Pastor Grogan was a dear friend. Still is. Without revealing his personal business, I helped him out of some financial situations. Also provided him with a new car when his old one kicked the bucket. I'd be willing to do the same for you."

Jake sat back and crossed his arms. "Mr. Knapp – sorry, Dewey – thank you so much for your kindness."

Dewey watched for a clue in Jake's countenance as to whether he would accept the offer of financial backing – that's the way Dewey looked at it. Of course, you could also say without dishonesty that he wanted the man in his pocket. The only visible change in Jake was a slight pulsing in his temples; the kind that came from clenching and unclenching one's teeth.

Jake looked down for a moment, then back up at Dewey. "I can't speak for Pastor Grogan, and I know I'm a lot younger than he is, but as nice as your offer is, I prefer to make my own way."

Jake's voice was neutral, conversational.

"Perhaps I'm a bit old-fashioned, but I would feel awkward taking that kind of help from you. I wouldn't want anyone to get the wrong idea. I'm not saying anyone in the church would, but you must see there could be the possibility of giving people the impression I could be bought."

Dewey started to protest, knowing he'd played too hard too fast, but Jake held up a hand.

"I'm not saying that's what you were intending. I'm only saying a pastor can't be too careful of appearances."

Dewey was quick to backtrack. Although it chafed him, it was now apparent Jake Wilson was not a man to readily accept help from others. Dewey had no intention of coming off as a manipulator, however accurate that might have been, and he had no desire to jeopardize his position on the council which had thus far remained intact since the pastoral change.

"I'm sorry, Pastor Jake," Dewey mustered as much sincerity as he could. "I understand completely. That wasn't my intention, and you're right. Ever since you've been here, I can't help but think you might be the age of my own son if I ever had one."

Jake's expression softened a little. There was a note of sympathy in his eyes, and Dewey congratulated himself. He'd been able to sway the conversation back in his favor – an old man trying to live vicariously through a child he never had.

Jake cleared his throat. "Well, I do appreciate the thought. And I cherish any wisdom you can offer on the council."

Dewey gave a placating smile and rose. "Of course. Of course."

Jake took the cue and rose opposite him.

Dewey stuck out his hand and shook Jake's vigorously.

"Please, as an old man to a young one, I'll be happy to help out in any way I can. Even if you just need someone to talk to some time," Dewey added this last as an afterthought, the offer of a confidant, a listening ear. "I'm so glad you're here. I know the church will flourish under your leadership."

As Dewey veered his Aston Martin from the parking lot and onto Watson Boulevard, he considered the meeting again. He needed to reevaluate his approach with Jake Wilson. He needed to handle the young man with kid's gloves, careful not to offend his softer disposition. Because what ultimately mattered was that Dewey retained his position of power. As much as Dewey led him to believe the church needed Jake to flourish, what they really needed was him. And that was what Dewey intended. It was his calling, God's higher purpose for him, and he would not let anyone stand in the way of that. Not even this upstart pastor. But ever since that first meeting, Jake had proved stubbornly resistant to doing anything that would allow Dewey sway over him. Dewey's annoyance for the young man had grown from frustration to dislike, to near hatred. Jake had made himself a nemesis in Dewey's eyes. The man lacked the proper respect.

CHAPTER 7

Sunday services at the Warner Robins Life Church were borderline extravagant. The church itself was an enormous, stately, modern facility on a sprawling ten-acre parcel of land on the southeastern side of the county.

Many modern churches in the vein of Elevation and Hillsong produced the equivalent of elaborate stage productions each week. Every service was a major undertaking. The music side alone was a massive conglomeration of moving parts, like a machine that needed to be tweaked and oiled constantly to keep it in its best condition. Life Church didn't have a choir, but they did use a praise team that included eight vocalists, the worship pastor who led from the keyboard, a drummer, an electric guitar player, a bassist, and a lead guitarist. Each one used in-ear monitors like the rock and country stars used, and for each of these, they had the ability to create their own sound mix using a smartphone app that interfaced with their soundboard. One of their soundboards, anyway. There were three.

The rear quadrant of the stage was a network of power and input/output chords laced together like an intricate spiderweb and concealed as best as possible through clever placement and subterranean pathways and outlets. Even so, it was impossible to completely eliminate the crisscrossing cables that resembled roads on a city map.

Then there was the media group. There were five people that manned the video cameras placed strategically on platforms throughout the auditorium. Behind and to stage right was a media room that could have passed for a small movie editing room. Here, Edwina Huff sat every service and managed camera shots through the headphones worn by the camera operators. Beside her, Nate Upton monitored the live internet stream, and to his other side, Patrick Holden supervised it all.

In the back of the auditorium, an elongated platform ran thirty feet long and housed the sound board that controlled the mix in the main auditorium. Here the sound engineer labored throughout the service making sure everything sounded just right. The written service map he received from the music pastor often read like a detailed instruction manual: raise mic number one for the first song, Rebekah will be singing that solo; on song two, the electric guitar will do a riff during the bridge, make sure he's loud enough to be heard, but not too loud; there will be no keys for the first song, it will be rhythm guitar driven, so Adam needs to be up for that one.

Beside the sound board were two more stations where volunteers managed the projection and lighting system. The light show was tailored for each service, always beautiful and expertly run. They had rows of spotlights and multicolored lighting rigs both on the stage floor and hanging high above. A fog machine kicked on a few minutes before service time, and once the band hit the stage, it was non-stop colors and strobes often synced to the beat of the music. There were streaking flashes during the upbeat songs, followed by interweaving pre-set patterns that waned and swelled with the ballads.

Then, it was Jake's turn to step on the stage for the sermon. He would be hit with a spotlight, and the sweating would begin.

Dewey Knapp made it his business to know all of this, just like he made it his business to know everything. Knowledge was power, and power was the honey of life; therefore, you could never have too much knowledge. The other thing Dewey loved about it all was that

Life Church's media team worked with admirable efficiency. They were disciplined and capable, even though they were all volunteers, and that was something to be proud of. That's one thing Pastor Jake did right. He got the best out of his workers. At least for that, Dewey respected him.

On stage, the jumbo, thirty-foot wide screen ran a pre-service mixture of announcement videos and prayer needs while contemporary Christian worship music played over the house speakers. All around the auditorium, people of all ages, colors, and financial strata mingled and made their way to their seats. It was still ten minutes before the Sunday morning service was scheduled to start, but Dewey had been seated now for a while. He always made it a point to be early.

"If you're on time," Dad would say, "then you're already late."

An elderly woman – Cora? Coral? Dewey couldn't remember – waved politely at him as she walked by. He gave a curt nod. He had to go easy with the encouragement.

Widows were in full supply here, like jackals on the African plains. Oh, sure. They talked a good game. Lonely and all that mess. But Dewey knew the truth. They were predators, each and every one. He was too old to have some grieving old mantrap devour his free time and wealth. *I'll be just fine by myself, thank you very much for asking.* Most of them spent their days with their pitiful stipends from the Social Security Administration watching soaps and gossiping with each other about who did what and why and with whom. Meanwhile, he was busy at the same age running multiple businesses and carving out his own little empire.

Then there were the others. Men and women of repute who knew that Dewey was a rich and powerful man. They were the ones who came by and shook his hand and gave generous compliments. People that knew his money kept this church going.

"...Mr. Knapp, it's so good to see you this morning..."

"...Dewey, I ate at your restaurant the other night, and everything was superb."

"Well, I'm just a blessed man," he would say, and so the niceties would go.

At ten o'clock sharp, the lights dimmed, and the music rose. The place came alive with anticipation as the worshipers got to their feet and sang along with the worship leader and praise team as they led the congregation through several rousing, upbeat anthems. At the end of the third song, there was a pause, and Pastor Jake Wilson, resplendent in boot cut jeans with polished black boots and a sport jacket and tie strode up the front stairs onto the stage.

Jake went through the customary greetings, popped a joke to everyone's great amusement. Dewey for the most part ignored all of this, waiting on Jake to get down to the real reason he was up there right now: the offering. That's what Dewey was really interested in, because as of late, Dewey was displeased with the way Pastor Jake handled it.

Jake finally rounded to the point.

"As always here at Life Church we're extremely thankful for all of you that give and help us keep the ministry and outreach going. Your dollars are what enable us to support missionaries all over the world, to do several important charity works here in our own community, and a whole host of other things all to be a light for Jesus.

"We want you to give today as you feel led by the Lord. I'm not concerned with you giving because you feel some obligation. I don't want you to give because you think it will earn you favor with God, nor do I want you to give because you think God will punish you if you don't. We believe here at Life Church that all the judgment we were due was poured out on Jesus at the cross, and He bore it all that we could live as free men and women under the new covenant of the grace of God. If you give, let it be because you feel the Holy Spirit leading you to give."

There was more, but Dewey had heard enough. As Pastor Jake finished, the musicians played another lively tune as the ushers went around and collected from the patrons. When the nearest usher came to Dewey, he smiled and put his offering into the basket. He was careful to let the two hundred-dollar bills be visible enough to be noticed by the usher. It earned him an appreciative nod, but after the usher moved on, Dewey sat down.

He was angry, but careful to conceal his emotion for the sake of the eyes that may be on him. Jake Wilson stood oblivious on stage, speaking to one of the musicians, smiling, laughing, as the offering finished up. Dewey Knapp watched with ever-growing irritation. Jake was being flippant with the people's giving, and that could threaten Dewey's investments. Both past and future. No, this would not do. Perhaps it was time to make a phone call.

JAKE WALKED UP TO THE child check-in/pickup counter in the lobby of the kid's church wing of the Life Church complex. As he approached the counter, a smartly dressed woman in her late twenties looked up and smiled.

"Hey, Angie." He held up a slip of paper with the number 29 printed on it. "Do you need my ticket?"

"No. She's the last one."

Jake grimaced. "You know how it is. The pastor is the first one to arrive and the last one to leave."

She gave him a wry look. "Isn't that what your staff members are for?" She was joking, of course. Jake would never go for letting people stay behind to do what he considered his responsibility, and everyone knew it.

Most of the time, in a church the size of Life Church, the opening and closing of the building were relegated to staff members, and these tasks – or anything considered similarly mundane – were seldom performed by the senior pastor. However, Jake's dad, himself a retired pastor, had always been there to open the doors and lock up afterward.

"Jake," Jim Wilson would say, "the pastor of the church should be the one with the biggest servant's heart. Do you know what Jesus did at Passover before his arrest in the garden? He washed the disciples' feet. Can you imagine, the God of the universe made flesh, stooping to wash the dirty feet of a bunch of commoners? Well, that's the kind of heart we" – he made a gesture to indicate himself and Jake – "want to have."

That lesson had stuck with Jake, and he'd done his best to live by it. He'd been around enough of the other kind over the years. Pastors who ruled their churches like dictators. My way or the highway, boys. If you don't like it, you can leave. The thought made Jake sick to his stomach. How had so many who claimed to be leaders drifted so far from the way Jesus had lived and behaved? Jake often spent a great deal of time wondering if many pastors were truly called, or if they were just people that had fallen in love with power.

Jake chided himself for his negativity. It wasn't his place to judge the heart of another. He was only responsible for Jake Wilson, and he was determined to do his best with what he had to work with. He was a preacher, a leader, but most of all, Jake wanted to put a spotlight on Jesus. If he could do that, even with something as simple as being the first in and the last out, he considered himself a success.

In front of him, Angie flicked a few keystrokes on the computer and entered the number from Jake's pick-up ticket.

"Alright. They should be up in a minute."

"Thanks. Hey, listen, why don't you take off? Don't let me hold you up."

She grabbed her purse from a drawer under the computer monitor and rounded the corner. "I'm gonna hold you to it. You know how it is if Chris doesn't get his favorite seat at the steak house."

"Can't have that. Not on my account."

She waved goodbye and left through the front double-glass doors.

Jake walked over to one of the benches along the side wall and plopped down, loosening his tie and pulling it off. He removed his suit jacket, placed it beside him, and proceeded to roll up his sleeves.

After a few moments, the door on the far wall opened and Boston walked out with a young woman Jake didn't remember, but he was instantly struck by her. The woman glided through the lobby with the grace of a swan, her movements lithe and efficient. Her skin seemed to shimmer under the usually harsh fluorescent lights like sunlight shimmering on grains of sand. But above all of this, was a smile that drew Jake in. It was a smile that never met a stranger. It was a smile that said, "I see you and you are important."

"Mr. Wilson! I had the bestest time."

"You did?" His brows furrowed as he rose to greet Boston. Her demeanor was so different from her typical quiet reservation.

Jake glanced back up at the young woman who had trailed Boston.

"Hi. I don't think I've met you yet." He proffered a hand which she took. Her touch was warm and soft and made it hard for Jake to concentrate.

Boston frowned and looked at Jake, confused.

"That's Jessica," she said. "How can you not know her? She goes to your church."

Jake gave a clumsy smile and answered while still looking at Jessica.

"Well, it's a big church, kid. Lots of new people come all the time and it's hard for me to meet them all."

Jessica gave Boston a radiant smile. "Right. We haven't met in person, Boston. Plus, I'm usually over here in the kid's wing during services while your...Pastor Jake preaches in the main service."

Boston wrinkled her nose and regarded Jake. "She's the best." She said the words as if telling him a secret. "You should do better."

Jake chuckled and cleared his throat. "Yeah. It's nice to meet you, Jessica."

"You too," she turned her gaze to Boston. "And it was especially nice getting to know you. I can't wait to see you again next Sunday."

Boston sparkled; Jake was struck by the change in the little girl. This was the most *alive* he had seen her. He wondered what could have affected her in this way, and if it was all the charming woman standing in front of him.

Boston gave a hearty wave.

Jake gestured at the doors. "Boston, why don't you go wait outside in the sunshine. I'll be right there, okay?"

Boston walked away and pushed open the double doors into the sun. Jake and Jessica both watched for a moment as Boston began singing to herself, her airy soprano notes slowly coming to a mute as the door closed behind her. Jake turned back to Jessica.

"Wow. Hey, um, I don't know what you did, but that's the first time I've seen her really look happy since she got here. Thanks."

Jessica smiled and stared wistfully past him through the glass doors at Boston who busied herself pirouetting. "Just give her time. Not that I'm trying to overstep..."

"No, no. Not at all. I'll take any help I can get."

They both watched Boston as she stopped spinning and began a balancing game on the edge of the sidewalk.

Jake realized how close Jessica was to him, and he could feel the warmth radiating off of her body, or so he imagined. Perhaps he was just feeling feverish. His tongue felt thick, and he was afraid to speak again. Afraid he would say something stupid. He couldn't remember the last time a girl had affected him this way.

"Nice meeting you," he managed stupidly.

"You too, Pastor Wilson."

Jake walked away, but not before glancing back over his shoulder one more time at the blonde who retreated the way she had come. It wasn't until halfway home that Jake realized he'd forgotten to stay and lock up the building.

JAKE LOUNGED ON THE couch in a t-shirt and shorts while Boston bounced around the room, throwing a deformed and stained tennis ball to Peaches who kept chasing it and bringing it back.

"And guess what the neatest thing is, Mr. Wilson? Her last name is Miracle."

"Really? That's an unusual last name."

Boston scoffed at him. "It's better than Wilson."

Jake threw his hands in the air. "What's wrong with Wilson? And I didn't say there was anything wrong with Miracle. It's just not a typical name. In fact, I've never heard of anybody named Miracle before. And by the way, why do you call her Jessica and still call me Mr. Wilson? Would it kill you to call me Jake?"

Boston shrugged, then threw the ball again for Peaches who was hopping with excitement. The dog took off after it, sliding in the foyer when her padded feet hit the slick tiles. She came to a skidding stop like a professional snowboarder, then made a quick U-turn. For a moment, her feet moved in place like a cartoon character as she tried to gain traction, but soon enough she caught some grip and streaked back into the living room, dropping the ball in front of Boston.

"Anyway," Boston continued, "she's really nice. She let me help with the Sunday school lesson, and she has this really cool board that's fuzzy and these Bible character pictures that you put on it and it makes the story like it comes alive."

Jake chuckled at Boston's raw enthusiasm. "That's even better than TV."

His sarcasm was completely lost on her.

"Right. And then she told me that since I was new she would go with me to kid's church and sit by me after our class was over, and she did *the whole time,* and then they had this contest where it was boys against girls, and this boy and girl both had to eat a donut that was hanging on a string without using their hands, and whoever got finished first won and it was the girl, and that meant every girl got ten tickets to use in the prize shop. I don't have enough to buy anything yet, but I can save up by doing memory verses and my Bible worksheets and stuff like that. I wish you could come to kid's church some time. Maybe somebody else can do your preaching one day and we can all go together, you, me, and Ms. Miracle."

Boston picked up the ball again and tossed it, but this time Peaches watched it go. She walked over to the couch and jumped up beside Jake, then blobbed onto her side as if to say she'd had enough playing for now.

Boston retrieved the ball and held it in the air for Peaches to see.

"Come on, girl. Come on."

She threw it again.

In response, Peaches closed her eyes and snorted.

"What about all the other kids?" Jake said. "Did you make any friends your age?"

Boston came and sat cross-legged on the floor in front of Jake.

"Friends my age are overrated."

"Overrated?" Jake squinted at her. "Has anyone ever told you that you talk like a grown-up?"

She paused, serious. "Mommy and Daddy used to tell me that all the time."

Jake kicked himself, but Boston's momentary lapse into contemplation passed quickly.

He prodded her again. "So, kids?"

"Not really."

"Hmmm."

CHAPTER 8

Jessica sat on the second-floor patio of apartment 305 of the Bradford Place apartment complex with her head leaned back. She savored the warmth of the sun on her cheeks and the opposing coolness of the Sunday afternoon breeze worming through her naked toes. On the patio table beside her, a glass of unsweetened iced tea reposed creating a sweat circle underneath itself as droplets of condensation tumbled down its side like so many infant waterfalls.

Below her the grass was overgrown – the landscaping company was having difficulty keeping up with the growth spurts that were the result of an abundance of recent showers – but Jessica found it charming.

The lawn was peppered by dandelions and Snodgrass and the effect was the appearance of a meadow outside her back door. Of course, there was only fifty feet or so if it before the wood-slatted fence and Osigian Boulevard on the far side, but if she pretended hard enough, she could imagine it going on for miles and miles. Between her building and the fence, a Bradford pear tree was rooted – hence the name of the complex; they were planted all over – and the leaves rustled in the wind like a brook cascading over rocks. Soon summer would be upon them, the air would be stifling and still, and the gnats and mosquitos would emerge like a pestilent army making being outdoors a miserable prospect. Jessica was determined to enjoy every day like this one for as long as she could.

She stuffed a wisp of hair behind her ear and closed her eyes, remembering the adorable child from her class that morning. Her first impression of Boston when she was dropped off by the pastor's secretary, Nancy, was that the child was too young to be in the class.

She recalled the moment.

Jessica had made her way to the door and spoke softly to Nancy as Boston ambled into the classroom and pulled out a chair three seats away from the nearest child at the table.

Jessica examined the child. "I think she might be in the wrong class, Nancy. This is the class for six to eight-year-olds."

Nancy epitomized the Southern grandmother type, and Jessica had no doubt everyone who met her got the same impression. She had been secretary of the church for twenty years, and Jake Wilson was the second minister she'd served in that capacity. Though Jessica was relatively new to the church, she had chatted with Nancy on a few occasions and was impressed with her straightforward wisdom and the ability she possessed to make anyone feel at home in her presence.

Nancy leaned in close and placed a warm hand on Jessica's upper arm.

"I know she's little," she said under her breath, "but she's nine."

Jessica looked over at the child whose petite frame had convinced her she could be no more than four and a half, maybe five, years old.

Nancy continued, her voice even lower than before. "That's Boston. Her last name is Evans, but she's Pastor Jake's new daughter." This last word she said with gentle emphasis.

Jessica understood. There were few, if any, of the churches' attendees that had not by now heard the tragic story of Boston's family and learned the role their pastor was taking on as a result, but Nancy spoke as if all of this was new to Jessica.

"This is her first Sunday with us and Jake's worried about her. She's a sweet little girl. Smart as can be, but..." she trailed off and cast that grandmotherly gaze at Boston who so far had not interacted with any of the other children.

Jessica nodded. "Don't worry, I'll take good care of her."

After Nancy left, Jessica strode over to where Boston sat with her face cupped in her hands. The girl watched the other children yammering and playing. She kneeled by Boston's chair.

"Hi, Boston. My name's Jessica. Jessica Maracle. I'm glad you're here this morning, honey."

Boston forced a smile. "It's nice to meet you, Ms. Miracle."

Jessica noticed the mispronunciation but said nothing. She was sure Boston would figure it out from hearing the other children call her name.

"Well, it's nice to meet you too." She was impressed with the child's manners. "You know, I was thinking, every week I get one of the kids to be my helper during Bible story time. Would you like to be my helper this morning?" When Boston looked dubious, she hurried to add, "You don't have to say anything. I just need you to put some pictures up on that felt board over there when I ask you to."

The corners of Boston's mouth turned up a fraction of an inch, and she nodded, causing her ponytail to bob up and down.

"Good." She stood up and walked to the front of the semi-circular table where the children sat. "Okay, everybody, let's get started. Boys and girls, I want to – eww, Kyle, don't eat that! – as I was saying, I want to introduce you to someone new. This is Boston," she indicated the blonde to her left, "and this is her first day with us. Can we all say hi to her?"

The kids said "hi" in a disjointed chorus, and Boston waved a timid hand in greeting.

"Boston, this is Katy, Talia, Ben, Kyle, and Dustin."

When story time came, Jessica ushered Boston to the front of the class and showed her the felt-backed pictures and the correct order. The story today was about Peter walking on the water to meet Jesus, and at regular intervals, she gave Boston a nod. Boston caught on with ease and placed each picture on the board in turn adding a visual element to the story. There was the Apostle Peter and Jesus in robes, a small fishing boat in heavy waves, and a couple of lightning bolts to signify the storm. Boston placed one of the bolts nearly atop Peter's head which drew laughs from all the children and Jessica as well. Boston gave the first big grin Jessica had seen.

At the end of class, Jessica asked Boston if she would like her to go to children's church with her. Boston agreed, so instead of going to the "big service" – as the kid's called it – she went and sat with Boston.

Jessica wasn't sure if Boston was so much drawn to her, as the other way around. She'd felt instant camaraderie with the girl, a camaraderie perhaps born of suffering. Though her own experience of pain had been much different than Boston's, there was no doubting the familiar haunted look in the child's eyes. It was a look that was recognizable to anyone who had endured loss, and Jessica's heart hurt to know the child was dealing with such a terrible thing at such a young age. Nevertheless, Jessica seemed to hit it off with the girl, and found herself unwilling to leave her side. This sweet child deserved someone to be there for her, to comfort her, and though she didn't want to overstep her bounds, she thought that sticking close to Boston on her first day was something appropriate for her Sunday school teacher to do.

She opened her eyes and took a sip of her tea. It tasted mildly bitter with a hint of lemon, the way she liked it, and she closed her eyes again letting her mind drift.

Painful memories came unbidden, and she steeled herself against the familiar assault of negative emotions, remembering the lead up to her own tragedy of sorts.

Craig Maracle had been a charmer. He was the kind of guy that appeared to tower above men taller than he was. And it was the first thing Jessica had noticed about him. He was fully at ease with himself and the world around him, and he drew women like a magnet.

It was the spring break of her senior year at the University of Alabama, and she had allowed her roommate to talk her into going to the redneck Riviera, aka, Panama City, Florida. The place was a tourist trap for beach goers, and come summertime, the city attracted a constant influx of party goers and sun worshipers from Georgia, Alabama, even Mississippi. It had food, bars, fun, and plenty of trouble to get into. The native Floridians didn't vacation there. They had better sense.

Jessica wasn't into the party or drinking scene, though at the time, she would drink on occasion. However, her college roommate, Lexi, drank most all the time and seldom missed any chance she could find to party hard. After agreeing to come with her, Jessica felt it was her solemn duty to keep an eye on the girl and make sure she didn't pass out in public or run off with some loser who would use her and abuse her. It was ironic now, looking back.

On the third night of their getaway, they decided to go to a beachside bar named Sharky's, a local watering hole and eatery established by a former local lifeguard. The sun had just creeped beyond the horizon and stars were already shining in the clear, moon-filled sky. In the distance, the waves rolled onto the beach, but they couldn't be heard over the blaring noise of the Michael McDonald wannabe blasting some blues tune from a Rhodes keyboard set on a stage and surrounded by enough speakers to suffice for a Led Zeppelin concert.

But the night was a tolerable, if humid, eighty-three degrees, and Jessica and Lexi reclined at a table near the tiki bar gossiping and laughing and talking about boys and annoying teachers.

By ten that night, Lexi was three sheets in the wind and could hardly speak without a slur. After some convincing from Jess, she had taken a cab back to the hotel which was only a couple of blocks away, otherwise Jessica would have insisted on accompanying her. But the night had grown cooler as the hours had ticked away, and the music had diminished to a tolerable volume as the artist chose more ballads than hard rock anthems or whining blues pieces. Jessica had no desire to leave so – perhaps against her better judgement regarding Lexi's safety – she had stayed.

She ordered a fresh Mr. Pibb, kicked off her flip-flops, and ran her feet back and forth lightly over the wooden deck beneath the table, allowing the grains of sand to roll under the balls of her feet like a gentle, exfoliating scrub. The waitress returned with the Mr. Pibb and asked if she'd like anything to eat as well. Jessica shook her head no, and the waitress walked off to continue her rounds with the other customers.

Jessica was busy contemplating her life choices and the benefits of the teaching degree she was seeking, when a group of young adults caught her attention. At first glance, she thought they were perhaps a little older than her, maybe early to mid-twenties, slightly past college age. The newcomers strolled to the bar, punctuating the air with their laughter and merrymaking. Jessica watched them long enough to see several of the women take seats on bar stools while the three men stood beside them talking and ordering drinks.

It was an odd little party, not for their behavior, but for their overall appearance. Each in turn was clean-cut, the women with expensive cocktail dresses, designer jewelry, and high-end hair dos. The men were a mirror to them, a couple adorned with ties and all three wearing sports jackets despite the heat. They were out of place amongst the other clientele clad in shorts, halter tops, and bathing suits. It was like they had stepped out of a magazine ad, and the notion was so compelling that Jessica momentarily considered it. After all, wouldn't magazines do photo shoots on beaches? Maybe they were all here for a shoot.

She smiled, amused with herself, and turned away, but not before her eyes made flicking contact with a dark-haired man in the group, the one without a tie. She thought nothing of it and stared out towards the ocean which now reflected the moonlight in luminous, undulating streaks where not blocked by wispy clouds. How glorious – if unlikely – it would be to one day own a cozy cottage on the seaside.

A shadow fell over her table.

She looked up, expecting the waitress, but instead met the eyes of the dark-haired man from the bar.

"Hi. I don't mean to interrupt your contemplation, but I think I saw you smiling at me earlier."

Jessica blanched, struck by his blatant forwardness. He had gotten the wrong idea. She started to protest, but he held up a hand before she could speak.

"No, it's okay. I get that a lot." His smile grew wider, revealing teeth so flawless she thought they had to be veneers. "I guess you want an autograph, and I'm happy to oblige. Do you have a napkin I could write on?"

Jessica's mouth fell open and she finally managed a couple of words in response.

"Excuse me?"

Jessica felt suddenly giddy and not a little off-balance. The guy was handsome, no doubt, but she was reasonably knowledgeable about pop culture, and she couldn't place his face. If he was famous, she didn't know it.

"Who are you?"

"I'm Craig." He held out a hand which she took without thinking. His grip was strong, yet gentle, and his hands were smooth, no marks of manual labor. Definitely a pretty boy, not that she couldn't tell that by looking at him.

She giggled and immediately hated herself for it. "No, I mean, are you famous?" She shrugged. "If you are, I don't know you. Sorry, Craig," she whispered conspiratorially, leaning forward for him to hear above the din of the nightlife, "I wasn't actually smiling at you."

She watched his face for a reaction, feeling pleased with herself. Whoever this guy was, a little bite to his ego would be good for him. But he didn't reveal the slightest offense. In fact, he laughed.

He pulled out a chair and sat without invitation.

"That's okay," he said. "I'm not actually famous."

Despite herself, she laughed. Jessica found herself charmed by this stranger. He was handsome, silly, and she had no idea if he was a man of good character or not. She had no plans to get together with anyone. She'd always been much too serious minded for shenanigans, and she'd sworn to herself from her first day as a freshman that she would complete her degree before giving time over to dating. No distractions, no silly boy games. If she worked hard, kept her nose in the books, and took enough classes to give Sir Isaac Newton pause, she could complete the core of her degree in two and a half years and be ready for a possible internship by the third. But that didn't mean she couldn't flirt, she reasoned. And besides, beach romances never lasted.

He spoke again. "Truth is, I just wanted to meet you."

She cocked an eyebrow. "You're not with any of the ladies from your entourage?"

He shook his head without looking that way.

"Heck, no. I prefer blondes like you."

Two of the girls he'd left at the bar were blonde, both lovely, and if she could read their body language correctly, all of them would be more than happy to be with Craig. In fact, a few of them had been shooting surreptitious looks over at her ever since he made his way to the table. And no matter how much they tried to conceal it, the jealousy peeked through.

She gave him an incredulous look. "Those two are blondes, moron."

The playful insult pleased him, and he sat a little taller.

"Right, but you see, there's a very specific shade of blonde that I'm attracted to, and they just don't have it. In fact," he made a square shape with his fingers as if framing her face, "I'd say you fit the bill just about perfectly." Now it was his turn to lean in and whisper. "Besides, I think theirs are dye jobs." He cut a mischievous grin, and Jessica felt her heart skip a beat.

"You're terrible."

"I don't deny it." His expression turned semi-serious but didn't lose the easy nonchalance that seemed to ooze from his pores. He placed his hands on the arms of his chair. "Seriously, though. I really did just want to meet you. I hope I wasn't too forward."

"You certainly weren't shy."

"No, I guess not. So, can I ask your name?"

For some reason, she thought about lying, but pushed the thought aside. Years later, she would wonder if it was some sort of self-protective instinct.

"Jessica."

"Jessica," he repeated. "I've always liked the name Jessica. It seems sort of – I don't know – regal, I guess. Like it should belong to a queen."

She scoffed. "Now you're being melodramatic."

He was quick to the defense. "No, I'm serious. It's a nice name."

"Thanks." She was surprised how at ease she felt with him in just a minute's worth of conversation. Surprised, and a bit nervous. "So, the truth. Why aren't you with any of the ladies you came here with?"

He laughed a bubbly, infectious laugh, and looked askew at them.

"They're nice girls, but not really my type. They're coworkers. And besides, they're all drama queens."

Jessica threw off the sexist remark for what it was, a farce. It was evident in his expression.

"What makes you think I'm not a drama queen?"

He shrugged. "I'm holding out hope."

"So, coworkers. Do you live here?"

He shook his head and raised a finger at the waitress across the deck. "No. We're here for a work conference."

"A work conference? Seriously? Who chooses Panama City for a work conference?"

"Exactly," he grimaced. "That's what I said, but my boss is kind of a wild party guy. We're from a small CPA firm in Atlanta, do mostly corporate work."

She thought of Lexi. "Yeah, my friend I'm here with is the same way. So, this boss of yours, does he only hire young, attractive people?" She regretted the words as soon as she said them.

But Craig nodded, then paused as the waitress strode up to the table. "Can I get a Diet Coke, please? And the lady?" he gestured at Jessica.

"I'm good," she said to the woman, who walked away with a "sure thing".

"Anyway, yes," Craig continued. "He has a habit of hiring young, attractive women. Terrible, I know, but like I said, he's an unconventional boss. That's him over there in the red tie."

Jessica examined the man. He was slim and athletic, probably Craig's age or younger. She had an instant impression of a rich kid straight out of business school that had found his niche in the accounting world and surrounded himself with pretty girls, fast cars, and all the luxurious accoutrements money could buy.

"I bet he drives a Ferrari," she murmured.

Craig smirked. "Corvette, actually. Mine's the Ferrari."

She laughed. "Are you for real?"

"No. I drive a Nissan. But he really does have a Corvette. What about you? You seem like the play-it-safe kinda girl. I'm betting you drive a..." he considered "...Prius." He tilted his head as if studying her like a police profiler. A moment later, he nodded. "Yep. Definitely a Prius."

She affected offense. "Please. I wouldn't be caught dead in a Prius."

Craig raised his eyebrows. "Mysterious. Okay, now you've *gotta* tell me."

"I drive a VW."

He moaned and made a show of covering his face with his hands. "Please tell me it's not a Bug."

"No, it's not a *Bug*." She said the word with distaste. "Don't get me wrong. I would happily drive a classic Beetle, but those new things are shameful replicas in my opinion." She puffed out her chest in mock pride and tilted her nose up with an air of sophisticated snobbery. "I drive a Golf."

He leaned forward, a twinkle in his eyes. "A GTI?" he said with respect.

But she shook her head. "Better. It's an R."

Craig flopped back, clutching his chest. "Oh, dear. It's a miracle. I've finally met a woman with great taste in automobiles."

"Be careful," she laughed. "Saying things like that will get you labeled as a chauvinist. Besides, I bought it used. I'm not a successful CPA. Just a broke college student, but my dad helped me buy it, and yes, I do love it."

He leaned forward and their eyes held. Jessica felt her heart flutter.

She sighed and forced the memory out of her mind. She was right about one thing. Beach romances never lasted, although the one with Craig had lasted longer that she would have thought.

Her eyes fell to the ring finger on her left hand. The empty ring finger.

CHAPTER 9

The following day dawned with the typical mad hustle and rush of a Monday. Jessica pulled into a parking space in front of Quail Run Elementary School at seven forty-five, exited her car, lifted her bag onto her shoulder, coffee in the other hand, kicked the car door shut, squeezed the lock button on her remote, and made her way inside feeling much like what she imagined a pack mule must feel like considering the weight of the books and materials in her bag.

She made her way down the hall to her classroom, deposited her burdens, clicked on the lights and set about preparing for the arrival of her fourth-grade students.

The morning passed in a blur of English and math, and by the time lunch arrived, she craved a good, hot meal. Unfortunately, she brought a sandwich from home – BLT – that she considered less than sufficient for her now rapacious appetite. Typically, she ate in her classroom, but today, her body was crying out for pizza, and the cafeteria at Quail Run had decent food. It was a no-brainer and she headed off to the cafeteria.

She passed through the line with the students, picked up a slice of rectangular pizza, a side salad – a choice singularly neglected by the students – and made her way to the register. She paid for the food and a bottle of water that she pulled from a bin next to the checkout and threaded her way through the students towards the tables reserved for teachers. She was about to sit down when her eyes fell upon a cute little waif with a sheaf of platinum hair sitting off to herself at the end of her class table. A half-eaten sandwich lay in front of her as she bent over reading a book.

Boston. Jessica recognized her immediately. They didn't discuss school yesterday and she had had no idea the child attended her workplace. She veered from the teachers table and crossed to where Boston sat.

"Hi," she stood in front of Boston who had yet to look up from her reading. The child did so now, and her face lit up with surprise.

"Hi." She folded her book closed and set it down beside the remains of her sandwich.

"Can I sit with you?"

Boston nodded vigorously. "Of course."

Jessica set her tray down and angled her legs under the bench seat. "Why are you sitting by yourself?"

Boston's countenance fell a little and she shrugged.

"Are you having a hard time making new friends?" Jessica asked gently so as not to be overheard by anyone else in earshot.

Boston shrugged again. "I just haven't felt much like it."

Jessica nodded. She didn't want to push. Boston had been through so much. Maybe she just needed time. Jessica changed the subject, nodding at the book that was face down on the table.

"Watcha reading?"

Boston lifted the book from the table to show Jessica the cover. "Percy Jackson. Have you read it?"

"I've seen the movie," Jessica winked.

"I got it from the library. It's pretty beat up." Boston looked morose as she examined the book. It was indeed in very poor shape. The paperback cover was faded, and the pages were yellowing from age and multiple stains. Even closed, it was evident that dozens of pages had been dog eared throughout its life at the Quail Run library.

"You like to keep your books in good condition?"

"Oh, yes," Boston said. "Everything has to be just right. No folds and no fingerprints and especially not bending the side."

"The side? You mean the spine."

Boston looked at the spine of the book as if considering this term. "Yes," she nodded. "Cause it holds the book together like the bones in your back."

Jessica grinned. "That's right. So, you like to read?"

The little girl nodded. "Mommy and Daddy read to me every night and they taught me how to read too. Reading was my favorite." She trailed off, a wispy sadness clouding her expression.

Jessica's heart broke and she grasped for something, anything to help Boston not sink into a melancholy reverie. "Do you know what my favorite book was when I was a kid? The Lion, The Witch, and The Wardrobe."

Boston sat up straighter. "I've heard the name, but I haven't read it. What's it about?"

Jessica leaned forward. "Well, it's about four kids that go to a magical land and have a big adventure with a lion that can talk. And you know what?" Jessica tapped the copy of Percy Jackson lying on the table, "Kids that like fantasy usually love it."

They finished out lunch talking about books and Pastor Wilson and what Boston's life was like now that she lived in Warner Robins. When the bell rang signifying lunchtime was over, Boston cleared away her trash and returned to the table.

"Thanks for eating with me, Ms. Jessica. I had a good time." She stood for a moment as if in a moment of indecision, then suddenly leaned over and hugged Jessica. Without another word, she turned and went to line up with her class, leaving Jessica staring after her.

BOSTON CLIMBED IN THE back of the Santa Fe, tossed her backpack in the opposing seat, and burst into immediate talk.

"I saw Ms. Miracle today, and guess what? She sat with me at lunch. Wasn't that nice?"

Jake perked up. "Really? Your teacher from church?"

"Yep. She's a teacher at the school, too."

"Huh." Jake scanned the Quail Run Elementary schoolyard in hopes of catching a glimpse of Jessica Miracle. He saw several teachers assisting children to their cars, but not the one he was looking for. He felt an immediate pang of disappointment. The car behind him tooted its horn and Jake realized the vehicle in front of him had pulled away. He put the Santa Fe in gear and accelerated towards the school parking lot exit.

"Hello?"

Jake snapped back to attention and glanced at Boston in the rearview mirror. He had to reach up and adjust it downwards to be able to see her petite face. She was scowling.

He turned onto Smithfield Church Road. "I'm sorry," he said. "What were you saying?"

Her voice was mildly chiding. "I said, Ms. Miracle told me all about the school codes today and what they all mean."

"What school codes?"

"You know, the code words they use when they talk over the speakers. They tell you when something's wrong."

"Oh, okay. I see."

"Right. So, do you want to know what they are?"

Jake looked in the mirror and grinned at her excitement. It was amazing what little things could brighten a child's day, and at this point, Jake was glad for anything that made Boston smile a little bit. The little girl had been through so much, more pain and sorrow than many adults, and there'd been so little smiling and laughter out of her since her arrival. The effect was a breath of fresh air, especially two days in a row. It seemed he owed Jessica Miracle a debt of gratitude.

"Of course," he said, his excitement now matching her own for different reasons.

"Alright. What do you think a code blue means?"

"Hmm." Jake thought. "I'm going to say code blue means they've run out of food in the cafeteria."

She giggled. "No, silly. A code blue is a kid that's hurt. And what do you think a code orange is for?"

He pretended to think it over. "An outbreak of the measles."

His joke fell flat.

"Orange means an active shooter."

"Okay, that's disturbing," Jake said.

If Boston thought so, she didn't say it. "Alright, now, a code black is a tornado warning. Do you have those here? Have you ever been in a tornado, Mr. Wilson?"

"Sometimes we have them. And no, I haven't been in one, but my parents have."

"Were they scared?"

"Oh, yeah. Terrified. At the time, they lived in a mobile home. They were pastoring a small church in South, Alabama."

"What city?" she broke in.

"That *was* the city. It was named South."

"That's weird."

He laughed. "I agree. Anyway, the mobile home was right beside the church, and one day the weather got really bad, and Dad said he glanced out the back window and saw the pine trees beyond the cemetery..."

"There was a cemetery?"

"The church had a cemetery behind it. Mostly for members. It wasn't very big, a couple of acres."

Her voice came back shocked. "I don't think I would like to live by a cemetery."

"Oh, it's no big deal. There was another time when I was eight or nine that we lived in another place by a cemetery. I used to go out and ride my bike all around the headstones and around the paved pathways."

"Don't you think that's kind of rude?"

He studied her briefly in the mirror. "Yes. Probably. Anyway, back to the tornado. Dad saw the pines back there bending so far, he thought they would snap in two, and that's when he heard the sound. Everyone always says a tornado sounds like a freight train, and Dad said that was exactly right. He yelled at mom to come quick – she'd heard it too – and they both ran out the front door to go to the church."

"Cause Jesus was there?"

He laughed. "Jesus is with us everywhere, not just at church. No, the church was brick. Mobile homes don't have a foundation like a house and they're light. They're more prone to damage from bad winds. But the church, though small by church standards, was still a lot bigger than the mobile home, and they knew they'd be safer there. They went out the door of the trailer and down the front steps from the porch, but by the time they reached the sidewalk, they both saw the tornado coming.

"Mom described it to me once. She said it was the most terrifying thing she ever saw. That huge funnel cloud spinning like a giant top, sucking up trees and debris and everything else in its path. Later, they found one of the county school buses that had gone missing in the storm. It had been parked outside the home of the driver – I don't remember the man's name. But the tornado picked it up and they found it two miles away lying on its top, a crumpled mess. The only thing left of that guy's house was the concrete foundation. Him and his wife had both been inside."

He glanced in the rearview mirror to see Boston's eyes were as large as saucers.

He continued. "It was right on top of them, and Dad did the only thing he could think of. He put his arms around Mom and said 'Jesus, help us'. He really thought they were going to die."

"What happened?" Boston's voice was nearly a whisper.

"A miracle," Jake said. "One of the real-life, true to God miracles Dad said he's seen in his life. When that tornado hit the edge of the church property, it picked itself up in the air like a giant pogo stick, swirled over them high in the sky, and sat back down on the other side of the cemetery."

Boston was dumbfounded. "Are you serious?"

Jake nodded from the front seat. "I promise. God protected them that day."

Jake expected a reply, but Boston remained silent. When he pulled up to a stoplight, he turned to see her staring out the window. She stayed that way for a long time. At last, she spoke.

"I'd like to see a miracle one day." Her tone was longing, almost melancholy.

"Maybe you will," Jake said.

Again, there was a long lull in the conversation.

"Mr. Wilson? Why didn't God protect my parents that day on the road?"

An agonizing sorrow seared Jake's chest, and he immediately regretted sharing the story. Her words crushed him, took the wind out of him. It was his turn to wait a long time before answering. Finally, he said the only thing he could.

"I don't know."

They were both silent after that for the remainder of the ride.

They arrived home and Boston went immediately to the back yard to play in her "fairy castle" with Peaches. Jake busied himself cooking stir-fry, all the while keeping an eye on them both through the kitchen window.

He expected the child to be sad after the conversation in the car, but by the time she and Peaches came inside, she was back to being cheerful. In fact, she went on and on about Jessica again until Jake made her go wash her hands for dinner.

His amazement at the change in Boston persisted. Ever since she had met this teacher, there had been a noticeable improvement in her demeanor. Jake was sure that for whatever reason, Boston and Jessica Miracle had formed a bond, and if that meant seeing Boston happier and dealing better with her loss, then he wanted her to spend as much time with Jessica as possible.

But he immediately questioned himself. *Is that really all you want?* He turned off the stove as the chicken in the pan sizzled, picked up the pan and set it on a burner that was cool. He considered the thought and his own motives.

Yes, that was all he wanted. There was no questioning his attraction to Jessica. She was lovely. Jake doubted there was a man in the world that wouldn't be attracted to her, but that didn't mean he had ulterior motives. Did it? He sighed. The truth was, she was way out of his league, but even so, no woman in her right mind wanted to be a pastor's wife without feeling a special calling for it. It was a tough gig. Jake had seen the stress of it that his own mother had dealt with for all those years of ministry.

No, Jake wouldn't wish that kind of life on anyone. Then he realized what an idiot he was being. Marriage? *You're in a dreamworld, dude. You don't even know the girl.*

He wiped his hands on a towel, pulled a couple of plates down from the cabinet and placed them on the table beside the glasses and silverware he had already laid out. He crossed to the refrigerator.

"Do you want juice or milk?" he called to Boston.

He heard her shut off the water in the bathroom.

"Juice, Mr. Wilson," she called back.

He opened the door and lifted the orange juice container from the inset shelf in the door. He also grabbed the pitcher of tea, closed the door with his elbow, and carried them both to the table as Boston skipped back into the kitchen, Peaches in tow.

Jake grimaced at the dog. *I think I lost my best friend,* he thought. Ever since Boston's arrival, Peaches was her constant companion.

They ate, Boston picking at the chicken and rice while avoiding the vegetables like all nine-year-olds. Afterward, they sat at the table, Peaches begging for scraps and Boston tossing her a few pieces of chicken when she thought Jake wasn't looking.

Jake stood and began to clear the table.

"Listen," he said. "I think you really like Ms. Miracle."

"I do," the response was immediate.

"Well, what do you think if maybe we ask her to do something sometime so you can spend some more time with her? I think it's good for you."

"Definitely," Boston said. Her voice was full of excitement, but there was something else. From the corner of his eye, he noticed Boston watching him carefully. Finally, "Maybe you like Ms. Miracle, too."

Jake paused in loading a plate into the dishwasher, made eye contact with Boston who was casting him a knowing smile, then looked away, his cheeks warming.

"I like all my members." As soon as he said it, he realized how fake the excuse sounded. *Only in it for the kid, huh? You're not fooling Boston and you won't be fooling Jessica.*

He wrestled with a bit of guilt, but it didn't last long. Boston could think what she wanted. She needed to be around Jessica, and he owed her that much. Besides, what was wrong with Jake enjoying the company of a beautiful young woman? Since becoming a pastor, he'd been on two or three dates at the most, and never with members. That kind of thing never ended well, and it certainly wasn't what he was after now, but that didn't mean he couldn't enjoy it. Pastors needed friendship too. And so what if he had a mixture of ulterior motives with the good? He knew that mostly it was about Boston. Yep, definitely about Boston.

CHAPTER 10

On Wednesday afternoon, Dewey Knapp picked up the phone and dialed the number he had obtained for the New Creation in God denomination state offices in Atlanta. He had to go through a couple of people before he got to the right office.

"William Tyndale's office. How may I help you?" the secretary said on the other end of the line.

Dewey cleared his throat. "Yes, I need to speak to Bishop Tyndale please."

"May I ask who's calling?"

"Just a concerned member," Dewey said.

The secretary paused on the other end and Dewey thought she might press him, but she didn't. "Hold one moment please," she said.

There was a brief pause as he was put on hold, a droning recording playing in the background which he ignored, then, "This is Bill Tyndale."

"Bishop Tyndale," Dewey said, pitching his voice higher and assuming a friendly tone. "I hope I'm not taking too much of your time. I'm sure you're a busy man."

"That's okay, Mr.?" he trailed off expecting a name.

"If it's okay, I'd rather not say." He kept it light, innocent.

Tyndale paused in the same manner as his secretary. "Alright, then. Is there something I can do for you?"

Dewey offered a melodramatic sigh. "I have to be honest, sir. I don't like to do this kind of thing, but I'm a little concerned about my pastor."

Another wary pause. "Oh? In what way?"

"Well, do you know Pastor Jake Wilson at Life Church in Warner Robins?"

Tyndale was instantly guarded. "Mm hmm."

"I don't think Pastor Wilson is acting in the best interest of the church financially."

"How so?" Tyndale said.

"You're probably aware that we've been approved for a new building program." Dewey knew full well that he was. He knew the procedures for getting such approval would have to pass through the Bishop's purview. "I'm a businessman, and money matters are what I do best. It's going to take a lot of capital for the project, and it seems to me Pastor Jake isn't pushing the people hard enough for money."

Tyndale laughed on the other end of the phone. "Really? You want him to ask for more money?"

"I'm not sure what's so funny about that," Dewey said flatly. Tyndale's response grated him, and he struggled to keep the annoyance out of his voice. He reminded himself that he needed to be ingratiating. He waited, not saying anything further, lest he betray his emotions.

After a moment, Tyndale finally spoke again. "I'm sorry. It's just that most people that complain about pastors and offerings say they're trying to get too much, not the other way around."

With Tyndale's apology, Dewey felt he'd gained control of the conversation. Now Tyndale was on the defensive and Dewey could be more forceful.

"Like I said, I'm a wealthy businessman. I take into consideration matters others may overlook or not consider of great importance. Frankly, Pastor Jake isn't insistent enough about the necessity of giving. The appeals he gives during the offertory give the people too much freedom to give if they *want* to. He needs to stress tithing and really push hard for financial backing."

Dewey could almost sense the other man's irritation, but Tyndale kept it in check, the mark of a wise man.

Tyndale said, "The State Council and I have been over your church's finances in light of the new building project. I assure you everything is well within the parameters we feel are necessary to keep any unnecessary burden off the church. I...appreciate...your call, but I think everything will work out just fine. Is there anything else I can help you with?"

So that was how he was going to play it. Dismissive. Dewey was impressed by Tyndale's ability to stay calm and downplay the complaint. Dewey would let it slide for now. When he spoke again, he resumed his friendly bearing.

"In that case, I feel much better, sir," he said. "Like I said, I'm just a concerned member. I love my church and my pastor, and I want the best for all parties involved."

"I'm sure you do," Tyndale said. Dewey knew the man was thinking just the opposite.

"Well, thank you Mr. Tyndale. I appreciate your time. I hope you have a blessed afternoon."

He clicked off the line without waiting for a response. Overall, he was pleased with the conversation. Tyndale might not be taking any action yet, but the seeds had been planted. Now on to phase two.

THE FOLLOWING SUNDAY, Jake made it a point to accompany Boston to her classroom early. He rapped on the doorframe of Jessica's Sunday school classroom. She looked up from her preparations with a smile. No one else was there yet. Boston bounded into the room and wrapped her in a hug before bouncing off to the table and grabbing a box of crayons and a coloring book from a stack laid out there.

Jessica came to him and offered her hand. Jake shook it, his fingers lingering a little longer than the socially acceptable norm as he pulled it back regretfully. He laughed the awkward laugh of a smitten schoolboy, and for all his self-talk, he knew in that moment that his interaction with Jessica was at least fifty percent for Boston and fifty percent for himself.

"Ms. Miracle, I never got to thank you..."

Jessica's nose crinkled and she offered a small chuckle. "Did you just call me Ms. *Miracle*?"

Jake's smile faltered. "Yes."

"Did Boston tell you my name was Miracle?"

He nodded, and she laughed harder than before.

"My name is Maracle. M-A-R-A-C-L-E."

Jake looked pointedly at Boston, his ears and cheeks warming. "Well, Boston was sure it was Miracle, and to hear the way she goes on about you all the time, I'm inclined to believe it."

Jessica glanced at the little girl and there was no mistaking the affection in her eyes. "She's a sweetheart. I just love her to death."

"Yeah. I never got to thank you for her first Sunday. She said you really took a lot of time with her and even sat beside her in kid's church. I'm not sure if you know how much that meant to her."

She leaned against the wall next to the door. "I know what it's like to be an outsider in a new place."

"Yeah? Did you move a lot as a kid? Military brat? Just about everyone around here is here because of the Air Force base. Not a lot of natives, I've found."

She waved it off.

"No. Not me. I came here for the job. Did Boston tell you I teach at her school?"

Jake nodded. "She did. And thanks for that, too. Sitting with her at lunch, I mean." He paused, glanced at his watch. Plenty of time before he needed to be back at the main sanctuary. "What about your husband?" he said.

She cocked an eyebrow and caught his eyes before looking down. "Subtle," she said.

Jake was immediately horrified. "Oh, my gosh. No, I didn't mean to...I'm sorry...that probably sounded like I was trying to hit on you."

She squinted, mischievous. "Weren't you?"

Boston had paused in her coloring and was watching the two of them with a scowl. "You hit her, Mr. Wilson?"

Jake found his tongue wouldn't work. Jessica came to his rescue.

"No sweetheart, it's just an expression."

Boston went back to her coloring, satisfied.

Jessica turned back to Jake, her expression more serious. "I'm not married."

He wanted to respond but was unsure what to say. He checked his watch again but forgot to actually look at the time. "Oh, I gotta go. Still some last-minute sermon prep to do for this morning."

Another little girl ran through the doorway, bumping Jake's leg in the process and pushing him a little closer to Jessica. He felt a fresh surge of heat in his face.

"Hi, Jessica," the newcomer called.

"Hi, Katie," Jessica said.

The girl joined Boston at the table, and they began to chat.

"Anyway, um...so...yeah, me and Boston were talking the other night and she really loves being around you and I think she needs positive female influences in her life. We thought maybe we could get together sometime and hang out. It would be good for her."

Jessica eyed him shrewdly. "I don't know. I love spending time with Boston, but I'd want to make sure *all* parties involved were interested in spending time together."

TAKING BOSTON 105

Jake sputtered, "Um...yeah...definitely." He backed away, bumping moronically into the door jamb in the process.

She giggled as he rubbed the back of his head.

"In that case," she said, "Boston already has my number. Maybe you can call this evening and we'll set it up?"

"Boston has your number?"

"Yep. She calls me all the time."

"She does?"

"Oh, yes. I know everything about you Jake Wilson."

"You do?"

But instead of answering, she pushed him away from the door and closed it softly in his face. Only at the last second before it fully closed, she said, "Bye, Jake. Talk to ya soon."

JAKE SPENT THE AFTERNOON counting down the hours until he felt it was okay to call Jessica Maracle. He had already gotten the number from Boston, but it had taken several hours for him to realize Jessica had been kidding about the kid calling her. Yes, Jessica gave the number to Boston in case she ever wanted to talk, but Boston didn't have a phone. She would have to have used Jake's, which she hadn't. The realization did nothing for Jake's confidence; he acted foolishly in front of her this morning, stammering, and klutzy. He could preach sermons in front of hundreds of people, but he turned into a yammering doofus in front of Jessica.

He sighed, frustrated with himself. At least she had been flirting with him, and that gave him hope. He didn't claim to be a relationship expert, but he knew flirting when he saw it, and that was *definitely* flirting, even if he'd made a mess of it on his side.

Not interested in a relationship?

The still, small voice caught Jake off guard. It was so like his own inner voice, but there was a subtle difference, one that he had grown accustomed to over the years. It was the same gentle prompting he often felt during sermons as the Lord led him with what to say. Did the Holy Spirit just bust a joke on him? Godly sarcasm? The idea made him laugh, then consider, then laugh again.

Okay. Maybe I was fooling myself a little, Lord. But she seems great, and it's for Boston, too. At least fifty-fifty. Or maybe sixty-forty. He could almost imagine God laughing at him.

Promptly at seven o'clock that evening, he dialed Jessica's number on his phone. He shifted his weight from one foot to another, swaying slightly as the phone rang. She picked up on the third ring.

"Hello?"

"Hi. Is this Jessica?" His stomach was all butterflies and churning dread.

"Hi, Pastor Wilson." Jessica's voice was smooth, collected, maddeningly calm.

"I was just calling like you said. You know, to set something up," he said.

"Of course. I had an idea this afternoon. I was thinking if you two are free next Friday evening, I could cook for us. Maybe play some board games or watch a movie? How does that sound?"

Jake faltered. She was talking funny, off somehow. He recovered after a moment. "Yeah. I...I think she'd like that."

"Good. Maybe you could text me some things she likes, and I'll see what I can do."

"Right." He hesitated again, unsure of himself. "Hey, is there somebody there with you?"

"No. Just me. Is everything okay?"

"Um, yeah." His brows furrowed.

"Great. I'll text you my address. How does seven sound?"

"Fine," he said.

"Alright. See you guys then, Pastor Wilson."

Jake hung up the phone, confused.

CHAPTER 11

Dewey Knapp exited a dark Mercedes and approached a posh-looking restaurant. The marquis read "A Touch of Italy". A small brass plaque inlaid in the brick beside the front door said: Owned and Operated by Dewey Knapp.

Dewey came to the front door, paused. Something on the plaque caught his eye in the shimmer of the pre-noon sun. He reached over and wiped away a smudge of fingerprints from the plaque with his sleeve, then unlocked the front door and went inside.

He took a moment to savor the aroma that still lingered after last night's dinner crowd. Of all the businesses Dewey owned, this was the place where he kept his main office. Mostly because he could order food any time he wanted it, and Dewey loved fine food. His protruding waistline was evidence of that.

He locked the front door behind him and marched through the restaurant, empty at this time of day. An hour from now, the eleven o'clock crew would be arriving to prep for opening at noon. But for now, he had the place to himself, and he basked in the peace and quiet as he did every day during the work week. Traversing a short hallway next to the kitchen entrance, he unlocked his office door and...

"Surprise!"

Dewey came to a startled halt as the door swung open to reveal most of the restaurant employees crowded into his office. Balloons and streamers decorated the office along with a large happy birthday banner. A man in his mid-thirties, Tanner Wallace, approached Dewey from the center of the group, his hand outstretched. The crowd behind him continued to beam. Dewey noticed a large cake sitting on his desk.

He ignored Tanner's outstretched hand as the young man stopped in front of him. Tanner hesitated, unsure of himself based on Dewey's scowling expression.

"I...uh...hope you don't mind," the young man said. "We knew it was your birthday and wanted to do something special for you."

Dewey offhandedly calculated the date and realized it was indeed his birthday, something which he never celebrated – Dad thought birthdays were superfluous – and dismissed the realization with some annoyance.

Now everyone in the room was staring at him with unease.

He spoke, his voice low and menacing. "How did you get in my office?"

TANNER WALLACE, HEAD chef at A Taste of Italy, stood with his chef's hat in his hands in front of the teak desk behind which sat a scowling Dewey Knapp. The office previously decorated resplendently with birthday decorations had been returned to its normal state at the gruff insistence of its owner.

"Mr. Knapp, I'm so sorry sir. We found out it was your birthday and...well, you've done so much for us all. You gave me a chance fresh out of chef school. We're appreciative. We wanted to do something nice for you."

Dewey's scowl deepened. "Do you know the problem with what you did, Chef Wallace?" It was obvious by his expression that he did not. "You showed a lack of respect for your employer."

Tanner was at a loss. "I...I don't understand, sir."

"How did you even manage to get a copy of my office key?"

Tanner hung his head. "Last week when you were interviewing for the new hostess position. I just swiped them from your desk when you had walked out to get someone else. Ran across the street to Lowes and was back before you even knew I was gone."

"So, you also cheated me out of time you were supposed to be on the clock?"

Tanner blanched a mixture of terror and offense. "Absolutely not, sir. I would never do that to you. I worked through my breaks the next day to make up the time."

Dewey considered this. It was a step in the right direction, but too little too late. It was improper to rearrange time without prior approval, and it still didn't excuse the main issue. He didn't even bother to address the time problem.

"Irrelevant," he said.

This earned a half-crazed look from Tanner that tempted Dewey to laugh, but he was teaching a lesson and had no desire to add mockery into the mix. This would be for the betterment of the kid's life, and ridicule would undermine the gravity of the lesson.

"The real issue is lack of respect. I care nothing for birthdays – I never celebrate mine – but I can understand the sentiment. I'm not *wholly* unfeeling. However, you took your employer's keys without permission and made an unauthorized copy of said key. You must see the problem with that."

It didn't appear that Tanner did. Dewey helped him out.

"It borders on criminal behavior," he said.

"What? You can't be serious, Mr. Knapp."

"I'm afraid I am. If you plan to succeed in life, I can give you no better lesson than to always respect those in authority over you."

Tanner opened his mouth to say something, shut it, opened it again, and shut it again. The motion made Dewey think of a fish. *An apt description,* Dewey thought. The kid had hooked himself with his own conduct, and now it was time to let him off the hook and back into the pond.

Tanner gripped his chef's hat so hard that it was crumpled into a tiny ball of fabric. He managed to speak at length.

"I'm really, really sorry, Mr. Knapp. My intentions were good. That has to count for something, right? Please, it won't happen again."

"That much you're right about. I'm firing you."

This time, Tanner didn't restrain himself. "This is total bull crap! You've got to be joking. Tell me you're joking."

Dewey narrowed his eyes. "I'm deadly serious," he said.

"But Mr. Knapp, I've worked my butt off to become a chef, and there's not a lot of opportunities for a chef in Georgia unless you live in Atlanta. What am I supposed to do? Be a cook at McDonald's?"

Dewey cocked an eyebrow. "I'm sure you're qualified."

"I have a family. My little boy is only a year old. You're going to kick me out of my job over me trying to be nice to you? That's the stupidest thing I've ever heard."

It was Knapp's turn to show his anger and he stood. Tanner cowered a bit, withered under Dewey's disdainful gaze, but he managed to draw himself up, a man desperate to fight for his livelihood and his family.

Dewey said, "Let me tell you something. My dad was a military man, then a civilian mechanic right here at Robins' Air Force Base. And he always taught me that the most important thing you can have in this life is respect. Respect makes the world go round. 'Get respect for yourself, son. Be the man that others look to for leadership. Be kind, and hard when you need to be, but above all, don't let anyone disrespect you'. You've disrespected me and the position I entrusted you with."

Tanner glared at the older man with undisguised hatred. He threw the chef's hat down on the desk and turned to walk out. He stopped and looked back when he reached the door.

"You're a jerk."

Dewey shrugged. "And you're unemployed. Come by tomorrow at noon. I'll have your last check at the hostess stand."

Tanner exited, slamming the door behind him.

AT FIFTEEN TILL SEVEN on Friday night, Jake and Boston walked up the sidewalk to the three hundred building of the Bradford Place Apartment Complex. Jake carried a homemade pecan pie in a tin with plastic wrap over the top while Boston chatted non-stop, hyper with excitement. Once in the pass-through, they took the stairs up to apartment 305. Boston rang the doorbell, bouncing with anticipation. After a few seconds, the door opened to reveal Jessica in a simple t-shirt and jeans and bare feet. She still looked stunning.

Boston lunged forward and threw her arms around Jessica, squeezing her. "Ms. Jessica!"

Jessica laughed, and her eyes flicked up for the briefest of moments, met Jake's, and fell back to the little girl. Was there something to that look? Jake wondered. Perhaps it was just his imagination, but it seemed almost – he struggled for the word – pained.

"Hi," she said, picking Boston's petite frame up with ease and cradling her close before pretending to drop her, catching her inches before her feet plopped back onto the floor.

"Ms. Jessica, I really like your apartment. Did you know you have a pool? I could see it through the fence. And when we passed by the dumpster, Mr. Wilson had his window down and it stank soooo bad. But that's okay because the trees are really pretty and everybody has trash so what can you do?" Her attention was drawn to the interior of the apartment, and she moved off looking around.

Boston kept jabbering as she moved away, taking it all in. Jake and Jessica shared a knowing smile.

"Thanks so much for this," Jake said. "She's been looking forward to this all week." He produced the pecan pie, which was already in plain sight, with a flourish. "I know you said just to bring ourselves, but I thought it would be nice to bring something sweet."

Jessica's face turned sour. "Oh, no. I'm allergic to pecans."

Jake balked. "Really?"

"Heck, no," she laughed. She took the pie from him and examined it closely, lifting the side of the plastic wrap to take a deep breath. "Mmm. Did you make this?"

Jake beamed. "One of the few things I can do other than preach is cook, so, yeah."

They had lasagna, one of Boston's favorites, and she proved it with her voracious appetite. Most of the meal was spent with Jessica listening between mouthfuls to stories from Boston about Peaches and her fairy castle – lighted gazebo Jake had explained – and tales of classes and school friends and every random thing that came to her mind.

Jake asked Jessica about her work as a teacher. Boston was in the fourth grade. Jessica taught fourth – though Boston was not in any of her classes – so their lunch hours were the same and Boston had taken to eating with Jessica every day.

Afterwards, they pulled out a set of Uno cards Jessica had in a kitchen drawer. It had been ages since Jake had played Uno, and it was a first for Boston. She had a blast making Jessica and Jake draw four, and though she didn't win until the third game, her laughter and joy were contagious.

At the end of the fourth game, Boston excused herself to go to the bathroom and Jake leaned back, stretching his arms over his head. Jessica got up and went to the kitchen to grab another diet Dr. Pepper.

"Want anything?" she asked.

He smiled. "No, I'm fine."

She pulled the can from the fridge and walked back to the table, popping the top in the process. She returned to her seat, deftly pulling the chair out a little with one foot and sitting across from him again.

For a moment, there was no conversation, just two adults sitting at a table.

Jake had spent his adult life with one goal in mind: become the best pastor possible. He always considered his flock to be his priority and as such, had actively avoided dating. He had no problem getting dates in high school and even college, but he never let anything get serious. His priority was always his vocation, something he considered the highest call he could have. So, he had always kept things platonic. And for more reasons than one.

True, there was the dedication to his call, but there was also a very real consideration. Temptation. There was no lack of what you would call American red bloodedness in Jake Wilson. And temptation had more than once reared its ugly head to go farther than would be Godly with a member of the opposite sex. Despite his dedication to amicable interaction with women, there were a couple of occasions where someone had made it obvious that they wanted more from him physically and Jake, especially in his twenties, felt the pull all too strong for human intimacy. Hormones could be a powerful thing, and in some ways, they terrified him. Nothing would derail a pastor's career faster than a moral failure of a sexual nature.

Now that he was in his thirties, his drive had diminished somewhat, but still, he took a page out of Joseph's book in the Bible who, when tempted by the wife of Potiphar, fled from temptation.

Although Jake had never actually run away, he had put up mental walls and emotional barriers.

But Jessica. He'd never felt so pulled to anyone in his entire life. He would never confess it to Boston, but ever since that first Sunday when he picked her up from kid's church, Jake couldn't stop thinking about the elegant blonde now sitting across from him. And now, so close, in her home, Jake wanted nothing more than to gawk at her, drink her in, be closer to her than he'd ever been to anyone.

JESSICA LOOKED UP AND their eyes met across the table. The connection was there. She could feel it as strongly as if it had been a live wire connecting them with electrical current. It had been the same when they had met eyes at his and Boston's arrival. In a flash, Jessica felt the pull to him, knew he felt it too, and had dropped her eyes from his.

Now, their eyes meeting again – something she'd been careful to avoid up to now – the pull was positively overwhelming. He was a handsome man. She knew that since the first time she'd seen him preach. Perhaps not in the Hampton's pretty boy way of Craig Maracle, but in a rugged and responsible way that had the effect of making him more desirable. That coupled with his dedication to his job and now to Boston, a child he had willingly altered his life to take in and raise as his own, only increased her attraction to him.

A flick of remembrance and fear pricked her heart, and she reminded herself it could never be. She crossed her arms and leaned back in her chair, creating more space between them. She was not suitable for Jake Wilson, and he was too good of a man for her to allow herself to be his downfall. He deserved better than that. Better than her.

She'd gotten carried away last Sunday allowing herself to flirt with him, to lead him on. She was so caught up in the moment that she didn't consider the ramifications of being with a man like Jake Wilson. It pained her that she had done it and that her coldness could now be a source of confusion for him, but it was better this way.

Her body language must have worked, because he leaned back as well, mirroring her movement. There was an awkward tension in the air, and she said the first thing that came to mind.

"How's Boston been handling things?" She kept her voice low so that Boston wouldn't be able to overhear should she approach unnoticed.

Jake's eyes met hers again, but without the underlying sexual tension he exuded previously. He was all business now.

"She's having nightmares. Almost every night."

"About the accident?"

"She won't talk about the details, but I think so. She wakes up screaming."

He rubbed a hand over his face and smoothed back his hair. Only now did Jessica notice that behind the handsome exterior, there was very real exhaustion. It shouldn't have surprised her. It had to be exhausting. Jake had a full-time job as pastor of life church, was a single man, and just inherited a troubled child dealing with the worst possible kind of loss. Jake was stretched thin.

Boston came back in the room and stood by Jessica's chair. Jessica put an arm around her.

"Listen, I have an idea," Jessica said. "What would you think," she gave Jake a pointed look, "if it's okay with Pastor Jake…"

"Just Jake," he said.

"…Jake, that you come over tomorrow afternoon and we can go swimming in the pool? Then you can stay over with me tomorrow night and I'll bring you to church Sunday morning."

Boston beamed. "Can I, Mr. Wilson?"

Jake hesitated. "I don't know, we wouldn't want to put Ms. Jessica out."

"Really, I'd love to have her," she said, giving Boston a squeeze. "Tell you what. Bring her by tomorrow at eleven and we'll go swim then have some lunch. What do you think Boston?"

"I think that would be *great*!"

Jake considered. Jessica watched him, hoping he would choose to take some time for himself, because no matter if she could never be with Jake Wilson, that didn't mean she didn't find him amazing. And one simple thing she could do, was watch his child so he could recuperate.

"Okay," he said. "I guess we can do that."

CHAPTER 12

Jessica stood next to a pot of chili simmering on the stove in her diminutive kitchen and examined the recipe for the tenth time. She counted off each step, drawing on memory to know she had followed the directions correctly. It was the moment of truth.

She decided on chili because it was another of Boston's favorites, though she'd never cooked it herself. Her mom had emailed her special recipe, always a favorite of Jessica's, and she'd gone through each step meticulously. Sure, it was a little warm out for chili, but who cared?

Jessica lifted the ladle off the spoon rest, gave the chili one last stir for good measure, then raised a scoop to her lips. She blew on it for a second or two, tested the temp with her finger, then took a large sip of the concoction. Immediately, her face twisted into a grimace, and she spit it back into the pot.

Okay, something got missed. That was most definitely *not* the chili she remembered Dad making, but she could have sworn she did everything right. It appeared they would be getting takeout. The doorbell rang, and she dropped the ladle into the pot, grabbed a hand towel, and wiped her lips as she went to the door.

Boston was radiant in a yellow sundress and matching sandals. Jake stood behind her, an easy grin on his face.

"Hi, Ms. Jessica. Are you ready to go swimming? There were a lot of people there when we drove by," Boston said.

Jessica shut the door behind them as Jake handed her a Target shopping bag.

"What's this?" she asked.

"Bathing suits," Jake said. "We bought several. Neither of us were sure what size she wore."

Boston sat on the floor and kicked off her sandals.

"She didn't try them on?" Jessica said, taking a seat on the sofa, Boston at her feet.

"No," Jake said. He meandered into the kitchen where the chili was still simmering. "I didn't think she could do it by herself. Some of those things looked complicated with all the straps and spandex."

"You didn't go in and help her?"

Jake turned and looked at her with horror. "Of course not. That would be weird."

Jessica rolled her eyes.

Boston interjected. "Yeah, Mr. Wilson. You gotta come in there too, silly."

Jake gave an involuntary shudder that drew a laugh from both.

He leaned over the chili and took a big whiff. Behind him, Jessica pulled swimsuits one at a time from the bag. She held up the first one to Boston who was now standing. It was enormous. At least three sizes too big. Jake couldn't possibly have thought it was remotely close to the girl's size.

She whispered so only Boston could hear. "What was he thinking?"

Boston shrugged and shook her head. She obviously thought Jake was just as crazy as Jessica did.

"What is this, chili?" Jake called.

"Yes..." she looked up just in time to see him pull the ladle to his mouth and take a big gulp of the chili that she had just spit in. She crinkled her nose in disgust.

"I think it needs a little cumin."

Boston noticed Jessica's expression.

"What's wrong?" she said.

Jessica began to chuckle. "I'll tell you later."

Jake rummaged through the spice rack until he found the cumin, then proceeded to pour a generous amount into the pot. He stirred it, then took another sip.

"Ahh. Much better."

Jessica didn't have the heart to tell him. "Knock yourself out," she said.

She took Boston by the hand.

"Come on. Let's go try these on." She picked up a couple of the best prospects, a bright blue one-piece, and a two-tone pink and black with a swim skirt, then led Boston to her room.

The pool at the Bradford Place Apartments was L-shaped with a medium-sized fountain in the crook of the L. Boston waded in the shallow end of the pool while Jessica lounged in a beach chair soaking up the sun.

It was a hot, humid Saturday, and the residents were out in force. More than a dozen children played in the pool and nearly every chair and table were occupied.

Jessica kept a watchful eye on Boston, but the little girl had assured her she was a good swimmer and had proved it upon their arrival by making a couple of expert laps around the shallows.

Jake had purchased a set of arm floaties and insisted that Jessica make Boston wear them. When Jessica pulled them out and began to blow them up, Boston looked at her as if she'd just sprouted two heads.

"I'm not a baby," she protested.

Jessica stifled a laugh at her diffident defiance. "I know, but Jake wants to make sure you're safe."

Boston crossed her arms. "I've been swimming since I was three and we had a pool at home."

Jessica sighed. She too thought Jake was being overprotective, but she didn't want to contravene his authority. Still, Boston looked so miserable that she couldn't help but cave a little.

"Fine," Jessica said. "I'll watch you really close, you show me you can swim fine, and we'll forget about these." She brandished the floaties, one half full and the other still flat and airless.

Boston gave a confident nod and hopped right over the edge of the pool into the water without even testing the temperature. As soon as she was in, she began swimming like a pro. It was dog paddling, but she was adept, and Jessica had no doubt the girl had spent a lot of time in the water. After a couple of quick laps, Boston swam to the edge where Jessica was watching her with a huge smile.

"Good?" Boston said.

In response, Jessica opened the valve on the half-filled floatie and squeezed the air out.

"It'll be our little secret," she told Boston with a wink.

Later, Jessica rose from the lounge chair she had been reposing in and walked to the side of the pool. She eased down, careful not to scrape her legs on the rough siding, and dangled them in the water. The water, chilled and refreshing, offered a welcome reprieve to the heat of the day. She scissored her legs in a figure eight, savoring the swishing of the water around her calves. Sighing with pleasure, she pushed her sunglasses up on top of her head and raised her closed eyes to the sun. The warmth washed over her face creating a satisfying counterpoint to the cold water.

After a moment, she lowered her head again and scanned the pool until she found Boston. The tiny girl splashed among some other children at the far end of the pool, still safely within the shallows away from the branching of the L where the deep end lay.

All around were the sounds of laughter. Families played, and from a distance came the delicious smell of someone grilling on one of the many barbeque grills located throughout the complex.

The thought of families caused her a pang of sadness, and she remembered Craig. There was a time when she felt her whole life was ahead of her. It seemed so long ago now, but here she was, thirty-one years old and divorced with no real prospects. She felt cliché thinking it, but it was true that she felt her biological clock was ticking away; and with each passing year, it moved down faster and faster. She knew she served a God of grace and mercy. She knew that Jesus was the solution to every problem and disaster life could throw, but in her dark moments, she struggled with questioning if her current predicament was God's punishment for the things she'd done. What if her lack of a family was just the harvest of the bad seeds she'd sown?

Overhead, a jet from the base cut a streak across the sky, triggering a sonic boom, causing many in the pool to jump, startled. Jessica shook off the jarring noise and was back in her reverie in a matter of seconds. Her thoughts turned to Jake, his gentle disposition, his drive to be the best pastor he could be. But he wasn't driven like Craig. He wasn't willing to step on others to accomplish his goals. No, he was completely unlike Craig. Where Craig had been a charmer and bad-boy type, Jake's personality was softer. Not less manly, and not overly mellow...just good.

In a perfect world, Jessica may have dreamed of what a future with Jake Wilson would have been like, but she didn't give it any serious thought or consideration. She just wasn't the person for him. So much of the church world looked down on divorcees. Especially when it came to holding positions of leadership. The stigma was a far cry from what it had been in days past, but there was often still prejudice there. Just being involved with a single pastor as a divorced woman could have negative repercussions on Jake's ministry. She admired him too much to ever allow that to happen. Then there were her own shortcomings and the accompanying shame. No. She would enjoy their friendship and savor the camaraderie they shared. But she dared not allow herself to hope for more.

BOSTON WAS REELING. She felt oddly out of place and time, her mind struggling to grasp reality. It was like she was experiencing the wreck all over again – rolling down the hill, the sounds of her parents' screams and her own.

You couldn't spend any amount of time in Warner Robins without getting somewhat used to the periodic sonic booms, but they could still be jarring, even for the most seasoned residents. Boston was not a seasoned resident. The crashing boom triggered something in her mind. Without warning, it was as if she was back in her family's SUV, and the explosive wake from the plane merged into the crashing sounds of trees smacking into their vehicle as it careened down the steep incline. She was there again. The fear, the terror, the disorientation; it all came back with a dreadful life of its own and paralyzed her with horror.

The other children had long since gone back to their normal play, but Boston remained with her hands clamped over her ears, her eyes squeezed shut, trapped in a living nightmare. She was desperate for the screeching metallic banging to stop. Desperate for her mind to be free from the torture of what had happened. She wanted to scream, to beg for help, but she couldn't release a sound. Her breathing came in fast gasps, and she bordered on hyperventilation.

Without realizing it, she slipped beneath the water, and somehow the cool liquid rushing over her head and the comparative silence of being underneath it helped to pull her a bit from the trauma. It was a shocking revelation, and for a moment she just stayed there. With little thought, she sprang to the surface, gulped in a deep breath, and plunged down again. With each breathless second of submersion the memories faded a little more and she regained some semblance of steadiness. Her young mind clung to the water as if clinging to life. She held her breath for as long as she could, until her lungs were burning for air, then popped back up at the last possible instant. It was a choice between breathing or sanity.

Gasping a large mouthful of air again, she dipped back under. Unable to keep herself under without expelling all her reserve oxygen, she allowed herself to float face down on the surface. It was easier that way. And finally, there was calm; only the sound of dull thudding and splashing as it came to her from underneath the surface. Her composure came back to her, and still she stayed there.

JESSICA, ABSORBED IN her thoughts, observed none of this. The scream, however, ripped her from her lull.

"Hey," an elderly woman shouted, "is that girl okay? Someone grab her!"

Jessica's eyes burst open, and she frantically scanned the pool as a flurry of movement started at the other end. Multiple adults and several of the kids in the pool moved towards a shape floating face down. Jessica recognized the blue swimsuit and blonde hair.

"Boston!" She heard herself scream the name as if it were coming from someone else and plunged into the water. She half swam half thrashed her way across the pool, fighting every inch for greater speed. It felt like it would take forever. Her emotions plunged into cold, hard desperation, a sinking feeling in her gut of utter despair.

A child nearby Boston, an older boy, realized all the commotion was directed near where he stood and he lunged for Boston, grabbing her by the waist and hauling her from the water. Boston's head came up and Jessica could see her eyes were closed. A new surge of panic smothered her.

Boston's eyes flew open.

"Hey, what are you doing?" Boston said. She shook the water from her face and hair, still in the boy's grasp. The boy dropped her, startled. Boston, free of his grip, plunged under the water again, but popped right back up, sputtering.

Jessica reached her and grabbed her up in a hug, squeezing Boston tight to herself.

"Oh God, oh God, oh God," Jessica muttered.

The crowd started to back away. Crisis averted.

Boston pushed hard against Jessica's chest so she could lean back a little.

"What's wrong, Ms. Jessica?" She looked frantically all around to see what the source of the commotion was.

"Are you ok!?" Jessica's voice was a breathless whisper.

Boston finally realized she was the center of all the attention.

"I'm okay." She looked around, her cheeks burning with embarrassment. "I'm okay," she said again.

Later, Jessica cast a sidelong glance at Boston. The little girl was dry, in fresh clothes, and sitting at the small kitchen table in Jessica's apartment. The child seemed okay. In fact, she seemed perfectly fine.

Still, Jessica was worried about her.

Jessica finished smearing peanut butter on the second half of the peanut butter and jelly sandwich she was preparing for Boston. She tossed the butter knife in the sink, then placed the two pieces of bread together. She paused, then mentally kicked herself for tossing the knife away since she hadn't cut the sandwich yet, pulled another from the silverware drawer, and cut it into two equal triangles on the paper plate already sitting on the counter.

She picked it up and walked over to Boston; sat down beside her. Boston was busy drinking grape Kool-Aid from the cup Jessica had given her earlier. On the television in the living room, cartoons played in the background, but the sound was down low almost to the point of being inaudible. Still, Boston watched with rapt attention.

Jessica took a moment to calm herself for the fifteenth time since leaving the pool. Ever since she saw Boston floating face-down in the water, her stomach had been in knots, and no amount of controlled breathing was helping her feel much better.

Boston looked over at her, then down at the sandwich. "Aren't you going to eat Ms. Jessica?"

"No, honey. I'm fine." She didn't think she could eat if she wanted to.

Boston shrugged, picked up half of her sandwich, and took a hearty bite, smearing a little jelly across her upper lip which she then wiped away with her hand instead of the napkin lying beside the plate.

Jessica watched as Boston ate. Finally, she couldn't help herself any longer. "Are you sure you're okay?"

Boston stopped chewing, then spoke through a mouthful of sandwich. "I *promise*, Ms. Jessica. I'm okay." She emphasized the word "promise", though it was hard to understand through the half-chewed bit of sandwich in her mouth.

"So, tell me again what happened."

They'd been over it three times already, but still, Jessica was unsettled – afraid there was more to the story.

Boston finished chewing, swallowed, and took a sip of Kool-Aid. She set the cup down and looked at Jessica as if she were the adult comforting the child.

"It just scared me, okay? The explosion."

"The sonic boom from the plane."

"Yes," Boston said. "I thought it was a big crash."

"And it reminded you of the car accident." Jessica wasn't questioning, just confirming details they'd already been through. Jessica hated saying the words. Hated even bringing up the painful subject.

Boston's intelligent eyes met hers. The whites were still bloodshot from the chlorine in the pool, and it had the effect of making Boston look like she'd been crying.

Jessica's heart ached for the little girl. No matter how brave a face she was putting on, there was pain behind her expression.

"It didn't remind me of the crash." Boston paused, considering her words. "It was more like...I was there again."

This was new. And troublesome.

"Like you were experiencing it?" Jessica said.

Boston shrugged.

"Has that ever happened before?"

Boston shook her head no.

"Well..." Jessica trailed off, unsure what to say. She'd lived near the base for long enough to recognize the similarity in Boston's experience and what soldiers went through with PTSD, and she worried that despite her protest to the contrary, Boston may have had flashbacks before.

She would have to tell Jake. Of course she would. The thought of telling Jake about Boston having a PTSD flashback on her watch terrified her. Not to mention having to describe why the entire group of residents at the pool had thought Boston had drowned – without floaties. But this was not about her. It was about a child that was going through a horrendously traumatic experience. A child that might be suffering more internally that what she was letting on.

One thing Jake told Jessica was that he had been hesitant to take Boston to a therapist, not wanting to further skew any normalcy which Boston may have felt with her new life, although he certainly wasn't against it. He had read several books about how kids dealt with grief, and one thing common was that kids could be much more resilient than adults. Boston appeared to be coping. But now, Jessica reflected, maybe it was time to take the step of going to a therapist.

Jessica intended to stay quiet, to let the conversation end for now and allow Boston to eat in peace. On television, Bugs Bunny pulled a fast one on Elmer Fudd. Boston watched and chewed.

The prompting of the Holy Spirit came unbidden, a gentle impression.

Ask her, daughter.

Her immediate thought was a firm *no*. She had zero desire to push Boston on this. It was bad enough that they'd already breached the subject of her parent's death. She didn't want to subject Boston to additional pain. Not after today.

The prodding came again, tender and soft.

Ask her.

Jessica clenched her hands in her lap, squeezed hard, then tried to relax them and allow the tension to seep from her body. She continued to fight the Lord for several minutes before giving up, knowing it was a losing battle.

"Boston. May I ask you something?"

Without looking away from Bugs, Boston said, "Sure Ms. Miracle."

That brought a smile to Jessica's face. Boston still insisted on calling her that from time to time, like a pet name, and suddenly, the tension left, replaced by a supernatural peace that now was the time for this conversation.

"You know, we've never really talked about what happened to your mom and dad. Would you like to?"

Boston turned to her and gave a sad smile, paused for a long moment, then began to unload.

CHAPTER 13

Jake started Boston with a therapist the week following the incident with the pool. Since then, she had improved significantly.

From how Jessica understood Boston's attempt at an explanation, the little girl was repressing her feelings about the crash and her parent's death. Boston also felt guilty, like it was somehow her fault – standard survivor's guilt. And she finally came clean about the dreams. Every night, she dreamed the same thing: rolling down the hill in the SUV, the jarring stop when they hit the final outcropping of trees, her parents mangled bodies, covered in blood, lifeless. She would call to them again and again, begging for a response. Nothing. They were just…gone. As fast as that.

The therapy had worked wonders for her. The therapist was a kindly woman in her mid-forties and a graduate of Boston College. She had suggested two sessions per week. One session was for Boston alone, and the other was for them both. It drew them closer together as they shared in a safe environment. And slowly, ever so slowly, Boston's nightmares began to subside.

Jake was thankful that she had no recurrences of flashbacks like the one at the pool, but the therapist was careful to warn them it was still a possibility. At least now, Boston would be aware of what was happening and be better equipped to deal with it. They would have to cross that bridge if and when it came.

They sat together in two armchairs in the therapist's office off South Houston Lake Road, Boston on the left, Jake on the right. Boston was all but swallowed by her chair, only her shoulders and head visible above the large, winged arms. Her short legs dangled from the edge, and she kicked them as she talked, performing a silent dance of her own contrivance.

The therapist, Dr. Donna Uling, spoke from her seat across from them. "You really like Ms. Jessica, huh?"

Boston nodded, her braid – it wasn't terrible, Jake was getting better at doing her hair – bounced in tandem with her nodding. As was often the case, the conversation had turned to Jessica Maracle. Jessica had been a Godsend for them both. She had bonded with Boston in a way that was truly beautiful, and she was always available to watch her, or to take her to the movies, or just to listen when the child needed to talk. In some ways, Jake felt jealous of her connection with Boston. Boston opened up to Jessica in a way that she didn't often do with him, and it pained him a little. Still, he wouldn't have it any other way as long as she had the support she needed. But in his deepest thoughts, he was also jealous of Boston. Of her connection with Jessica.

From the beginning, he had been attracted to Jessica, and his affection for her had only grown over the subsequent weeks and months. But although Jess was amazing with Boston, and although she had grown to be a good friend to Jake, there was something unmistakably standoffish in her behavior towards him. He didn't know why, but she kept him at arm's length emotionally. There were times when Jake was convinced that the attraction was mutual, but like a wisp of vapor, it would disappear as if blown by the wind.

Jake and Jessica had taken Boston to Wild Animal Safari in Pine Mountain a couple of weeks back. Jessica had been there before, but it was Jake and Boston's first time. They spent the afternoon riding through a "safari" enclosure several miles long in a rented park van painted like a zebra with bars instead of windows on the sides. Through these came a constant bombardment of lolling tongues from a plethora of exotic animals anxious to be hand-fed from the large souvenir cups full of food – some kind of grass or hay pellet – that you could purchase at the ticket counter. Boston was wracked with fits of hysterical laughter every time an overzealous goat, bison, or watusi would overshoot the food and slime her fingers or palm instead.

"Hand sanitizer, hand sanitizer," she cried out gleefully until Jessica would pass it back to her, rinse and repeat, rinse and repeat.

But the incident that stood out to him that day happened within a segregated section of the park where exotic animals were housed in individual enclosures. A cinder block stone wall roughly four feet tall surrounded a sunken pit where various species of rattlesnakes were kept. Leaning over the top, one could look down upon the slithering occupants without fear of them being able to reach you. Jake had leaned in next to Jessica to see a particularly hefty timber rattlesnake sunning itself and his hand had brushed against hers where it lay on the top of the wall. It was an honest accident, but she recoiled as if shocked and immediately turned away. The reaction was so strong, it gave him pause. Indeed, he felt rather belittled for the rest of the afternoon, until he was able to convince himself he was being ridiculous. Perhaps she hadn't noticed the brush and was just turning away at that moment – *yeah right dude, if you believe that you're an idiot.*

Furthermore, he was perplexed with her cleverly disguised, yet noticeable reticence to reveal details about her past. Any time he would try to make conversation about it, he would get the bare basics, which of course had the effect of making him more curious than ever. But no matter how much he pried, her responses were shaded.

"You don't want to know about me. I'm boring," she would say. Or, "You've been a good Christian man all of your life. I could never equal up to you. I prefer to think my true life began when I was saved five years ago." Or even, "I'd much rather hear about you. Tell me again about what it was like starting as a pastor at such a young age."

Stonewalled every time. Still, that day had been magical for Boston. *My little girl was happy that day.*

His little girl. It had been so easy to think of her that way. Something beautiful and scary and magical had awakened in Jake Wilson, and it was more powerful than anything he could ever have imagined. Before, he seldom gave thought to having children. It was one of those nebulous possibilities of the far future that he had no real plans for. Maybe in another time and another place. But now, he had grown to love Boston as his own. And like any parent, he knew that nothing she could do would ever cause him to love her any less. He would give up anything for her, even die for her.

Dr. Uling was speaking again, and Jake realized he drifted for a moment from the conversation. He forced himself back to the present.

"So, being with Ms. Jessica makes you happy, but you also feel guilty about that?"

Boston stared at the floor and shrugged. Her legs had stopped bouncing and her brows wrinkled in thought.

"Why?" Dr. Uling said.

It took a few moments for Boston to find the words to convey what she felt.

"I don't know. It just makes me sad. Like, maybe it hurts my mommy."

Dr. Uling offered an understanding smile. "Do you think spending time with Ms. Jessica makes you feel like you're betraying your mom because you're finding affection from another woman?"

Boston was sullen. "I don't want Mommy in heaven thinking I left her behind."

"Ah." Dr. Uling considered this for a long time. "How about Jake?" she finally said. "Do you feel the same way about Jake and your dad?"

Boston looked askance at Jake who smiled encouragingly.

"No. Not really. Well, I just...I think...see Mommy and Daddy wanted me to be with Mr. Wilson. You know what I mean? So, it's kind of okay."

Jake was amazed by the logic behind her reasoning. It was flawed, but nevertheless something that might upset the sensibilities of a child.

"What do you think your mom would say about that if she were here to ask you right now?" Dr. Uling said. "Do you think she would want you to be happy, even if that meant spending time with Jessica?"

Bravo, doctor. Jake thought it was a brilliant response.

Boston worked it all out in her head, viewing the idea in a new way.

"I think Mommy would want me to be happy no matter what. Because she loves me."

Dr. Uling gave a gracious smile. "I think so too. I know your mommy loved, loves" – she changed the word to the present tense – "you." Dr. Uling was not a believer. She'd said as much to Jake, but she was respectful of their beliefs, and though she didn't hold to the idea of an afterlife, she had assured Jake she would do nothing that would undermine Boston's belief system.

"You know what else?" she continued. "In that way, your mom and dad live on through you. Everything they ever taught you lives inside you, and the choices you make, the paths you choose, are part of them. So, in that way, they're always with you."

Boston took a surprised breath, "Just like Jesus lives in my heart, Mommy and Daddy do too."

Dr. Uling smiled, but Jake saw her immediate discomfort and indecision. He took over for her.

"You know what, sweetheart?" he said to Boston, "I think that's a wonderful way of seeing it."

Dr. Uling gave Jake a slight nod of thanks.

JAKE LOUNGED ON ONE of the sofas across from Jessica in the "fairy castle" while Boston sat on the bridge; Peaches curled against her hip. She dangled her legs through the slats in the railing, her feet under the bubbling water up to the ankle. Boston had discovered that if she put her feet in the water, the koi would usually come and nibble her toes. It had become one of her favorite pastimes, always accompanied by giggles and a detailed description of every move to Peaches who stayed by her but was otherwise indifferent and usually kept her eyes closed, snoring softly.

Summer was ending and the night was hot and humid, but the ceiling fan in the gazebo did an adequate job of cooling them as well as keeping the gnats and mosquitoes at a minimum. Jake was not an outdoor man in the traditional sense – he had no love for hunting or fishing or camping for that matter – but he'd always liked being in the fresh air and lounging on a beach or under a canopy of trees, and this was as close to an ideal evening that he could ask for without a reprieve in the temperature.

Jessica reclined on the oversized cushions of the opposing sofa, nearly lying down, her legs crossed Indian style, her shorts revealing long, slender muscles in her thighs and calves. She took a sip from the frosted San Pellegrino bottle in her hand then replaced the cap. Jake watched her movements, but mostly he watched her legs – that is until his eyes met hers. She had in turn been watching him which meant she'd noticed his inability to focus above her waist. His ears suddenly burned, and his face tingled with a rush of blood.

He tried to cover it as best he could.

"I was noticing you're in really good shape. You must work out a lot."

She smirked, and Jake had no doubt she saw right through his pitiful subterfuge.

Good job Pastor Jake. You big dufus.

She studied him and her smirk became a full-blown smile. "I do cross fit."

"Ah. The workout of the self-flagellant."

She laughed. "You should try it. You'd love it."

He shook his head adamantly. "Oh, no. I have no desire to see how long I can go until I pass out or puke. I'm quite content to move as little as possible and keep the contents of my stomach."

"Sissy," but her tone was playful.

They both watched Boston as she gave some inaudible detail to Peaches who cracked her eyes just long enough to oblige the child, then went immediately back into her slumber. But Jake also watched Jessica out of the corner of his eye.

Nights like this had become common place, the three of them together, and Jake savored the time with Jessica. She'd become a close friend, and although he knew that she did it primarily for Boston, he wouldn't have traded his time with her for anything. He wasn't a fool. He knew she kept him at arm's length emotionally, but there was still a part of him that hoped one day that would change.

"Tell me about being a pastor, Jake Wilson."

He straightened. "What do you want to know?"

"What's the worst part? What do you hate the most?"

"Like I'm gonna tell a member."

"Come on. I'll be your confidant." She stretched out her legs and crossed them at the ankle. With great effort, Jake was able to not focus on them.

"Well, to be honest, there's nothing I *hate* about it. I mean, yeah, it can be rough sometimes, and probably the worst thing is dealing with drama. Someone's always got some kind of drama going on. This person doesn't like the music we sing, or that person doesn't like the way I preach, or they don't like my tie, or they want us to do more outreach to the community. It's silly the things people get uptight about." Jake rolled his eyes. "Just recently, the State Administrative Bishop called me because he got an anonymous complaint that I wasn't asking for enough offerings."

Jessica offered an incredulous laugh. "Are you serious? Who complains about that?"

Jake's laugh echoed hers. "That's what the Bishop said."

She tilted her head back in thought, her eyes following the spinning fan above. "You know, I think all of that pettiness would drive me nuts."

Jake sat back and examined Boston for a few seconds as she stroked Peaches' ears. The dog made kicking motions with her feet as she slept, maybe dreaming of chasing her mortal enemies – squirrels.

"It can. It used to bother me a lot more in my younger days, but I try to remember that we're all flawed. I have to give other people the same grace God has given me. We have right standing with God through faith in Jesus, not our own ability to be good, or agreeable, or anything else."

Jessica studied him. "Have you ever had a hard time giving *yourself* grace?"

Jake weighed her words.

"Oh, absolutely. I think sometimes that's harder than giving it to somebody else. I believe we're predisposed to self-condemnation.

There's stuff from years ago that still comes back to haunt me. I know God has forgiven it, but that's the thing about sin. You don't forget.

Her expression had taken on a seriousness that wasn't there before. Jake realized Jessica wasn't asking a hypothetical question about how *he* dealt with his past. This was personal to her. With the realization came a sense of weighted responsibility, and he prayed for wisdom to say the right thing.

A sad smile tugged at the corners of Jake's mouth. "I wish it was easy – forgiving oneself. But it's usually not. We just have to keep reminding ourselves that if God has forgiven us, who are we to hang on to condemnation. Jesus knew what He was getting when He saved us, and if He sees us as right, it's our job to try and see ourselves the same way."

She smiled at him then, and he got the distinct impression she knew he was addressing her insecurities. The smile masked her pain, but not quite enough to fully hide it.

"Jess," he said softly, "is there something you want to talk about?"

Her response was too quick. "Me? No. I was just curious." She rose. "I've got some papers to grade. I should get going."

Jake rose as well, but he didn't press her. He had told her the truth, and if there was something that needed to be dealt with from Jessica's past, something that was eating at her, he would leave the Holy Spirit to work on it.

Jess said her goodbyes, hugging Boston and rubbing her nose against Peaches' who'd perked up at her leaving. Jake waved as she pulled from the driveaway.

Lord, be her healer. Let her know it's okay for her to let go of what you've forgiven. With that, he turned and went inside.

CHAPTER 14

Jake sat on the couch with his laptop, legs outstretched onto the ottoman. He was supposed to be working on his sermon for Sunday, but he was mostly watching television and thinking back on his conversation with Jessica.

She was a strong woman. Anyone who met her would know that. But given the abruptness of her departure tonight, he was willing to bet whatever she was harboring was really eating at her. He wanted to help, wanted to be there for her, but experience told him pushing could be a move in the wrong direction.

Boston bounded down the stairs with Peaches in tow, breaking his train of thought, went straight to the back door and unlatched the deadbolt.

Jake eyed her. It was past bedtime and he'd already tucked her in. "What are you doing?"

Boston, already opening the door and stepping out with Peaches, yelled over her shoulder. "I left my tablet at the fairy castle."

His first thought was the tablet could wait, but that's not what came out of his mouth. "Turn the lights on so you can see where you're going."

But it was too late. The glass weather door had already swung shut and he doubted she heard.

Jake set his laptop on the cushion beside him, shoved the ottoman out with his feet, and got up, giving a good, old man groan in the process. He was only thirty-five he thought with some regret. He shouldn't be getting stiff backs and cracking knees yet.

He trundled over and peered out the weather door. Sure enough, he couldn't see Boston at all in the looming darkness, but he could just make out Peaches' white haunches receding in the distance. He flipped on the lights, and the back yard lit up like a small village.

Boston had crossed the bridge and picked up her tablet, turned on her heels, and made her way back towards the house. Peaches had gone to the edge of the water on one side of the gazebo and was busily sniffing around the edge of the pond.

Boston was almost back to the house-side of the bridge when it happened.

Out of the corner of his eye, Jake saw a flicker of movement. Something silvery gray scampered along the northwestern edge of the fence in the corner of the property. Jake could make it out clearly under the string lights along the fence line. An opossum. They were not infrequent visitors to the yard.

The houses on this side of the street backed up to a large, wooded area uninterrupted for a half-mile or so before running into the houses on Avondale drive. The area was a haven in the city for all forms of wildlife and it was not uncommon to see opossums and raccoons. Sometimes coyotes could be heard in the distance offering their jackal-esque calls to the moon or whatever it was they went on about.

Peaches had never been trained as a hunting dog, but there was no denying her nature. She was still very much a pointer, and years of breeding had left a strong prey instinct in her. She immediately perked up at the same movement that drew Jake's attention, and, in a flash, she was up and charging back across the bridge to give chase to the emboldened little invader that dared to trespass on her property.

Peaches and Boston hit the far end of the bridge at the exact same moment. Boston, alarmed by the sudden commotion, spun awkwardly to see what was going on, right into Peaches' path. With no time to veer, Peaches slammed into Boston's legs at full speed, sending them both sprawling. Peaches recovered almost immediately and continued her wild chase of the opossum that was already scrambling over the beck fence to safety. However, Boston went down hard, and her head smacked the handrail with a heavy *thunk* that was audible through the thick glass of the weather door. Jake flew into action.

Four hours later, Jake tucked Boston into bed for the second time that night. It was three in the morning. Boston fell asleep on the way home from the emergency room, and he had carried her up to her room with little more than a stir. She had cracked her eyes sleepily as he laid her down in her bed and pulled her fuzzy cat blanket over her. Jake tucked it under her chin and gave her a soft kiss on the cheek. There was still some blood residue in her hair. The ER nurse had only been able to wipe away so much. He would help her with it tomorrow.

It had taken eight stitches to seal the gash near her hairline. She had taken the numbing shot like a trooper. Jake had thought the bleeding would never stop. He had fairly soaked a hand towel with her blood while on the ride to the emergency room. But in the end, the ER physician said she showed no sign of a concussion or any lasting damage. A little fix up and instructions to keep the area dry for several days – Boston would have to wear a plastic cap in the shower – and she would heal up just fine.

The following morning, Jake woke Boston at nine. She went to the church with him every day during the summer and Jake set his own schedule, but today he had to be at the church at 10:00 for a council meeting, otherwise he would have let her sleep in.

The group arrived for the meeting in the same way all congregations arrive for services: some early, some right on time, and some who are always late and would be even if Jesus had called the meeting personally.

Boston, being the adorable child that she was, was fussed over by everyone. Everyone except Dewey Knapp who seemed uninterested in her accident. They insisted on pampering her and treating her like a princess, bringing her donuts – a regular at council meetings – and even some decaf coffee upon Boston's request. She tried it and promptly decided for orange juice instead.

Nevertheless, Boston ate up the attention, greatly exaggerating her "near death" to the oohs and ahhs of the council members.

Nancy took Boston to her office to hang out when the meeting started.

Jake greeted everyone and followed with prayer in their typical fashion. Then there was a bit of catching up and joking around the table. Jake then called the meeting to order. "There's something exciting I want to share with you guys today."

He walked over to a filing cabinet in the corner of the conference room and pulled a rolled-up piece of parchment with a red ribbon tied fancifully around it out of the top drawer. He came back and set it on the table.

He untied the ribbon and spread out the parchment for all to see. Each in turn stood and leaned in to better view the paper on the table.

"Of course, this is just a fancy copy to show to you guys. The actual originals are still digital, but this is the completed blueprint of the family life center."

They took their time walking around the blueprint, pointing out things of interest, making comments about certain additions or subtractions based on what could actually be built in lieu of suggestions that had been proposed. All in all, everyone was pleased.

The family life center had been a project on the docket for more than a year now. It had been a slow, painstaking process, and after the

State Office had given the go ahead at the first of the year, everything had been put on the backburner with the death of Boston's parents and Jake taking custody of her. Little had been done other than Jake telling the church council that they were approved to begin searching for financing, but before that, Jake wanted to get the blueprints drawn. He had finally received them that week.

After they had looked over the blueprints to everyone's satisfaction, Jake spoke once they were again all seated around the table.

"The next step is to find the financing. We've put out some feelers, but now we're going to get down to business and work out the details. Once that's done, we'll hire a contractor – with the help of the denomination – and break ground."

"Why do we need the denomination to get a contractor?" This came from Dave Wilkes, one of the younger council members.

"Technically we don't, but I promised Bishop Tyndale I would at least consult with them. Thing is, they have churches going up or adding additions all the time, so they have connections with lots of contractors from all over. May be able to get us a better deal or someone with more experience for a comparable price."

The council nodded in approval.

By the end of the meeting, Jake was feeling great about everything. Despite Boston's hiccup last night, her nightmares were improving, and their relationship grew stronger every day. The church was prospering, and apart from his wistfulness that Jessica Maracle would show more than a friendly interest in him, life was good.

CHAPTER 15

The phone rang and William Tyndale's secretary picked it up.

"This is William Tyndale's office; how may I help you?"

Dewey Knapp's gruff voice traveled across the line. "I'd like to speak to Mr. Tyndale, please.

The secretary paused and took a deep breath. "May I ask who's calling?"

This question was completely unnecessary. She knew exactly who it was. His calls had been annoyingly frequent as of late and he'd given up any pretense of anonymity. She also knew Bishop Tyndale had no desire to speak with the old codger.

"This is Dewey Knapp from Warner Robins. I'm calling regarding Pastor Jake Wilson."

The secretary made a motion of clawing her own throat, but when she spoke again, her tone was perfectly professional.

"Sure. If you don't mind holding, Mr. Knapp, I'll see if *Bishop* Tyndale can take your call."

In his office at A Taste of Italy, Dewey Knapp puffed on a Cuban as the line clicked and Christian Muzak began to play. He hated being kept waiting, but at least he was in his favorite place. He chewed a little at the end of the cigar and blew out a couple of smoke rings through pursed lips.

A lot of Christians frowned on smoking, but frankly, Dewey didn't see the problem. Still, for the sake of appearances, he usually didn't indulge in public. But here in his office, he could do whatever he wanted without the worry of nosy busybodies interfering with his personal liberties.

He watched the second hand on his Patek Philippe wall clock tick by. At a full minute and ten seconds, the line clicked again.

"Hello, this is Bill Tyndale."

"Mr. Tyndale, Dewey Knapp from Warner Robins."

A hesitation from Tyndale. "Mr. Knapp. I trust you're feeling better with the situation we previously discussed."

Dewey took a long draw before answering. Smoke drifted out of his mouth in spouts as he spoke. He put on his best attempt at concerned innocence.

"Actually, no. I'm still concerned about the finances of the church, but that's only part of the reason I'm calling."

In his own office, Tyndale pinched the bridge of his nose.

"Really, Mr. Knapp. Being on the church council doesn't make you privy to these types of conversations behind one of my pastor's backs. And frankly, your concerns over the finances of your church are noted, but honestly beyond your purview."

Knapp scowled and held the phone away from his ear long enough to mouth a few profanities. This was the first time Tyndale had taken an aggressive tone with him. He regained his composure and spoke again, his tone conciliatory.

"Yes, sir. I understand, but as I've said before, I know how to conduct a successful business and my concerns are valid. I just want us to face this new project with a strong monetary foothold. You know, we still owe over a million dollars for the sanctuary expansion."

"Sure. I know it's a lot, but again, the State Council assures me everything looks fine. I don't think the church will be overburdened."

"Yes, well anyway, the other thing," Dewey's tones were measured, "Pastor Wilson has taken quite a bit of time off recently.

I'm not sure he's juggling this new fatherhood thing and the church too successfully. He spends far less time at the office than he used to according to my contacts."

"You're contacts. Are you spying on Jake Wilson?"

Dewey gave a noise of shocked offense. "Of course not. But one notices things. Like I said, I'm just concerned."

"Mr. Knapp, don't you think you're being a bit hard? The man lost his best friends and took on the duties of being a single father. Jake's a good man and I'm sure he's doing the best he can."

Dewey Knapp turned on the false empathy. "I understand responsibility. It's not always easy takin' care of necessities, but it's part of life. I recognize Jake Wilson's special situation. I just want what's best for him, and he seems overwhelmed. I love him too much to let him fail."

Tyndale was silent and Dewey could imagine him trying to gauge him from the other end of the line. "Mr. Knapp, have you talked with Pastor Jake about any of this? If you're so concerned about him, maybe he could set your mind at ease, or you could offer to help him in some way."

"Maybe that would be best," Dewey said. "I thought I'd come to you first. I don't want to offend him. I thought maybe an encouraging word from his superior, placed in the right way at the right time, might help him to snap out of his slump."

"I'm not seeing anything to be concerned about, myself." There was a pause. "But I'll keep an eye out. Like I said, though, go to Pastor Jake. I'm sure he'll be happy to address any of your concerns."

The conversation ended and Dewey sat back in his chair, gazing at the ceiling, replaying it in his mind.

JAKE FLIPPED THE PROPOSAL over on his desk and straightened it. The man across from him waited, his expression unreadable.

"Dewey, I was surprised to find out your bank gave the loan for the sanctuary upgrade. Honestly, I didn't even realize you owned a bank."

Dewey affected humility. "I've been blessed. I don't like to make a show of the things God has given me."

Jake doubted that very much.

"I want to thank you for this proposal," Jake lifted the corner of the document with a finger. He cleared his throat. "It's kind of you to...uh...be willing to take a risk with your own business to...um, help us out with a new loan for the family life complex."

Dewey gave a slight nod, his heavy jowls bouncing under their own bulk, the crow's feet at the edges of his eyes furrowed as if squinting into the sun.

"However, I have to say I have a couple of concerns." He watched Dewey for a poker tell; something to clue him in on what was going through the other man's mind, but there was nothing. He may as well have been watching the side of a mountain. Since he offered no response, Jake continued.

"My first concern is the lack of a fixed rate option in your proposal. I understand that loans for churches are considered commercial and from the bank's – your – standpoint it helps your profitability to have an adjustable rate. I'm no expert, but I think we can get financing at a fixed rate for the term of the loan through some of the banking connections the denomination already has in place."

Still no reaction from Dewey. He remained as stony as a hangman. No counter proposal.

Jake went on. "Next is the term-to-amortization ratio. The term is listed at fifteen years, but the loan payments are spread out over twenty. Doesn't that mean that at the end of fifteen years we would be responsible for paying the remainder of the balance in a lump sum?"

There was a crack in the façade. Dewey began to smile, but it was not a friendly smile. There was something cold and calculating about it. It was like a chill had seeped into the air of the office.

"I assure you Pastor Wilson that this is all quite common for this type of loan."

But Jake had done his homework, and he wasn't finished.

"Then there's the issue of these 'other third-party fees' addressed on page ten. I've gone over it several times to make sure I understand the premise. I think it's actually referring to prepayment penalties and termination fees which would prevent us from paying off the loan early or refinancing with another lender at a better rate." A pregnant pause. "Am I correct?"

In all the time Jake had known Dewey Knapp, he had never trusted him. Always, there was something about the man that stirred misgivings in his spirit. Even in council meetings, and despite the usually cheery demeanor the man displayed to others, Jake could sense something unpliable underneath the surface. Now, Dewey Knapp released that hard part of himself, and made no effort to conceal it. When he spoke, his words were laced with a venomous ferocity that unnerved Jake.

"Are you calling me a cheat? I come to you as a businessman with an offer to help you out with a large loan that you need to further your vision of this congregation, and all you do is insult me and accuse me of selfish ambition?"

Jake attempted to remain respectful. After all, the man was an elder, and that was how the Bible told him to behave when dealing with an older man, do so as with a father. He stamped down his growing frustration and annoyance.

"I apologize if you feel I am accusing you. Would it not be prudent of me to seek the best possible deal for our people? Doesn't that make me a good businessman as well?"

But his efforts at easing the older man's hurt pride were a wasted effort.

"You're not a businessman. You're just a young, upstart preacher who thinks he knows more about the business world than someone who's made millions in business over more years than you've been alive. Don't try to sit there in your smug, self-effacing pretense, and act like you weren't accusing me of being a crook. That's exactly what you were trying to do."

"Whoa, come on now, crook is a hard word."

Dewey Knapp stood suddenly and, despite being only 5'9 or so, Jake thought he looked much bigger. For a moment, he believed Dewey might come over the desk after him, so indignant was his appearance. Jake had a fleeting image of Knapp pummeling him with meaty fists. Knapp leaned on Jake's desk with both hands, coming uncomfortably close. Jake resisted the urge to slide his chair back.

"Do you have any idea how much money I've given to this church, Jake Wilson?" He said Jake's name like a curse word.

Extra, extra, read all about it. Pastor of Warner Robins church arrested for throw down with member after insulting him over loan terms and conditions. That's all Jake needed now. But thankfully, Dewey spun and stomped for the door.

"You've made a mistake," he called over his shoulder. "You'll regret this."

Jake was flabbergasted. True, he'd always felt something was off about Dewey, but the man's reaction today was an absolute shock. Something arose in Jake, then. A boldness beyond himself and an authority that he recognized as coming only from the Holy Spirit.

"Stop." His voice came out with authority, surprising Jake and turning Dewey on his heels, though the man still looked like he craved a brawl. "Mr. Knapp, I have known you for a while now. We've always been amiable, but I must say your behavior here today has been unacceptable. I love you, and want what's best for you, but frankly, I'm not going to allow you to take advantage of this church or to think you can treat me so disrespectfully and not stand up for myself.

"Even if I liked the terms of your loan, I still wouldn't accept it. In my opinion, as a member of this church, it would be improper for us to go with your bank. Kind of like insider trading. That being said, I don't want there to be any hard feelings between us. Truly, I am not trying to offend you." Jake felt the veracity of his words. As is so often the case in a confrontation, his anger was mingled with regret, and he perceived the soul of the man standing there. He was concerned not about losing a member, but about the state of Dewey's heart. He spoke in earnest. "Please, don't leave like this. You're a member of my council and beyond that, a person that God loves. A person that I love."

For a moment he thought Dewey might consider this. Thought he might sit back down. Maybe the man would realize he overreacted. But instead, all the anger drained from Dewey's face to be replaced by an icy stoicism. Jake could *see* him reigning in his emotions. It was creepy to watch, and somehow more imposing.

"I believe we're done here," Dewey said, then turned and left.

DEWEY KNAPP PLOPPED into the driver's seat of his late model Mercedes Benz S400 and shut the door with all the calm reserve of a monk. Once he was inside, however, and hidden by the way-over-the-legal-limit window tint, he slammed both hands onto his steering wheel with enough force to cause bruises. Part of it was directed at Jake, and part at himself.

He gritted his teeth until his jaws ached. He had underestimated the kid. He hadn't expected Jake Wilson to be a shrewd contract reader and it had backfired. Dewey should have been slyer in the contract wording to obfuscate the way the contract bent strongly to his benefit. The kid had seen through it, and now, the contract was lost. There was no way Jake would capitulate, and that meant Dewey had lost a great deal of money.

Worse than that, he had been humiliated. Talked down to by that arrogant young punk. And he had lost his temper. Broken his composure – something he *never* allowed to happen. There was only one option left now. He would make Jake Wilson wish he had never met Dewey Knapp. Yes, the kid would pay. It was time to show him just how ruthless he could be.

CHAPTER 16

Jessica bounded down the stairs of her apartment towards the waiting headlights. The night was a pleasant seventy-four degrees, and a breeze caressed her bare legs below her sundress as she stepped off the bottom step and walked the rest of the way to Jake Wilson's Santa-Fe, which, for the record, was sitting in the handicapped parking space.

She grabbed the door handle and swung it open, her eyes meeting Jake's. Again, that chemistry, that connection; it pulled at her like gravity. Every time they were together, it was harder for her to fight.

"I don't see a handicapped sticker on your car," she said seriously.

"I told him not to do it, Ms. Jessica," Boston said from the back seat. Jessica peered over the headrest to smile at the little girl before hopping inside.

Jake was playfully defensive. "There was nowhere else to park. Besides, in all the times I've been here I've never seen anyone park in this spot."

Jessica pulled her door shut as he began to back out.

"And you call yourself a pastor."

Jake shrugged and laughed.

"Ms. Jessica, you look so pretty. That's what Mr. Wilson said when you came down the stairs."

"Boston!" Jake said in horror.

Jessica's face flushed and she was glad for the semi-darkness inside the car.

"Why am I not supposed to say that?" Boston protested. "I think she looks pretty, too."

Jessica watched from the corner of her eye as Jake squirmed in his seat. His lips worked as if he wanted to say something, but nothing came out.

Jessica made a quick turn in her seat and looked back at Boston. "You know what? You look really pretty too. What about Pastor Jake? Does he look pretty?"

Boston wrinkled her nose. "Boys aren't supposed to be pretty, but even so, he's too scruffy."

"Hey," Jake said. "I like my stubble."

Jessica looked at the new growth on the side of his face and chin and decided she liked it as well. Without thinking, she reached up and ran a hand across the right side of his face. The reaction was instantaneous. Jake's body stiffened and he looked at her quickly then turned back to the road as he turned out of the complex onto Tom Chapman Boulevard. She pulled her hand away and tried to play it off.

"It's not that scruffy. I think it looks good on him, Boston."

"I'm gonna call him sandpaper face," Boston said.

"Hmm. Me too." But Jessica barely heard herself say the words. Her hand still felt tingly from where she had touched him, and again without thinking, she pulled her hand to her nose and breathed in the husky-sweet scent his cologne left there. Realizing what she was doing, she mentally kicked herself for the second time in half a minute and tried to pretend like she was just scratching her nose.

Jake still seemed stiff and stilted, and he cleared his throat before speaking again.

"Boston is sooo excited about the fair. I've been telling her all the cool things we're going to do there."

"But I'm not going through the haunted house," Boston said. "Sandpaper face said I can have all the junky foods I want tonight, so we have to try everything."

"Sounds like a plan, sandpaper face," Jessica said, nudging him on the shoulder. "Pastor Sandpaper Face." They all laughed.

By now, they were heading south down Highway 41 where they would connect with Russell Parkway and subsequently 75 South to Perry, about fifteen minutes from Warner Robins.

The Georgia National Fair was an eleven-day event held each October at the Georgia National Fairgrounds and Agricenter in Perry, Georgia. It was a massive event yearly drawing a half million visitors, replete with livestock shows, rides, games, fair food, fine arts competitions, and multiple concerts. The eleven-hundred-acre sprawl also housed the Reaves Arena, an 8,520-seat complex where many of the regional high schools held their graduation ceremonies each year.

Jake, Jessica, and Boston laughed and joked all the way to the turnoff. Jake joined the line of cars and eventually pulled into the massive grass field surrounding the fairground. He followed the directions of a parking worker who waved a flashlight with an orange cone on the end and pointed them towards a section of the field labeled as parking area H. They were on the west side of the grounds and the nearest entrance was the main gate straight ahead.

Even at eight p.m. there was a steady stream of patrons moving from the parking areas to the various gates for entry, and by the time Jake's group reached the front entrance, they were fifty people back in the line. But the ticketing agents worked quickly, and the time passed in a flash, Boston and Jessica pointing at things they could see from where they were and discussing plans for what to do first and what would be the scariest ride and so on. Jake, who participated in the conversation most of the time, still found himself drifting and just watching the two of them together.

The way Boston clung to Jessica, and the way Jessica sheltered her and kept her close; it was beautiful to watch. *They* were beautiful to watch.

Something felt different tonight with Jessica. The shield she normally placed around herself was not there, or at least seemed weaker to him. She had already touched him twice – he recalled not only her touching his face, but her nudging his shoulder – something that he couldn't ever recall her having done before. And he wanted her to touch him. Wanted it more than anything in the world. Jake Wilson may have been a pastor, but he was still a man, and he couldn't keep his eyes off her.

He paid for the tickets – Jessica stubbornly insisted she pay for her own, a battle which she ultimately lost – and they alternated passing through the turnstile, Boston first, then Jessica, then Jake. As Jake exited the far side, his upper thighs depressing the bar until it rolled forward, Boston stopped suddenly in front of Jessica to tie her shoe.

Jessica braked to keep from running into the child, which in turn caused Jake to smash into her. The turnstile had already locked in place, and he couldn't back up if he wanted to. The effect was that it pressed him harder against her and he reached out and wrapped his arms around her stomach to keep from toppling her.

The feeling was unlike anything he had ever imagined. He'd been close to girls before, hugged them, kissed them, but with Jessica, the woman who had been possessing his thoughts since the moment he met her, the curves of her body pressing against his was hypnotic. His arms tightened as she regained her balance and leaned back against him, steadying herself. For a moment, he couldn't let go. The soft contours of her stomach beneath his hands, her hair pressed to his nose, her slender shoulder blades pressed into his chest…

"Thanks," she said.

"No problem," he mumbled.

"Boston, keep moving honey. There are people behind us," Jessica said.

Boston sprang up and Jessica went to move forward, but she was still locked in Jake's embrace. She giggled a little, then put her hands lightly on his and pried them apart.

"You can let go now, I'm safe," she said. But her words weren't chiding. There was something gentle and sweet about them.

Jake briefly considered not letting go, just standing there, holding her close, getting drunk off her nearness...

"Hey buddy, move it would ya?" a gruff voice said from behind him as the next man in line tried to enter the turnstile.

Jake finally let go and they both moved away from the entrance to rejoin Boston who was now finishing with her laces several paces away.

Jessica smoothed out her dress as Jake tried to get his breathing under control. He turned away and pretended to watch the passersby so she couldn't see his face. His heart was beating so fast he could hear the blood pumping in his ears.

A hand grabbed his, and at first, he thought it might be Jessica – thought, or rather dreamed – but the hand was little, and Boston was pulling him forward pointing excitedly to something up ahead. It was so loud around them, and she was talking so fast, that Jake couldn't understand her.

"Hold on, I can't hear you," he laughed.

Boston stopped pulling and turned around to him. "I want to go ride the sky lift. Can we ride the sky lift?"

Jake hesitated and gawked at the sky lift. Heights were not his thing. He used to get dizzy climbing on his jungle gym set as a child. He came with no intention of riding anything high tonight, but he estimated the lift was only fifty feet from the ground at its tallest point and he didn't want to appear like too much of a wimp in front of Jess, so he conceded. "Whatever you want."

Jessica came up and Boston took her by the other hand and pulled them towards the sky lift with the baby-blue chairs. And so, they walked, looking to anyone who noticed like they were a beautiful, happy family. And that's what Jake found himself pretending. A grown man, pastor of a huge church, pretending that Jessica was his and Boston was theirs and they would spend the rest of their lives in this perfect moment never growing old and never having a care in the world.

They gave the conductor of the sky lift two tickets each, stepped forward, and waited for the next chair to come around. As it swung in behind them, the conductor stalled it just long enough to help them sit down without getting smacked in the back of the legs, flipped down the lap bar, then they were moving forward and rising into the night sky.

THE LIFT ITSELF WAS just a transport system from the west end of the midway to the far side of the fairgrounds. Its maximum height was fifty feet, but from above, the lighted midway below looked like a magician's wonderland in a dazzling array of every possible color of lights. The scrumptious smells of funnel cakes, pizza, and pretzels wafted up to them like a tantalizing advertisement for the olfactory senses. To Jessica, the sounds of laughter, and music, and clanking rides, and ringing bells punctuated the night with a strange yet lovely mishmash that congealed into something akin to an auditory smile. The atmosphere was heady.

Boston, seated between Jessica and Jake, was beside herself.

"I want to go on the Ferris wheel," she all but shouted.

"Oh, no, no, no. No way," Jake said. "I'll let you and Jess have that one. I'm already a bit higher than I like on this thing, much less that crazy wheel that's been taken down and put back together a billion times. I bet they lost at least one bolt or screw every single time. It's probably held together by duct tape."

"Oh, come on you big chicken." Boston bounced happily, and Jake clung a little tighter to the lap bar as the chair bobbed in time to Boston's movements.

Jessica's eyes met his, and she saw the hardly concealed fear.

"You said you didn't like heights, but you weren't kidding were you? Don't worry. I'll protect you," she said. "It's my turn to return the favor."

As soon as the words left her mouth, she felt like an idiot. What a stupid, cheeseball thing to say. I'll protect you? Had she lost all her self-control in one evening?

Maybe. Possibly yes. Likely yes. She couldn't get the feel of his arms around her out of her mind. It had been instinctual for him, probably as much to keep himself from falling as her, and though it only lasted a few seconds, his closeness had charged her senses like a battery. Her skin came alive with goosebumps that had nothing to do with the cool night air. She had leaned into him, the back of her head against his face, his breath on her neck, his strong arms tantalizingly snug across her belly, warm through the light fabric of her sun dress.

She found herself staring at him and forced herself to look away. When she breathed out, her breath was shaky. All the while, the nagging, bitter truth picked away at her conscience, reminding her that she was not good for him. He was everything she could ever want, but to allow him to be with her would be the most selfish thing she had ever done.

But still, she was so tired of fighting it. So tired of resisting the desire. Just for a little while tonight, she wanted to know what it was like to be with Jake Wilson, not as a friend, but as someone whose feelings coincided with the ones she knew he had for her. She wanted those arms around her again, that breath on her skin, those piercing eyes gazing knowingly into her own with an animal desire to dispel all space between them.

God, why do I feel this way? You know it's not good for me to be with him. You know it can never happen. So why don't I have the strength to resist right now? Won't You help me? For his sake if not mine.

There was no answer. Only silence. No calming whisper in her soul. And with each passing moment, her resolve kept melting away.

In the end, they did get Jake on the Ferris wheel, but not without a considerable amount of cajoling and outright shaming. By the time he got to the top, however, he was no longer concerned with saving face. Jessica almost felt bad. He was as pale as a ghost.

"I don't care what any of you think of me," Jake complained, "I hate it up here and you're both trying to kill me."

Boston thought this was the funniest thing she'd ever heard gauging by the level of her laughter. They were suspended at the top of the Ferris wheel as the worker unloaded and reloaded a car at the bottom. The cars were circular and open, and Jake was leaning into the middle, his head between his knees, refusing to look out.

Jessica took pity on him a little, but not enough to hold back her sarcasm.

"Just think of it like this," she said, "you believe in God, and right now, you're closer to Him."

Boston was wracked with a fresh bout of laughter. Jake looked up long enough to glower at Jessica, who also laughed.

His voice was gruff through clenched teeth. "If you weren't so pretty, I'd chuck you over the side of this thing."

His words made her breath catch. That was the first time he'd paid her an unabashed compliment. Sure, it was done in a joking manner, but the declaration of his attraction was not part of the joke.

Boston, sitting on the other side of the car, scooted around until she was next to Jake and put her little arm around him. She waved

Jessica over with the other hand. Jessica slid closer until she was nearly up against him.

"Now you put your arm here like mine," Boston said.

Jessica did as she was told.

"Now we've got you, Mr. Wilson. You don't have to be afraid anymore."

However, the added weight of all of them being on the same side very much had the effect of tilting the car in that direction, and Jake peeked up long enough to verify they were no longer level, popped his head back down, and started to pray for his life to be spared.

"Mr. Wilson, don't be a baby."

After what must have seemed an eternity for Jake, they completed several more revolutions and were deposited safely back onto the ground. Jake was unusually quiet, and when pressed, confessed to feeling a bit sheepish about his behavior, which, of course, guaranteed that Jessica and Boston would mock him the rest of the night. Eventually, even he joined in the laughter, and made light of his fear.

Jake did redeem himself, though. Although he obstinately recused himself from anything else more than thirty feet off the ground, he rode everything else possible with Boston, including things that spun and flipped and caused people to revisit whatever contents had been previously deposited in their gullets. Jessica was thankful Jake could ride them. Heights didn't bother her, but those things certainly did, and she had no desire to spend the rest of the night puking.

At one point, Boston *did* throw up, retching pitifully into the grass along the midway, but Jessica and Jake thought that had more to do with the inordinate amount of junk food she had consumed than motion sickness, because consume they had done. They ate like pigs until they were all stuffed beyond comfort: cotton candy, pizza, tater tots, and sodas. Once it was all out, and after a few minutes of forced repose on a bench for her to catch her breath and rest, Boston felt much better and tackled the next phase of the night – games.

Boston loved them all, but by far her favorite was a game in which she had to throw darts at a board covered with inflated balloons. If you popped five balloons, you got a prize. The problem was that she was dangerously inaccurate. After the first round, the game worker had taken to hiding behind a very large stuffed bear lest the only thing to get popped would be his head.

Now, they sat on a bench beside the Red Baron, a kiddie coaster that was a large oval with four small "hills" and once-fiery-red carts that had devolved over years of weather and abuse to a shade of dull, faded pink. It had been Boston's favorite ride of the night because Jake allowed her to ride it alone. She assumed it was because she was a "big girl", but the carts were so small neither he nor Jessica could fit in them.

"I wanna ride it again," Boston announced.

"How many tickets do you have left?" Jake said, setting down the oversized grilled corn on the cob he had been eating.

Boston counted them out. "Twenty."

They were only a few feet from the entrance, not far enough for her to get lost. "Take off, sport."

She sprang away, leaving Jake and Jessica alone. She stood behind a group of taller kids, patiently waiting her turn, then handed the ride attendant the required number of tickets. She walked onto the deck and boarded a cart with another little girl roughly her age. Typical of Boston, she and the other girl were chatting away.

Jake laughed. "She's got all the extroversion of an infomercial salesman."

Jessica's eyes followed her.

"The therapy's helped so much," Jessica said.

"You've helped," Jake replied. "I can't thank you enough for being there for her, Jess."

She shrugged. "I like it as much as she does." Jessica took a bite of her grilled corn on the cob, then turned to face him.

"How are *you* doing Pastor Jake Wilson?"

"Peachy."

She cocked her eyebrows.

He said, "No, really. I'm good. I think I'm doing alright with her. Church, though. That's another story."

"What do you mean?"

He picked up his corn on the cob, wrapped it roughly in its paper wrapper and set it between his feet to throw away later. "I had a not-so-pleasant run in with a member the other day. One of my council members. It got kinda ugly."

Her face showed concern. "What happened?"

Jake shook his head, remembering the encounter. "I've got this guy; he owns a bank. He brought me a proposal for a loan on the new family complex."

"The council member? That seems a little inappropriate."

Jake nodded. "Yeah. My thoughts exactly. Still, I wanted to give him the benefit of the doubt. I looked everything over, got a little help from Ed Kilgore. You know him? Red-haired man in his mid-fifties? Wife is Eva. She's a member of the praise team. No? Anyway, he pointed out some areas that were keyed to benefit De...this man. I mean, I get that banks are in the business of making money, but he's a council member, and this deal was really skewed in his favor."

"To take advantage of the church. And you called him out on it?"

"Yup."

"And...?"

"He pretty much threatened me."

"Wow. Did he threaten to beat you up?"

"No. He just said, 'You'll regret this', whatever that means."

"Hmm. What are you going to do?"

"I don't know," Jake said. "I thought about talking to Bishop Tyndale, he's the State Administrative Bishop, but...," Jake looked down at his shoes, "I don't know. I guess I'm hoping the guy'll come around. I don't want there to be any bad blood between us."

Jessica took another bite of corn, working it over. "You think it could be the same guy that complained about the offerings?"

Jake shrugged, but he knew that in a way, it fit. If Dewey had planned to give the church a loan, he would want to make sure the church wasn't going to default on it.

Across the midway, the Red Baron made one of several turns in its rotation and Boston came into view. She waved from her seat, all smiles. They both waved in return, and when Jessica looked at him again, he broke into laughter.

"Hey, you've got a piece of corn stuck in your teeth."

"Oh, God." She cupped her hand over her mouth, turning red, and dug with a fingernail. After a moment she removed her hand and bared her teeth, growling like a rabid animal. "Better?"

"No." He reached out to her. "Here, let me."

"Eww, no way."

"I was just going to point he said," laughing at her. Instead, he opened his mouth and pointed to the corresponding place in his own teeth. "Right there," he said.

She turned her head and covered her mouth with one hand while she dug at the spot with a fingernail. Eventually she turned back and gave him a quick peek.

"You're all good," he said. "As beautiful as ever."

Their eyes locked. He lowered his hand, and as he set it down on the bench, it brushed against her knee. It was no accident. He knew it and she knew it. Jake realized he wasn't breathing, and he started to inch towards her, painfully slow, as if they were two celestial bodies in a collapsing orbit, the draw irresistible.

"Mr. Wilson! Ms. Jessica!"

Jessica drew back a little, the moment lost.

Boston skipped towards them from the rollercoaster entrance. "Guess what, guess what? I rode the whole rollercoaster with my hands in the air. The whole time!" She bounced forward with excitement, but as she did, another pedestrian crossed her path. Boston's foot caught against the man's shoe. She tripped and went down in a heap.

JESSICA SAT ON AN EMERGENCY room bed, cradling Boston in her arms. Boston's eyes were red and puffy from crying. A few feet away, Jake sat on a rolling stool intended for the doctor, but presently under Jake's requisition since there was no doctor present.

"I'm starting to worry a bit about your coordination," Jake teased Boston. She, in turn, stuck out her tongue. Jake reached over and laid a hand on her foot, giving it a tender squeeze.

Jessica kissed Boston on the head. "Leave her alone you mean old Mr. Sandpaper Face," she said, causing Boston to laugh and brighten a little.

A middle eastern physician in a white lab coat with the requisite stethoscope around his neck, knocked briefly before entering. Jake rose, but the doctor motioned him to remain seated. In his hands, he carried a rugged looking portable computer, the kind you might expect on a commercial about the military. He set it on the top of a storage cabinet and angled it for easiest viewing.

He moved over and introduced himself as Dr. Patel, bantering with Boston and coaxing a smile from her. He asked a couple of questions about the fall then moved back to his computer. "What you've got, young lady, is a clean break of the ulna." He tapped a couple of keys on his computer and a television screen on the wall that previously had been running wellness messages and advertisements for the hospital changed to show the x-ray of an arm.

Doctor Patel reached up and indicated a spot on the x-ray. "You see here, this little line?" He indicated a spot with an up and down motion, tracing across one of the bones with his finger. "This is the break."

Jake strained, but he couldn't tell any difference between the rest of the x-ray and where Dr. Patel was indicating.

"I'm not sure I see anything," Jessica said.

Jake was relieved it wasn't just him.

Doctor Patel turned back to them. "It can be hard to see sometimes. If you're not trained and know what you're looking for." He made a gesture at Boston. "Especially with these little ones."

"I have to get a cast?" Boston said.

Dr. Patel nodded solemnly. "I'm afraid so. But the good news is, you'll heal up just fine in about five weeks. Thankfully," he turned back to the x-ray again pointing at the invisible crack, "we won't need to do any reduction of the fracture."

"You mean set the bone," Jake said.

"Yes. The alignment is good, so we just need to place the cast and you'll be free to go. I recommend children's Tylenol and ibuprofen for any soreness, but that should subside after a day or two."

He hit another button and the x-ray image disappeared from the screen.

"You've been a brave little girl," he said to Boston. I'm going to get the nurse to come in and let you pick out what color cast you want, then we'll get that arm wrapped up." He winked at her and glanced at his watch. "It's late, but tell your mom and dad they need to treat you to ice cream tomorrow. How does that sound?"

Boston nodded happily. Jessica's eyes met Jake's at being referred to as Boston's parents and her look was tinged with something akin to sadness. For a moment, it made Jake's heart hurt, but then he told himself he was reading too much into it.

Later that night, as he tucked Boston into bed, her left arm outstretched with a pink cast on it, he thought back over the night. It had been eventful to say the least. And apart from the end, it had been perfect. They were memories Jake would cherish forever, and for the first time, he was truly honest with himself. He allowed himself to admit what he'd been afraid to admit. They were memories he only wanted to share with one other person. Memories meant to be shared for a lifetime. He knew without a doubt that he was falling in love with Jessica Maracle. He only wanted to be with her. And after tonight's "almost kiss", he was now convinced she cared for him too.

CHAPTER 17

It had not taken long for Jessica's marriage to Craig Maracle to devolve into the realm of Greek tragedy. They'd been married for less than a year when Jessica began to expect that the same charm he had with her, he still used to woo any and every willing young lady that crossed his path.

It wasn't until the end of their marriage that she was able to *prove* his infidelity, but the signs had all been there. The surreptitious looks from across the room, the late nights at work, the emotional distance, all were telltale indicators as sure as if she'd been watching them on a soap opera.

Now, lying on her bed, she restlessly replayed it all in her mind. She didn't want to but was unable to stop herself.

She had gotten home late. By the time they were done at the emergency room and Jake and Boston had dropped her off, it was after four in the morning. She had showered, not bothering to dry her hair, and slipped into bed, all while thinking of Boston and the poor child's ordeal. But she'd been brave and had assured Jessica that she would be okay, concerned that Jessica was upset over her injury more than she was.

But by the time Jessica's head hit the pillow and she extinguished the bedside lamp, there was only one thing she could think of – the kiss. Or near kiss would be more accurate. She had come so close to doing what she had promised herself not to. And rather than feel guilty for it, she felt exhilarated. It was a fool thing to do – to allow the evening to pass while ignoring the warnings in her heart. To allow herself to imagine, even if only for an instant, that she was with Jake Wilson as anything more than a surrogate mother-companion to Boston. This line of thinking led inexorably back to – Craig.

It wasn't Craig's unfaithfulness that ate at her. It wasn't the fact that he didn't love her, or that he betrayed her that was such a source of agonizing pain for her. That is not what caused her feelings of unworthiness. No. She could only wish that were the case. Because in the end, she was just as bad as him. And that was why she could never be with Jake Wilson. She could never be with such a man, a pastor, without putting a blackened sinful tarnish on his reputation, and that's something she could not allow herself to do.

Yet, despite her best efforts, she had failed miserably to keep her emotions in check. Jake Wilson was everything she had ever dreamed of. Despite her afflicting conscience, she could see no easy way out of the snare she'd allowed herself to be drawn into. What would it do to Boston for her to pull away from Jake? Could she continue to be around him even if she could keep their relationship platonic? She didn't think so. What was worse, she didn't want to.

When it came to Jake Wilson, she wanted him in every way, and it all felt so right, minus the nagging voice in her gut. She closed her eyes and allowed his face to paint her memory. The way he leaned in, his breath sweet and husky, his eyes locked on hers with shared desire. Even now, her body craved him, as only someone who had known the throes of marital ecstasy could understand. There was a draw that someone untouched didn't experience. It was a deep, animal pull to be one with another person.

She hated herself for it. It had gotten her into trouble before.

She opened her eyes, doing everything in her power to will away the image of Jake, the longing the thought of him caused in her stomach.

Jesus, please. I'm not strong enough. Please help me. I can't do this to him. I can't ruin him. Please, please, please.

The last word of the prayer ran over and over and over through her mind, each one a begging plea for God to rescue her from destroying Jake. She cared too much for him to do that. She lov—

No! She shut the thought down, tears forming in her eyes, and she clamped them tightly. *You're not worthy of that. You don't deserve that, and you don't deserve him.*

Trust me.

The soft whisper in her soul came as it often did. Just two words. But it didn't help. She didn't feel better. Trust Him how? To make her feelings go away? To help her not break Jake's and Boston's hearts? Even now, she knew she was powerless to resist Jake Wilson. She knew she couldn't just step away. That's why when the text came from him at five in the morning, she had only one response.

The text simply said, "I have to see you tonight."

Her reply was equally as simple.

"Okay."

JAKE HAD SET EVERYTHING up the following morning by text. The plan was for her to be picked up by Jake and Boston at a quarter to seven, and they would spend a quiet evening, a welcome respite from the flurry of the night before, having a bonfire and roasting marshmallows for smores by the fireplace in Boston's fairy castle.

It only took a moment, however, to realize something was up when she came down the stairs promptly on time and Jake met her at the sidewalk. He led her back to his Santa Fe and opened the car door for her. He had never greeted her in this manner before, and though it surprised her a little, she hadn't quite caught on. But when she leaned into the car to say hi to Boston, the child was not in the back seat. She was not in the vehicle at all.

"Where's Boston?" she said before he could shut the door behind her.

"Babysitter." He gauged her expression, then cautiously added, "I hope you don't mind."

Jessica felt a nervous flutter deep in her belly, like her insides had decided to do a gymnastics routine. She caught Jake's eyes and they held. His face was flush, but he smiled.

"I may have led you on a bit," he said.

Jessica knew. Jake intended this to be a date. He had tricked her, deceived her, lied to her – in the most innocent way possible, of course – and it was thrilling. He quickly shut the door before she could respond and rounded to his side, crawled in and started the engine.

"So, what *are* we doing?" she said.

Instead of answering, Jake put out his hand in a bold, fluid, singular movement and wrapped it around hers. In response, and with no need for thought, she slid her fingers through his until they were intertwined. It was exciting, and beautiful, and frightening all at the same time. No questions. No declarations. It was two people coming together as nature intended. It was inevitable. And as they pulled out of the complex and onto Watson Boulevard, Jessica knew all her resistance to Jake Wilson was gone.

A Taste of Italy was teeming with patrons, even for a Thursday night. The restaurant had solidified its reputation as a fine dining establishment after being featured for its authentic Italian cuisine in Southern Living Magazine in the summer of 2011. Since then, it had garnered praise in every respected food magazine in the Southeastern United States as well as favorable editorials by vetted food critics from the Atlanta Journal Constitution to the Columbus Times. As a result, they never lacked for a crowd.

As a high-end restaurant, they catered to the tradition of table reservations for elite clientele – or in this case – those who were willing to pay a premium. Reserving a table on such short notice had cost Jake more than he'd ever spent on a single date in his life. And that was just to get the table. But by the time they arrived and there was an enormous line waiting halfway around the building, it was worth it to be able to usher Jessica right inside – past the ownership plaque with Dewey Knapp's name on it that was hidden behind a waiting patron – and be pointed to a candle lit round top nestled comfortably in an out of the way corner of the restaurant.

The interior of the restaurant itself was a masterclass in Italian design replete with midnight-ebony marble countertops, mosaic floor tiling, and a charming blend of metal and wood accents for a mixture of old and new world styles that transported the diner from Middle-Georgia to the likes of Rome or Venice.

A host in black tuxedo pants and a crisply starched white dress shirt with black bowtie ushered them to their table, pulled Jessica's chair back, and assisted her in sitting. He laid a menu in front of each of them, then stepped back and crossed his arms behind his back in a well-rehearsed, almost militaristic show of pomp.

"It's an honor to receive your patronage tonight Mr. Wilson, Ms. Maracle," he said as they settled in. "Have you dined with us before?"

They both shook their heads in the negative, and off the host went into a flurry of details including everything from a brief history of the restaurant to the specials on the menu to the dishes of highest acclaim by food critics and Yelp reviewers. After his brief monologue, he assured them a waiter would be with them momentarily and dashed off to help the next party.

"Oh, my gosh. He knew our names," Jessica said as she pulled the menu to herself.

An equally proficient waitress showed up and filled their water glasses. After taking their order for drinks – no thank you, we don't need any wine – she moved away to give them time to peruse the menu.

Jessica took a few moments to gaze around the restaurant in amazement. The lightning was intentionally low key, and the primary source of lighting was the oversized candle on the table and wall sconces with real, gas-lit flames that made the entire place seem to dance with life. She wondered if that had been difficult to get by whoever passed for restaurant regulation committees or whatnot. And the smells. The smells were a mouthwatering assault on the senses. She had not recalled being very hungry when they arrived, but as soon as they entered the building and the aromas wafted over them, she felt famished.

Across from her, Jake was watching her. His hand crept across the table and the tips of their fingers met, probing gently. Overhead, some ambiguous Italian music played ethereally through the hidden speaker system pumping out the tinkling strains of a mandolin.

They'd said surprisingly little on the drive over from Jessica's apartment. It was as if by unspoken agreement, they had put off serious conversation for later, both content for the time to live in the moment.

The waitress appeared again, and after no small amount of deliberation on Jake's and Jessica's part, took their order. When she was gone, Jessica leaned in close, her voice velvety soft.

"How did you manage to get a reservation with all of those people waiting outside? It must not have been easy."

Jake laughed. "It was super easy. Just expensive."

Her mouth turned down in a guilty, pouty frown.

"No, no," he said. "It was absolutely worth it." His expression grew serious. "I'm sorry I lied to you. I was afraid if I told you my plans, you might not come. We've never done anything that didn't revolve around Boston."

He was so sincere, his words so tender, that it made her heart skip.

"I don't think I could ever turn you down." It was the most honest thing she could say, even though it brought a twinge of guilt; but she pushed that aside, unwilling for now to consider the past or allow it to hold sway over this moment.

He continued. "I think I've been lying to myself for a long time. I wish I could claim purely altruistic intent. I wish I could say I only did it for Boston. I told myself that. I really did. Over and over. But the truth is, even without her, I would have wanted you around. Since that first time I met you, I haven't been able to stop thinking about you."

He dropped his head, then, and she felt his fear of rejection.

"Do you think I was any different?" she said. He looked up at her. "Do you think I would be here with you" – she indicated the romantic place in which they sat – "if I didn't feel the same way?"

AT EIGHT P.M. ON THE dot, as was his custom, Dewey Knapp pushed back his Zuri ergonomic high-backed office chair with premium lamb-skin leather and stainless-steel base, heaved himself up – something which was more difficult by the day – and loped around his desk. He pulled open the door and ambled out of his office to his usual spot, a junction between the short hallway to his office and the kitchen entrance, sheltered by a low wall, where he could oversee the comings and goings in his restaurant unobserved. He stuck out a pudgy hand and stopped Eddie Marsden, one of his most seasoned waiters, who happened to be passing by at that moment.

"Ed. Get that new chef to whip me up a couple of cannelloni, stat."

"Sure thing, Mr. Knapp. Coke?"

Knapp shook his head. "Sprite. I'm easing off the caffeine."

Eddie shot off like a cannon to do his bidding. Such a great kid. Always respectful, hardworking, and ready to please. Just the kind of kid Dewey liked. The kind of kid that one day might be promoted to a managerial position if he kept up his go-getter attitude.

"God helps those who help themselves," he muttered under his breath.

He let his gaze drift from the workers in the kitchen, to the host and hostess busy welcoming and seating guests, to the diners that were filling their faces and lining his pockets. Life was good. Mostly. Something he was reminded of when his eyes fell upon a familiar face. One he was neither expecting nor wanting to see.

Jake Wilson – that pompous little windbag – sat in a corner table. Across from him was a pretty, blonde woman. Though Dewey didn't know her name, he did recognize her as someone he'd seen at the church before. It appeared Jake Wilson was branching out into the dating world. How interesting.

Dewey spun to head back to his office, was briefly stopped by Eddie who handed him his Sprite. He nodded his thanks and went into the office, closing the door behind him and locking it. He didn't want to be disturbed. He went immediately to his chair, set the Sprite down on a coaster so the antique wood of his desk wouldn't be stained with sweat rings, and picked up his phone. He knew the number by heart and dialed it without thinking. A deep voice spoke from the other end.

"Dewey."

"Barton."

"To what do I owe the pleasure?" the deep voice said.

"That thing with your wife a couple of years ago. You used a private investigator, didn't you?"

"What's that gotta do with anything?" Barton said.

"Nothing, except I might have some work for him. Still got his contact info?"

Barton was silent on the other end. Dewey pictured him flipping through an old-fashioned rolodex. "Yeah. Got it right here. I can text it to you."

"Sounds good. Thanks. Let's do golf soon."

Barton swore. "Dewey, you know my hip can't take that no more."

"Of course, I do," Dewey said with a grin. "That's why I want to play. Cause you can't keep from betting on yourself, and that's easy money for me."

"You got enough money, you old jackass."

"No such thing. Thanks Barton."

"Don't mention it."

He hung up the phone as his cell on the desk chimed a message notification. He opened it, pickup up the desk phone again, and dialed the number on the screen of his cell.

Three rings. "Hello?"

"Good evening. Is this Harley Wright?"

"Maybe."

Dewey rolled his eyes.

Harley must have reconsidered his approach because he said, "Sorry, man. This is my private phone, not my business line. I wasn't expecting a call. If I may, how did you get this number?"

"I'm a friend of Ed Barton."

"Ah. In that case, how may I help you?"

"I'm in need of your services," Knapp said. "I've got a couple of people I'd like to dig up some dirt on. Does that sound like something you could help me with?"

"Hey, dirt's my middle name. Are you in Atlanta?" Harley said.

"No. I'm in Warner Robins, and the job would be in Warner Robins. Is that a problem?"

"It depends. If I need to be there regular like see, the price goes up. You know, hotels and all that."

"If your work delivers, price won't be an issue," Dewey said. He could almost feel the smarmy critter smiling on the other end of the phone.

"Alright, then. When do I start?"

Dewey didn't hesitate. "Tomorrow."

DINNER ARRIVED, AND as the waitress set the plate in front of Jessica, the rich fragrance of the dish drifted up to her with an enticing zest that made her mouth water.

She had chosen the bucatini with lemony carbonara, something she'd never had before, but the description on the menu made it look too good to pass up. The pasta was a rich, earthy yellow with thinly-sliced garlic cloves, a generous amount of grated parmesan, and guanciale – something the waitress had identified as salt-cured pork jowl. And of course, it contained fresh lemon juice as the name implied, something attested to by the Michelangelo-level artistry of the finely grated lemon zest and thinly sliced peel decoratively arranged around the outer edge of the plate. On request, the waitress added a sprinkling of crushed black pepper tableside.

Jessica looked from her plate to Jake's with amusement. Unlike her adventurous delving into an entrée she'd never tried before – after all, how often did one get to try something new from an acclaimed restaurant? – Jake had opted for a pepperoni flatbread pizza with a small side salad.

"You don't want to try something fancy?" she'd asked him after the waitress had memorized their order and removed their menus.

He had smiled sheepishly. "I'm a simple guy. I like good food, but not too fancy. Guess I never outgrew my childhood pickiness."

They spent a good fifteen minutes saying little while they ate. The food was fabulous. Jessica's bucatini perfectly blended the rich, creamy pasta with the mildly- caustic bite of the lemon. Jake happily declared his pizza was the best he'd ever had. As they began to wind down, both of their bellies pleasantly full, Jessica gazed across at Jake, watching the way his hands moved, how his jaws worked while chewing. She took him in, the way his early-stage crow's feet crinkled as he smiled, and the cow lick that managed to make itself known on the left side of his hairline despite the obvious attempts to tame it and the relative shortness of his hair.

As dinner wound down – "No thanks, we don't want any dessert tonight" – their conversation began to morph from the relative small-talk of the evening to more serious issues. They spoke more of the church, and Jake's challenges as a pastor. They talked of Jessica's childhood and of Boston's parents and the time Jake had spent with them at school.

The conversation lulled, and they stared at each other for a moment. Jessica smiled, trying to gauge the man sitting across from her.

She said, "What are you thinking?"

He grinned and looked away for a moment. When he looked back, he didn't meet her eyes. Almost shyly, he picked up his glass and swallowed a mouthful of water. When he set it back down, he leaned in towards her and shrugged.

"Just how beautiful you are. I can't imagine how you've never been married. I'm sure men were beating your door down."

Jessica felt her smile falter, but quickly forced it back into place. They had never discussed past loves. It was an intentional decision on her part. She had no desire to traverse that minefield, and though she should have expected it, the statement had shocked her back into reality.

For a while, a beautiful, blissful couple of hours, she had managed to forget the past and live only in the moment with Jake Wilson. Now she realized she'd been a fool. She looked away at the families happily eating dinner at neighboring tables, couples sharing laughs and stories, and she wondered if she was doomed to never have that again. No husband, no family to call her own. When she looked back, her smile was gone.

"Jake, I..." She knew she had to tell him. Knew it had to be now. But when it came to it, she was terrified. What would he do when he found out she'd been married before? Up until yesterday, it hadn't mattered because she had not allowed any romantic interaction between them. But that had changed. She had foolishly allowed herself to pretend that for this one night, the past didn't matter.

Jake's expression had changed, aware of her reticence, the turn of her countenance. He put a hand across the table and grabbed hers, squeezing softly.

"Hey. What's wrong?"

She steeled herself and spoke the words, each one leaving her mouth like a nail in her coffin, sealing her into the awful truth of what could never be changed.

"I'm so sorry, Jake. I've never told you. Never thought any of this would happen." *God, help me.* It was so hard.

Jake's brows furrowed, but he remained silent; allowed her the time she needed.

"I..." She suddenly felt like a fool. *What are you doing? Why are you making a big deal out of this? You're acting like you're going to marry this guy. At best, this is just a first date. Anything could happen. What makes you think any of your past matters?* She felt her nerves calm. Was she reading way too much into a fledgling relationship? Surely.

She decided to just tell the truth; at least part of it.

"I've been married before, Jake."

He remained silent, processing the information. He didn't get up and run away. That was a good sign.

"Okay," he finally said. "Is it okay for me to ask what happened?"

"Short version, my husband cheated on me, so I divorced him and took a teaching job here to get away from him."

There. She'd said it. *No, you haven't. You left out the worst part.* She realized she was gritting her teeth and forced her face to relax. *It's not important,* she told herself. *I'm allowed to date. If things get too serious, I'll tell him. I'll deal with it then. But why not enjoy myself for now if he's willing?*

He ran a finger over the back of her hand that he was still holding. "How long ago?"

"Four years."

"Did you think that would matter to me?"

"Yes. No. I don't know, maybe."

That wasn't the truth. Not really. It was the other thing that worried her. The thing she didn't want to think about and especially not say out loud. But her being married, sure, that was a bit of a concern. Maybe that would be an instant deal breaker for a minister, or at least for Jake. Jessica had heard stories of pastors and Christians that believed divorce was wrong no matter the circumstances and would never marry a divorced person or perform marriage ceremonies for people that had been in prior marriages. She'd even heard of some denominations that demanded couples return to previous spouses if they'd been in a prior marriage. Jessica was still new to Christianity and was certainly not a theologian, but that seemed extreme even to her.

He nodded. "I think I understand. Biblically speaking, you had every right to divorce a cheating husband. I certainly think that falls within the parameters of what is acceptable. If you're worried that it would be a turn off to me just that you'd been married before...well..." he met and held her gaze. "It's not."

Part of the constriction left her chest, and with those words, she allowed herself to lock away the other part, to put it in a dark place and refuse to think about it. For now, it was all about Jake. She was losing herself. Losing herself to the moment. But she no longer cared.

JAKE AND JESSICA WALKED up the staircase to her apartment door hand in hand, like two high-schoolers on a first date. The climb was punctuated by silence, a nervous excitement circulating between them like an electric current. As they reached the door, Jessica pulled out keys from her pocketbook, chose the correct one, inserted it into the lock and turned. The deadbolt gave a slight clunk as it slid back into the door.

"Jessica..." Jake started at the same time Jessica turned and said, "Come in."

His grip on her hand tightened, their fingers sliding together. Her hand was warm and moist, and Jake's eyes locked on hers. He couldn't know for sure, but he imagined she saw in him the intense desire bubbling underneath the surface of his calm façade. After all these months, the connection that he'd hoped for and dreamed of seemed to be coalescing into reality. How many times had he convinced himself of her indifference? How many times had he fallen asleep dreaming of what it would be like to touch her hand, to kiss her lips, only to despair at the thought that she didn't see him that way? And now, after all of that, here they were, seeing each other in a new and deep way that promised the budding rose of romance.

Jake considered the invitation with every intention of accepting it.

It's time to go home, son.

The inner voice came with a clarity Jake didn't often experience and it was enough that Jake let go of Jessica's hand. But was it really

God? What harm could there be? He would just go in for a few minutes. He didn't want to leave her yet.

"Please?" she said. "I'll make some coffee. When do you have to be back?"

Jake consulted his watch. Ten thirty. He'd told Amber, the teen from his youth group keeping Boston, that he'd be back by eleven thirty. He still had an hour.

He felt another caution in his spirit, but this time, he squelched it. He had no intention of doing anything wrong, and after all, he was a grown man. Jessica was an adult and there was nothing wrong with them being alone. Besides, he hadn't even kissed her. They could spend some time and continue to talk, delving into the newness of the relationship and the possibilities that lay ahead.

"Okay." As he said it, the insecure feeling dissipated, and Jake blew it off as his own conscience instead of an actual warning from the Lord.

She smiled, pleased, and took his hand again and pulled him inside. Her fingers lingered on his for a moment, then she gestured with her left hand toward the kitchen. "I'm going to put the coffee on."

He nodded. "I'll be back." He headed down the corridor to the restroom and shut the door behind him. Once inside, he stood at the sink and stared at himself in the mirror.

AS JAKE MOVED TO THE bathroom, Jessica shut and locked the front door behind her. Her breathing was shaky, and she forced herself to take long, slow breaths.

Moving to the kitchen, she pulled the bag of Starbuck's dark roast from the cabinet above the sink, grabbed a filter, and placed them both into the coffee maker. She turned it on, and it beeped happily like a small robot coming to life.

She walked back to the living room, kicked off her shoes – immediately sinking down several inches in height – and turned off the overhead in the connected dining area. Now there was only the lamp in the corner giving off a soft glow. She turned to take a seat on the couch when Jake appeared down the hallway.

Their eyes met and again she felt the pull. He came to her. His expression was serious in the dim light and though he walked slowly, it was with purpose. She knew it was going to happen. Knew it as sure as she knew her own name, and she knew she wouldn't resist.

Jake stepped up to her, reached out, and tenderly pushed the hair on both sides of her face back behind her ears.

"Jess." His voice was a husky whisper. He took her chin in one hand and gently lifted her face towards his. Their lips met in an explosion of sensation that rocked her to her core and made her knees weak. It lasted maybe ten seconds that felt like a lifetime, and when he pulled away for a breath, she was panting for more. She didn't have to wait long.

His arms curled around her and pulled her closer than before.

Jake whispered into her ear. "I think I'm falling in love with you."

A wave of guilty regret washed over her, and her mind flashed to her determination of a couple of nights ago that she was no good for Jake. It wasn't fair for her to stain his life and ministry because of her misdeeds. But at the same time, his words caused an excited stirring in her abdomen, and warmth flooded her in a way that had not happened since intimate moments with Craig.

She quickly shoved the thoughts of Craig away, and as much to banish him from her mind as to slake her own desire, she pushed her lips to Jake's again. This time was even more passionate, and she felt it in the way his body tensed and hers responded. His arms dropped around her waist, and he pulled her hard to him, dispelling any remaining breathing space between them. She felt herself moan a little, and with that sound, she could feel his desire increase.

Warnings began to sound in her mind like gunshots, harsh and foreboding, but she was helpless to stem the oncoming tide. They were caught in the throes of the moment now, like a riptide drawing them in with treacherous purpose.

He pulled her across the room, his arms still around her waist, smothering her neck with kisses, his lips like the caress of velvet across her skin, causing goose pimples to rise where they landed. In a simple move half-instigated by him, half-by her, he placed her on the couch and laid his body on top of hers.

The warnings were like cannon shots now, and something grew in her spirit, a warring power that was strong, desperate to break through. Despite the yearning of her body, the delicious feel of his weight on her, a light began to break through the deepest part of her mind.

Still, the physical pull was sooo strong. Her mind was screaming. *Help! Help! Help! Not like this. Not with him. It'll destroy him.* But at the same time, her arms tightened around him, desperate for intimacy, longing for all barriers to be gone. It had been so long since she'd had intimacy with a man, and it all came flooding back with a vicious vengeance, punctuated by the very real and intense emotion of...love? Was it love? Yes, she loved him. Loved him with everything in her. Loved him with her heart, mind, soul...her body...*Oh, God!*

His hand drew along her hip, up her side and came to rest on her left breast. Two things happened at once. First, a burst of pleasure weaved through her like tendrils of fire. Second, the light that had been pushing back against the temptation broke through in a sudden, terrible, wonderful wave of power that could only have come from the Spirit. In an instant, all her resolve to protect Jake Wilson, to love him enough not to destroy everything he had worked for, everything he stood for, solidified into a determination that instantly cooled the burning sexual desire that had threatened to take them both.

She put her hands against his chest and pushed. Surprising herself with her own strength, she raised his upper body from hers.

"No!" It was a strangled cry of anguish. "Jake, I don't want this."

The effect was instant. It was as if a terrible realization had dawned on Jake, and he quickly rose.

"Jessica, I'm sorry. I'm so, so sorry!" He began to pace back and forth across the living room, his hands gripping his temples like a man in the throes of a horrendous headache.

She sat up, tears already spilling down her cheeks. Her face felt hot and puffy as if she'd been crying for hours, and a sharp pain seared through her stomach. She thought she might be sick.

Jake was still pacing. He turned suddenly and looked at her, took in her tears and anguished expression. He took a large step towards her, fell on his knees, and grabbed her hands.

"What have I done? What have I done?"

She wasn't sure if he was asking her, or God, or himself. But she was sure his misery matched her own judging by the way his voice broke with emotion.

She tried to speak, but the words caught in her throat. She tried again, and finally managed to find her voice.

"Please leave," she said in a tortured whisper.

He recoiled as if slapped. "What?"

"Please," she said again. "I need you to leave."

"No, no, no. Jess, please no. Don't make me go. I need to fix this. I need to..."

"You can't fix it," she said, raising her voice. She didn't mean to shout at him. In truth, she wasn't even angry at him. Her anger and disgust were all aimed at herself. But she couldn't say that. Not right now. The pain was too great, because she knew that this would be the last time she would ever allow anything to happen between them. She had awakened from the fantasy. How could she have been so selfish to lead him on like this? How could she have let him risk everything in his ministry for her? And because of her, he had allowed himself to go beyond a boundary she knew he didn't want to cross. A wretched sob escaped her.

JAKE DIDN'T KNOW WHAT to do. He would do anything if he just knew what. The excruciating despair of what had occurred ripped through him like razor tipped arrows.

All his life he had been careful not to give in to sexual temptation. Knew the cost it could have for his ministry. And now, when he finally found love, what he believed to be true love, he had immediately crossed that line and felt totally powerless to stop it. The condemnation was instant and crushing.

She'll never want you, now. She trusted you and you took advantage of her. You just blew it. You just blew your first real shot at not being alone. You're disgusting. I hate you.

The inner voice sounded so much like God that it stunned him. Had he been wrong about Jesus' unconditional love and grace? Surely not, but his heart screamed otherwise. Did it even matter? How could he forgive himself? Above it all, was the guilt and pain of hurting Jessica that was drowning him. The look on her face made him want to die.

When she screamed at him, it had an awful note of finality to it. The despair he heard there was unbearable. He tried one more time, his words a suffering appeal.

"Jessica. Let me..."

She rose then, abrupt and decisive, and pushed him towards the door. She was sobbing openly now. He realized with shock that he was too. Could this really be happening? *Oh, God, let this be a nightmare.* But her words tore him apart as she forced him to the door and opened it.

"...this never should have happened," she was saying. "This has all been a mistake. It's not right. I don't want this. I don't want...don't..." she struggled through the words like quicksand. She braced herself and looked deep into his eyes. "I can't be with you, Jake. Not like that. This will never be."

He stepped backwards through the doorway, battling for comprehension, longing for understanding.

"I don't believe you," he protested. "How can you say that?"

She hung her head, not meeting his gaze any longer. "Because it's true. Whatever this was, it's over."

With interminable slowness, she shut the door in his face. Jake stood alone in the pass-through, staring at the shut door. In that moment he was aware that some part of him had died, and he didn't see how it could ever be revived.

CHAPTER 18

Jake had taken to spending nearly every waking minute of every day wondering where Jessica was and what she was doing. He would conjure her image in vivid detail picturing her in front of her classes at school, or lounging at home in the evenings, or reading a novel before bed. And always, despite his best efforts, she carried a look of pained disappointment. Disappointment that he had caused through his actions and selfishness.

He could only imagine what she must think of him. He was supposed to be a pastor, a man of God, and he had fallen prey to the most basic of temptations at the first opportunity. Jake's guilt was overwhelming, and despite his constant teaching on the grace of Jesus, for once it seemed like he was beyond its reach.

The first couple of days after the incident, he had called at least ten times each day. Each time he left a message begging her for forgiveness, pleading for her to call him back. But each time, he was met with nothing. No return calls. No messages. Only the most painful silence he'd ever known.

He recalled their time together at the restaurant. The conversations they'd had. What a hypocrite he was to go from talking about how much he loved being a pastor, to using her for his own sexual gratification. If only he'd listened to that warning. But no. He had rejected the prompting of the Holy Spirit and look what had come of it.

When Joseph in Genesis had been tempted by the Potiphar's wife, he had fled, literally run away from the temptation. Jake didn't do that. Even worse – in this story he was the tempter, and Jessica the tempted. He had taken advantage of the only woman he had ever loved and fondled her in the most inappropriate way. How could he stand in front of his congregation and be a witness when his own sin consumed him?

Jesus, where are you?

The first Sunday came and passed. Jake had never prayed so hard before he went out on the stage to preach. He'd never felt like such a failure. Nothing before even came close. This was on a whole new level. Moral failure by his own making.

Everything he said from the pulpit seemed to fall flat. When he looked at the faces of his congregation, all he saw was condemnation. It was like they knew. Maybe they did. Maybe they could feel his betrayal, like a wound to the spirit. Somehow, he made it through his sermon points, bypassed the invitation, and closed the service a full twenty minutes sooner than normal.

He'd gone immediately after service to the children's church wing, excusing himself from conversations as he passed dozens of members and visitors.

"I'm so sorry, I have to catch up with someone..."; "Forgive me, can I get back with you?"; "Thanks, I'll give you a call this week. Sorry for the inconvenience."

It didn't matter. Jessica had not shown up that day. A substitute had taken her place for Boston's Sunday school class. The next Sunday was a repeat, and Jake feared the worst. He feared Jessica would never return.

A thousand times he considered going by her apartment and knocking until she had to answer the door, but every time he was on the verge of going, he thought better of it. She could call the cops, and then where would he be? He'd be a pastor labeled an adulterer *and* a stalker.

Oh, Jesus, I can't do this. I'm dying inside. She doesn't deserve to be hurt like this. Please, help me make this right.

But it couldn't be made right, could it? How do you take back what's done? So, he sank deeper and deeper into despair and self-loathing, until the crushing weight of his failure threatened to destroy every good thing he'd ever thought about himself. All the while the voice of the enemy kept ringing in his ears: failure, adulterer, hypocrite, vile, selfish, pervert.

JESSICA BUMBLED THROUGH the next two weeks as well as she could. She relied heavily on makeup and sunglasses to mask her puffy, bloodshot eyes, but even with her best efforts, she was unable to avoid at least a few inquiries into her emotional or physical state. She blamed it on allergies – "I've been doing some jogging and I think the great outdoors have decided they don't like me" or "Probably just the weather changing for the fall" – and that had been sufficient to appease whoever was asking. Of course, then she had the guilt of being a liar on top of it all, but at this point, she almost didn't care. She was so miserable without Jake that it was hard to do anything other than exist. And she'd already told the worst lie she could tell. She told Jake she didn't want to be with him. She had hurt him instead of admitting her own failures, and that made her a coward.

She no longer had any doubt that she loved Jake Wilson. Loved him more than she'd ever loved anyone or anything in her life. Much to her surprise, she had taken this harder even than the ending of her marriage. And through it all, she blamed not only herself, but God. Because why would God ever put Jake and Boston in her life in the first place if he knew she would fall for him and be unable to do anything about it without destroying his life?

Then there was Boston, the sweet, angelic child that had come to mean as much to her as Jake in her own way. Jessica grieved for her loss as well. She still saw Boston at school every day. They talked, and Boston would sit with her at lunch on occasion. Jessica tried to hide her fragile state from Boston, and thankfully, thus far Boston had not asked why they hadn't done anything recently outside of school. By now, her pink cast was full of the fledgling signatures and drawings of her fellow students offset by the practiced smooth lines of the John Hancocks of teachers and church adults. But no matter how well Jessica hid it, the truth remained that their relationship would forever be marred by what had happened between her and Jake.

Saturday morning, she sat on her couch watching You've Got Mail, wrapped in a fuzzy throw blanket sans makeup, un-showered, and in need of fresh deodorant. She wore the pajamas she'd donned as soon as she arrived home from school on Friday afternoon. Her hair was pulled up in a half-hearted attempt at a bun, just to keep it out of her eyes. Had she looked in a mirror, she would have cringed at the creature staring back at her. A half-eaten takeout box from Steak-Out sat on the table along with her school bag containing unfinished lesson plans and ungraded tests. She hadn't brushed her teeth the night before or this morning, and they felt as fuzzy as her blanket; she could smell her own breath when she sighed too hard. Jessica had gone full-blown pity party. She knew it, and she wallowed in it.

This was the state she was in when the doorbell rang. She jumped like she'd been caught doing something wrong, then decided whoever it was, she would pretend she wasn't home. She climbed out from the couch, dropping the blanket on the floor, and tiptoed over to the front door to gaze out the peephole. Whatever she expected, it wasn't the person she saw.

A handsome woman, likely in her forties, stood in front of her door waiting patiently. She knocked again, then rang the doorbell. Jessica had never seen the woman before, but she was dressed nicely, at least from the waist up, the part Jess could see, with a smart-looking light gray business jacket. She held a folder of some sort in her hand. Saleswoman? Possibly, but that was prohibited within the complex, not that a few entrepreneurial spirits didn't try it anyway sometimes. For no other reason than curiosity, she cracked the door open to the length of the chain and peeked through.

"Yes?"

The handsome woman smiled. "Are you Jessica Maracle?"

Okay. Not just a random salesperson.

"I am. And you are?"

"Ms. Maracle, my name is Emma Flannery. I'm from the Department of Family and Children's Services. I wonder if I could come in and talk with you for a few minutes?"

Jessica processed the information. Why would a DFCS representative be coming to see her? Did this have something to do with Boston? Did something happen to Jake? Her stomach lurched and she was hit with a wave of nausea.

"Um, sure. One moment, please." She closed the door, ran back to the couch, picked up the blanket from the floor and wrapped it around her tank-top like a bathrobe. She went back and removed the chain to allow the woman entrance.

"Thank you," Ms. Flannery said walking in without further invitation.

Jessica directed her to the recliner.

"Please don't mind the mess," she said, glancing around with some dismay at the state of her apartment.

"Please, Ms. Maracle. I know I was not expected. You wouldn't believe some of the places I see in my line of work."

Jessica wasn't sure if that was supposed to make her feel better or not. She sat back down on the couch, still feeling uneasy.

"What's this about?" she said.

Ms. Flannery leaned forward in the recliner. "Can you confirm that you know a man by the name of Jake Wilson and a child in his care, Boston Evans?"

Jessica stiffened. "Yes. Is something wrong? Did something happen to them?"

Ms. Flannery held up a hand. "Nothing like that, per se."

Jessica folded her arms tightly around herself, still filled with dread.

Ms. Flannery went on. "You've been named as a character witness in a matter concerning the welfare of the child. We received a tip that she might be getting abused by her guardian, Mr. Wilson."

"What?" Jessica was stupefied. The statement pulled her out of her self-indulgent malaise. "That's ridiculous. Jake Wilson would never hurt that little girl. Who said such an awful thing? Whoever it was, they need to be strung up by their toes."

Ms. Flannery was obviously taken aback by Jessica's forcefulness, but she managed a smile. "Ms. Maracle, I understand this type of thing can be emotional, but we're required to investigate the matter. If you don't mind, I'm going to ask a few questions if you could just answer, then I'll give you plenty of time to add anything you wish."

Jessica nodded.

"Are you aware of an incident on June seventh in which Boston had a laceration to her forehead that required stitches?"

"I am."

"And to your understanding, what were the circumstances of this injury?"

Jessica thought back for a moment. It had been several months, but she still remembered what had happened according to Boston and Jake. "She was in the backyard, and their dog, Peaches, took off after a raccoon or something knocking Boston down. She hit her head on the bridge over their koi pond."

"And you were not present at the time?"

"No ma'am."

"You were, however, present when Boston's arm was broken on October the ninth?"

"I was, yes," Jessica said.

"Could you describe what happened?"

Jessica said, "We were at the fair in Perry and Boston had just gotten off one of the kiddie coasters. She was running back to us and, well, she just tripped."

Ms. Flannery flipped open the folder in front of her, consulted it for a second, and shut it again. "What's your relationship to Mr. Wilson?"

I wish I knew, Jessica thought. "We're friends. When Boston first moved in with Jake, I was her Sunday School teacher. She took a liking to me, and we started doing stuff together."

"Just you and the girl?"

"No. All three of us." Jessica was starting to get frustrated again.

"Would you say you've been around them both frequently since Boston came to live here?"

"I would." Though not so much recently.

The worker paused before the next question. "Have you ever seen Mr. Wilson mistreat Boston in any way? Do anything that might make you suspect he abuses her?"

Jessica huffed. "Of course not. Really, Ms. Flannery, Jake is one of the sweetest men I've ever known. He turned his life upside down to take Boston in."

Ms. Flannery nodded. "Do you think given the situation – like you said he gave up his freedom – maybe he could be frustrated and taking it out on the child?"

Jessica gave the other woman a piercing glare. "Never."

Ms. Flannery smiled again as if she had not been asking extremely personal questions of a stranger. It occurred to Jessica that she had no idea if the lady was even who she said she was.

"Do you have some identification?" Jessica said.

Ms. Flannery pulled a badge out of her pocket indicating she was a social worker with DFCS. She handed it to Jessica to look over.

"Ms. Maracle, you may be surprised to find out I'm a member of Pastor Jake's church."

"You are?" She looked up from the ID still in her hand.

"I am. And I personally don't believe a word of this complaint. I believe the same as you do about Pastor Jake. I would trust him with my life, but I'm afraid that's not good enough for the state, though, so I had to follow procedure."

Jessica felt like she could finally breathe, realizing the woman in her home was an ally and not an enemy.

"We had to go through the process just like with anybody that's reported. Everything in the evidence lines up with the complaint being ill-informed at best, and outright deceptive at worst."

Jessica's brows furrowed. "You think somebody was out to hurt Jake by making a complaint?"

Ms. Flannery sighed. "It's possible. That's certainly how it appears to me. Either way, everything you told me corroborates what Jake and Boston have told me about both injuries. A little accident prone, perhaps, but nothing abnormal at all."

"Who gave you my name?" Jessica said.

"Pastor Jake did."

Jessica thought that must have been hard for him to do considering the current state of their relationship. Still, he had trusted her to be honest and supportive with something as important as Boston and that at least made her feel a little better.

But the problem seemed clear to Jessica. Someone wanted to cause trouble for Jake and Boston, and she thought she might know who. Not a name, but the person Jake said had threatened him. The question was – what was next?

AFTER JAKE DROPPED Boston off at school, he went straight to the church. The rest of his staff wouldn't be there until nine a.m., and he wanted the extra time to spend in prayer. He locked the front door behind him, placed his things in his office and went to the sanctuary.

Jake had always enjoyed walking and praying, and often – especially in his younger pastoral years – came to church early or stayed late to walk around the sanctuary while he did so. Now, he set the lights at a dim setting then went to the sound booth and turned on the speaker system. Pulling his phone from his pocket, he chose a worship album on Amazon music and ran the cable from his phone to the system. He hit play and set the volume low as the first strains of music began to permeate the sanctuary.

He began to walk in large circles from the back to front. Immediately, his mind and body fell into the familiar rhythm, and he spent the first couple of songs in worship, thanking God for His goodness, for His Son, and for salvation, but try as he may, it felt flat and lifeless. After the second song, he sat down on the front row. He wasn't really praying, not worshiping. He was just trying to spend time with the Lord.

Bishop Tyndale likened spending time with God to spending time with his wife. "Jake," he would say. "It's like this. Me and Sarah don't constantly jabber at each other when we're together. In fact, most of the time we don't say much at all, but we enjoy being in the same room. When you pray, son, it's not about all the words you say or all the requests you have. It's just about being with Him. He already knows it all anyway," he would say with a wink.

Jake did that now. He allowed himself to sit, to ponder, to remind himself that the Spirit of God lived inside him regardless of how he felt. He reminded himself that he didn't live based on his feelings, even if the guilt of his actions was eating him alive. He reminded himself that in the Bible, God had considered Abraham righteous because Abraham believed the promises of God, not because Abraham was without sin. In fact, when examined closely, Abraham was at times quite a sketchy character. The thought made him laugh out loud, but it also gave him pause.

Jake knew there would be consequences to his actions. Repercussions from sin. But he also knew that in God's eyes, he was as clean from his sin as it was possible to be, because nothing could make him holier than the blood of Jesus already had. It was time to let go of the guilt and shame. Time to deal with the issues and move on.

CHAPTER 19

The first week of November was unseasonably cold for Middle Georgia. By the second week, morning temperatures were in the thirties and didn't get much above forty in the afternoons. Typically, Warner Robins experienced warmer weather throughout most of the holiday months and didn't get colder extremes until late January or February. But not so this year.

Jessica pulled into the Bradford Place Apartments, amazed at how many of the residents had already put up Christmas decorations on the balconies or patios of their apartments. Personally, she never could bring herself to put out decorations before Thanksgiving, but even so, she loved to see them on other dwellings.

She wondered if Jake and Boston had put up decorations yet. It had been nearly a month now since she'd seen them, and Jessica was desperate for interaction with the little girl. After parting ways with Jake, she at first had still spent lunches at school with Boston. But the last week of September had thrown a curveball into her schedule. Mrs. Patois – Denise to Jess – had gone on maternity leave. That had been expected. What was not expected, was that her planned replacement substitute would have to move suddenly due to her husband being transferred from Robins to Holloman Air Force Base in New Mexico. Unable to find another substitute on short notice, several of the teachers had to take on extra duties until a suitable replacement could be found. Jessica had to cover third period math which took place at the same time as Boston's lunch, effectively cutting the opportunity to see her each day. She was also desperate for interaction with Jake but knew that would be a mistake. Knew that it wasn't possible. Still, none of that was Boston's fault and Jessica didn't know how to rectify the situation without making matters worse.

She pulled into a parking space in front of her apartment block, turned off her car, and exited. As she shut the door, a sudden gust bit sharply into her skin and she tightened her scarf, making her way quickly to the walk through. It was even colder there as the wind channeled through the open space like a tunnel, and all she really wanted was to get inside, but she forced herself to check her mail knowing that she had bills coming due soon.

Most people hardly bothered to look at bills in the mail anymore; at least that's what her teacher friends from school told her. Most of them had their bills set up on automatic recurring payments, and Jessica agreed that would have been more convenient. But Jessica's pay was stretched thin. The apartment rent was expensive and on a single income, between that and her car payment, credit card bills, and food, there was little left over by the end of the month. She had to be careful, so she preferred to keep a close eye on her bills and tracking the paper statements helped her to do that.

Jessica pulled the mail out of her box in a wad and stuffed it in her bag, too cold to care if it was neat or not. She could uncrumple it later. She quickly popped the box closed, locked it back, and turned to go up the stairs.

Jessica had never been very good with the cold, and she half ran up the staircase, regretting for the hundredth time not wearing her Timberland boots today and instead wearing the flats that left most of her ankle and the top of her foot exposed. What a stupid thing to do. She got to the landing, hefted her bag up higher on her left shoulder, all the while fiddling with the keys in her right hand, until she found the correct one for the door. She shoved the key in, clicked back the deadbolt, and went inside as quickly as possible, savoring the warm seventy-one degrees she had set the thermostat to that morning.

She moved inside quickly and shut the door, giving a shiver, thankful she was out of the wind. Moving to the kitchen table, she tossed her bag in one of the chairs, then pulled the clump of mail from it and tossed it all on the table. She was sorting through it, smoothing out the wrinkles, when she noticed a small pink envelope that seemed out of place among the rest. She bent over slowly, suspicion working its way through her. The envelope was face-down so she didn't see an inscription. She gently lifted the corner like it might be a snake and tilted it up until she could see the writing on the other side. It simply said "Jessica", but the handwriting was unmistakably Jake's. Over their time spent together with Boston, she'd seen him write out enough sermon notes to recognize the awkward scrawl. There was nothing beautiful about Jake's writing, but it was distinctive.

As she lifted the letter, a fragrant trace of his cologne split the air. Her stomach tightened painfully, the smell immediately catapulting her back to that night in October only a few feet from where she now stood when Jake had first held her in his embrace, smothered her neck with kisses, the soft scratchiness of his beard tickling her flesh. She kicked herself, ashamed how quickly she fell back into that mindset. She backed away from the table and the letter as if it might spring to life and pounce on her.

Jake's calls had been sporadic over the past couple of weeks, totaling three or four at most. As had been her habit since that terrible night, she never listened to them. She deleted them right away, knowing of a certainty that if she gave in the slightest bit, she would call him. If she heard his voice, heard the anguish there, she would run to him like a schoolgirl. She loved him too much for that.

God, help me to get past this. Even if I never find love again, help me to do what's right for Jake. Help me to be a strong, Godly woman that supports him by giving him his freedom. Touch him, heal his heart, and help him to move on. Let him... She could barely bring herself to say it, and even when she did, she knew she didn't really mean it. But she felt like it would make her a better person. Felt like saying the words would mean she was doing her part to let him go. *God give him someone else.* Tears began to stream down her face, hot and thick, and yet she continued. *Lord, give Jake a loving woman who will be there for him, be a great mom to Boston, and exactly what they need. I know You love him and want what's best for him. Help me to want that too.*

She gazed at the letter and picked it up, cradled it to her chest. With a great effort, she set it back down. When she reached for it, her intention had been to throw it away, to discard it just like all his voice messages. She knew she couldn't take the words; couldn't stand to see whatever he'd written inside. But still, for some reason this physical, tangible piece of him, piece of his heart, she couldn't bring herself to throw away. Not yet. She set her bag down in one of the chairs beside the table, trudged to the bathroom, tossed her clothes on the floor, and pulled a towel from under the sink.

During all of this, the letter consumed her thoughts. It was a siren call beseeching her, tempting her, begging her, calling for her. She sighed heavily and ran her hands through her hair, trying to will the draw of the letter from her thoughts.

She moved to the tub and turned on the water. She knew the exact place to stop the lever so the water would be as hot as she could stand it without scalding her skin. She reached in and plugged the old-fashioned stopper into the drain, letting the tub begin to fill. She sat on the edge and watched the water rise. Once it reached a sufficient depth, she stepped in and laid down, putting her ears underneath the water level as it continued to rise. The sound of the water filling the tub was loud from underneath, and she tried to concentrate on the sound rather than thinking about the letter in the other room. Eventually she had to stop filling up the tub and she lay there in confusion and torment.

It occurred to her that God had been silent recently. It seemed like ever since that night, that gentle prodding and leading of the Holy Spirit that she had grown accustomed to was non-existent. *God, what's going on? Where are You? I know You promised never to leave me or forsake me, but I feel like You have. I feel like You're so quiet in one of the worst times of my life.*

She lay there letting her mind drift until the water began to get cold. She had no idea how long she'd been there, but she had a sudden flash of clarity. It wasn't that God wasn't speaking. She wasn't listening. The truth of it reverberated in her heart, and with the realization, the words came. It was different from the voice she was used to hearing, and yet somehow, she knew it wasn't her own. Because it flew in the face of everything she'd been telling herself all these weeks.

You're looking at this all wrong, daughter.

It seemed to keep repeating in her mind over and over, and as it did, it became stronger and stronger and closer to the familiar voice that she was used to. And then, she heard His voice stronger than anytime she could ever remember in her life. It wasn't audible, but there was something so sure and powerful about it that it immediately made tears spring to her eyes. Not tears of pain, not even tears of joy, but tears from knowing that He loved her, and He was still there for her. The voice said the last thing she expected:

Read the letter.

MY DEAREST JESSICA,

I've tried to write this letter a dozen times. I've written hundreds of sermons, but this is the hardest thing I've ever had to write. I know you must think me the biggest hypocrite in the world and that I took terrible advantage of you. You'd be right. There's no excuse for what I did that night. I was wrong. I allowed myself to get carried away and I'm not even sure how it happened. It was all so fast. I know it's a lot to ask, but can we please talk? At least let me explain face to face. Let me apologize to you and beg your forgiveness. If you still want nothing to do with me, I'll understand, but at least I can go on knowing I faced it like a man. I need to know that you've heard my regrets and that I've repented of my actions.

Boston misses you. She doesn't understand. I don't know how to begin to explain it to her. She loves you so much. Even if you don't want to speak to me, would you consider calling her? If you tell me that's why you're calling, I won't hold you or interfere. You know where I am.

Yours Truly,
Jake

JESSICA READ THE LETTER twice more through, then walked to the couch and eased down onto it. She crossed her legs and placed the letter on her lap. She read it one last time, trying to see the meaning *between* the lines.

It was obvious Jake blamed himself. He saw the dissolution of their relationship as related to him touching her inappropriately. That had never been her intent. She was trying to save him, to save herself. Had Jake been inappropriate? Yes. But she had been just as much a willing participant. It didn't really matter who pulled away first, only that God was able to get through to one of them and keep them from going farther than they did.

But now. Now. The weight of her decision hit her like a wrecking ball. What had she even said to him that night? She was so emotional at the time. She couldn't recall the words. She just remembered the overwhelming feeling of her selfish failure and that she had to get Jake away from her, because if he stayed, she would have fallen back into his arms. She would never have been able to let him go, and that was something she would not have been able to live with.

Rather than feeling sorry for herself, she finally placed herself in Jake's shoes and realized that she was being a coward. If she really loved him, and she knew that she did, the only real thing to do was to tell him the truth. To let him know that it wasn't because of what happened that she stepped away. No, that was just a reminder of how unworthy she truly was, and it had jarred her from inaction. He had to know the truth, otherwise it would haunt him forever.

Ten minutes later, Jessica grabbed her car keys, pulled on a jacket, and locked the front door behind her. She took the stairs as quickly as she dared, her breath puffing in little vapor clouds. Now that the decision had been made, it was like a switch had been flipped. She needed to see Jake. Needed to tell him the truth. And she couldn't wait another night. Not another hour.

As she pulled out of the complex, she whispered a prayer for the right words. She paid no notice to the dark sedan that exited the complex a hundred yards behind her. People came and went all the time. And when she turned onto Osigian Boulevard and the car followed suit shortly thereafter, she had forgotten it was even there.

JAKE SECURED THE DOOR of the dishwasher and hit the button twice to start the 2-hour cycle. For the life of him he could never figure out how he and one little nine-year-old girl could go through so many dishes in a couple of days. Honestly, he felt like all he ever did was wash dishes. Boston sat on the couch on the other side of the kitchen island, entranced by some bizarre kids show that Jake was pretty sure had to have been written by people on LSD. He rolled his eyes and chuckled at the silly antics taking place on the screen, walked around the island, and sat down on the couch beside Boston.

The sweet little girl leaned her head over on his arm and yawned. Her breath smelled of chocolate milk. He put an arm around her and pulled her close as Peaches came and nestled at his feet. Jake was suddenly struck by how blessed he was sitting here in this room, at this time, with Boston. At the beginning of the year, he never would have imagined that the horrendous tragedy that had brought them together would have brought so much beauty into his life. Of course, it was a beauty that was also tempered by grief. Grief for the loss of Boston's parents, and now Jake's grief for the loss of Jessica Maracle. Not a day went by that he didn't think of her constantly.

He mailed the letter a couple of days ago. It was a last-ditch effort. Everything he had tried so far had been fruitless. Jessica had not responded at all. He had prayed over the small letter before slipping it into her mailbox. *God, please let her call me. Please just let me hear her voice and tell her the truth. I need to know that she's heard and understands my regret.*

Peaches had just begun to snore when the doorbell rang.

Boston looked up at the door then at Jake. "Who's that?"

Jake frowned. "I don't know." He checked his watch – five after seven p.m. "Maybe somebody selling Girl Scout cookies," he quipped.

Peaches perked up, having had enough experience with Girl Scout cookies to equate the words with the boxes that showed up frequently for several months every year. Jake would often give her Trefoils as treats. It was amazing she wasn't a butterball.

Jake pulled his phone from his pocket and swiped a finger across the screen. The Ring app was already showing a notification and he clicked to join the video. His breath stopped cold in his chest.

"Jessica."

"Jessica!" Boston sprang up like a top and sprinted for the front door. Jake was almost too stupefied to move but he managed to say "Boston, wait for me, hang on." But Boston was already unlocking the door. The door swung open and there she was just as beautiful as the last time he'd seen her. He felt his heart skip a beat and more than anything he wanted to run to her and take her in his arms and hold her close.

But he didn't move. His legs stayed obstinately still, planted like the roots of a huge oak. Jessica bent down and picked up the little girl, hugging her tightly, squeezing her eyes shut as she did so.

"I've missed you so much," Jessica said, and as she did, her eyes briefly made their way to Jake's.

"Where have you been?" Boston said.

Jessica set her back down and squatted so she would be at eye level with the girl. "I'm so sorry honey, there's been some things that I've had to deal with. I'm sorry I was away from you."

Boston cocked her head to the side and placed her hands on her hips and said very stubbornly, "Just don't let it happen again."

Jessica gave her a smile, then leaned forward and kissed her on the forehead, making an exaggerated smacking sound in the process. Jake was still frozen, unable to fathom that she was actually here. It had to be because of the letter. There was no other reasonable explanation. A dozen questions and thoughts ran through his head at the same time. Was she here for an apology? Did she come to reconcile? He dared not hope that. It was too much to hope for, and if it wasn't true, he didn't think that he could bear it.

Peaches, who stood by waiting with the patience of a saint, finally decided she'd had enough and nudged Boston out of the way to demand Jessica's attention.

"Peaches," Boston said in mock exasperation.

Jess bent down and rubbed the dog behind her ears and under her chin. For her part, Peaches gave Jessica several kisses on the nose, her tail thrashing in a state of doggy euphoria.

Jessica stood again and their eyes met for the second time.

"Hi, Jake." she said softly.

"Hi, Jess."

Boston watched them with curiosity, understanding perhaps in a childlike way that something was passing between them that was more than just what she could see on the surface. But it passed quickly, because she grabbed Jessica by the hand and started tugging her towards the stairs. "Come on come on come on, Ms. Jessica. You have to see what I've got, and you have to see what I've done to my room."

Jessica left and shot Jake an awkward glance. Jake gave her an understanding nod, a silent acknowledgment that he would be here for her when she was ready.

"Do you want me to take that jacket?" he asked her.

Jessica pulled Boston to a stop for a second and slid out of her jacket. She handed it to Jake. As she did, their hands brushed for the slightest instance, and for a moment, Jake once again felt like he was whole. But it was brief and quick, and something that he knew was unlikely to last. As Boston dragged Jessica upstairs, chatting all the while, Jessica laughing at her enthusiastic ranting, Jake turned off the television and sat down on the couch to wait and to pray.

CHAPTER 20

Harley Wright sat in his dark car parked on the side of the street a block away from Jake Wilson's house. He already knew it was Jake Wilson's house. He was a good detective, and he'd checked the address and been here multiple times previously to keep a watch on the man. Harley would rotate every so often between watching Jake and watching Jessica. The old man wanted results, and results were Harley's specialty.

Unfortunately, not much had happened over the last month except for the big fat checks rolling into his bank account every week. *Dewey must be freaking loaded*, he thought. Harley may not have looked like the most upstanding guy, heck, he *wasn't* the most upstanding guy, but he made enough of a reputation with his services to charge a premium, and Dewey Knapp hadn't batted an eyelash at his fees. That being said, the old man was starting to get anxious. Harley had discovered some things about the girl, but Dewey still wanted more, and it was taking time. Harley wanted to get done with the job and get back home. He didn't mind the travel and he certainly didn't mind the checks, but he did have a life of his own, places to haunt, bars to visit, chicks to see. Well, he would stick it out because that's what he was good at. Who knew? Maybe something would happen tonight. He waited.

TAKING BOSTON

AFTER MAYBE THIRTY minutes that felt to Jake like twenty years, Jessica came back down with Boston and Peaches in tow. She saw Jake sitting on the couch and gave him a shy smile.

"Mr. Wilson guess what?" Boston said excitedly. "Ms. Jessica thinks they may have a new fourth grade substitute in a couple of weeks and she'll be able to eat lunch with me every day at school again."

"That's great, honey," Jake said. "Can I get you anything?" he asked Jessica. "We have some sodas, of course there's water, milk – Jake made a nasty face, he wasn't a fan of milk; he wouldn't even eat cereal, he only bought it for Boston - whatever you like really," he said.

"No thanks," she said quickly. She turned her attention back to Boston. "Hey, Boston, listen I need to talk to your dad for a little while okay?" Boston gave her a question glance. "Alone. Is that okay?"

Boston raised her eyebrows. "Oh, you mean grown up talk. Okay, but can I watch tv while you talk, Mr. Wilson?"

It was getting close to Boston's bedtime, but Jake knew there was no chance of her going to sleep this early tonight. "Sure," he said.

She flopped onto the couch and picked up the remote. Peaches took up residence beside Boston on the couch as Jake walked around to the back door and put on a pair of worn slippers sitting beside it. He opened the back door and was preparing to go through the storm door when he looked back, noticing Jessica was not following.

Jessica cocked an eyebrow at him. "Going outside? It's freezing out there."

Jake smiled. "Nah you'll be fine," he said. "I've made some additions."

Jessica shrugged, picked up her jacket from where Jake had left it on a chair, and followed him out into the backyard.

Boston's fairy castle was already lit, and Jessica immediately noticed two new additions. There was of course the fireplace that was always there, but there was no fire blazing in it. However, there were two industrial-sized outdoor heaters like the ones you often see at sidewalk restaurants. Jake led the way down across the yard and then the small bridge. Jessica was amazed to see the koi in the pond still quite active. She wondered if that was heated as well.

Jake fiddled quickly with both heaters, and they flamed to life, the heating elements quickly turning a warm orange red.

The pleasant swish of warmth coming down from each heater was more than enough to take the chill out of the air underneath the gazebo, and Jessica, who had slung her jacket over her shoulders as she walked out of the house, now found that she didn't need it at all. She slid it off and set it to the side as Jake took a seat across from her on the opposing sofa.

She was amazed at how normal it all seemed, and how quickly they slipped back into the old familiar ways. She had so many wonderful memories of sitting out here just like this with Jake as Boston played with the fish or with Peaches or sat snuggling with her or Jake as they talked into the night. Funny now, or sad really, how through all those times of deep discussions and thoughts she had managed to completely avoid the discussions about her past that should have come up in any normal relationship.

They sat across from each other, and she started to speak, but Jake raised a hand and cut her off.

"No, no, no, please let me start if that's okay. Jessica, I'm so sorry for the way I treated you. I want you to know that it was never my intent to take advantage of you. If there's any way..."

"Jake, please," she interrupted. "I got your letter today, and it broke my heart. But probably not for the reason you think. I realized how incredibly selfish I've been." She noticed her hands shaking and clasped them together, forging ahead. "You seem to think the reason

I've stayed away from you is because I was offended, or because I thought less of you for what happened between us. But you're wrong. You're so wrong."

Jake waited with a confused look on his face, his attention focused on her, his toes tapping nervously on the concrete floor.

Jessica took a deep breath to focus her thoughts, to think of the perfect words, but in the end she didn't really know how to say it the right way, so she just said it the only way she could. "Jake, what happened between us was on both of us. The only reason I stopped you was because it reminded me of what I am, and what I've done."

Now Jake definitely looked confused. "Okay," he said. "I guess I'm going to need more than that."

She gave a harsh, bitter laugh, then lowered her eyes in shame. "I wasn't honest with you. I mean, I was, but not completely. Yes, I was married, and yes, my husband cheated on me, but I left out the parts of the story that I thought were too terrible to talk about." Her momentum was building. The edge of the cliff was near, and she would jump over it regardless of the outcome. "See, I had known for a while that Craig was cheating on me. I'd suspected it for longer than that, but I found emails, pictures, texts, and plenty of other evidence that he was sexually involved with more than one other woman. I was devastated. I loved him. When we met and got married, I wasn't a Christian. I believed in God in a general way, but I had no relationship with Him. I didn't understand what it meant to be a new creation in Christ until the last year we were married. That's when I got saved."

"Well, that's good," Jake said. "So far I'm not seeing anything so bad."

Jessica felt hot tears stinging her eyes and struggled to keep them in, but it was no use. They spilled over and trickled down her cheeks. The heater still blew the warm air down upon them, but as they blew against her tears, it had a cooling effect which accentuated the chill of the night and caused Jessica to shiver. Or maybe she was just shivering because of the part of the story that came next.

"There was a guy, Jake. Another guy. Someone from my church. He was a good guy, and he meant well. I was new to the church and didn't have a lot of friends. It was a small congregation and the only other person close to my age was him. His name was Tim, and he was easy to talk to. I should have known better, but he was the only person in my Christian sphere that I felt like I could go to.

"At first we would talk after church. He encouraged me, helped me pray for my marriage. I was angry, but I thought maybe if Craig got saved, he would change. But as time went on and Craig got worse, I started to call Tim on the phone. I wanted someone to talk to not just on Sundays or Wednesday nights."

Jake nodded solemnly.

"On top of it all, Craig was doing a lot of traveling at the time, so he wasn't around much. I was heartbroken and bored. Just a real mess, you know? Tim suggested we go out to a movie, just to kill some time as friends. And that's all it was. I was never really attracted to him. He was cute, but my thoughts were on my failing marriage. We did the movie. Then we started going to dinner sometimes. Then there was this thing, or that thing, and..." she took a breath, dreading the next part.

Jake said, "You found yourself seeing a lot of each other."

She nodded. Her tears had stopped, but her emotions were still raw. "I..." she tried, the words like poison in her mouth. "I...I didn't mean for it to happen..."

Jake rose from his seat and crossed over to sit beside her. He sat gently and angled in her direction to listen, but he made no attempt to get closer.

Why would he? Jessica thought. He could probably guess by now what happened.

"Did you sleep with him?" Jake's question was quiet, careful.

She nodded in misery, and a single sob escaped her before she managed to choke it back. "I think it was more to do with loneliness than anything else at first. But then, it was an escape. See, it wouldn't be as bad if it were just a single time, a momentary terrible decision; but it wasn't." She looked away and gazed into the night, too ashamed to meet his eyes or say anything more.

JAKE RELEASED A SILENT breath and prayed for the right words. Nothing came, so he stayed still, afraid to say something wrong. He didn't know if she was waiting on him, or if she just needed time. At last, he simply reached out and placed a hand on her back. As soon as his hand made contact, a wretched moan escaped her, and she began to sob uncontrollably. He couldn't stand it any longer. In one fluid motion he slid near and put his arms around her.

He let her cry for a long time. At least ten minutes must have passed. Her sobs subsided, but her tears remained, and all the while, Jake thought about the revelation she had made and what it meant to him and how it might affect them.

"I was no better than Craig," she said, her head still against his shoulder. "I'm an adulterer."

Jake closed his eyes, her pain nearly tangible in its dreadful efficacy. "Jess, there's so much wrong with that statement. You are not your past. Do you really think God hasn't forgiven what you did?"

She sat back a little so she could see him. "You still don't get it, do you?"

"I guess I don't."

She smiled then, a sweet and sorrowful smile. "I'm not afraid I haven't been forgiven. I've since learned so much about the grace of God; and I've learned even more in my time with you. It's not God I'm worried about. It's you."

"Me? Do you think any of those things would make me care any less about you? Did you think I would stop loving you because you were human? Because you fell prey to temptation at the most fragile point in your life when you'd been betrayed by the one person that was supposed to care for you more than any other?"

She looked at him then and he saw the truth behind her eyes. That's exactly what she feared. Not a lack of God's forgiveness, but a lack of his, and perhaps the inability to forgive herself. He remembered then the conversation they'd had right here so many months ago, and he realized with dawning wonder that God had been planting seeds of healing for Jessica Maracle even then.

"You're such a good man, Jake. Why would you ever want to be with a woman like me? Someone used and abused, who turned to their flesh for gratification. That's why...don't you see? That's why I pushed you away that night. I wasn't angry at you. I knew I let things go too far. I *wanted* them to go too far. My past came back to haunt me, and I can't put that on you, Jake. For you to be with someone like me, it could destroy the ministry you've built. That night just reminded me of how wretched I am."

Insight poured through him, and he spoke as the Spirit put the words on his heart. "There's nothing wrong with wanting emotional *and* physical intimacy with someone you care about, Jess. That's the way God made us. It's just about keeping it in the right place. And don't you dare think that was all on you. I let myself get way out of control. I knew I shouldn't have come in. Knew it would be dangerous if anything happened." Jake measured his next words, aware of how they could sound; how they could come across. "I want you more than any woman I've ever known. I want you emotionally, and spiritually, and yes...physically. My body craves intimacy with you, and that of itself doesn't make us wrong. It makes us real. What we choose to do with that is what's wrong or not."

"You would really forgive me of all of that? All the terrible things I've done?"

Jake smiled as the Holy Spirit prompted him. "Have you forgotten David slept with another man's wife then had him killed to cover up her illegitimate pregnancy?" He cocked a quizzical eyebrow at her. "Have you killed anybody yet?"

She couldn't help it. She chuckled and shook her head no. "But your church. What if they knew? Even just knew that I'm divorced? It could hurt you, and I can't live with that."

He weighed her words. The truth was, he didn't care what anyone else thought, but he took a different approach. One he also believed to be true. "I think you're underestimating the people of God." He took both of her hands in his and kissed her sweetly on the forehead. "I know there's a way to do this, and I'm messing all of that up. But I *know* that God brought us together. I'm sure of that, now. I may be overstepping, but I love you, Jess. I love you more than anything in this world, and I want to spend my life with you."

Fresh tears spilled from her eyes. "Jake. I'm so scared."

"I get that. All I'm asking is for you to trust me when I say God has a plan for us. His plans aren't always clear, and sometimes they're scary, but He always does right by us in the end."

JAKE TUCKED BOSTON into bed, pulling the covers high up to her chin. Her left arm stuck out, its bright pink cast looking a little worn for the wear.

"How's that, sweetie?" he said.

Boston nodded. Behind Jake, Jessica watched it all.

"Okay, we'll be right downstairs if you need us."

Jake leaned over and kissed Boston on the cheek, then turned to leave with Jessica.

"Jessica?" Boston said.

Jess turned back. "Yes?"

Boston pointed to the spot on her cheek that Jake had kissed. Jake and Jessica shared a smile. Jessica walked back to the bed and placed a kiss on Boston's cheek as well. Jessica's hair hung down and brushed Boston's nose. Boston giggled and scratched at it with her right hand from under the covers.

"You remind me of her," Boston said.

"Of who, love?"

"My mommy."

Jessica smoothed Boston's hair back from her face, then kissed her again, this time on the nose. When she looked up, she saw Jake wipe away a tear.

Jake turned out the light and they walked back down the stairs, took a seat on the couch. On the television, Jake put on a soft-Jazz music station to play in the background. They sat that way for a long while, hand in hand, talking sporadically during long stretches of listening to the gentle strains of John Coltrane and Cole Porter.

Jessica leaned over and gave him a kiss. It was unspoken, but they both kept it short, unwilling to give place to further temptation, especially not after last time.

"I should be going. I have to work in the morning."

Jake gave her an odd look.

"It's a Saturday," he said.

"Tutoring. I do it once a month on Saturday mornings."

Jake made an "ah" motion with his mouth.

"Listen," Jake began, but he was interrupted by a scream from upstairs. Immediately, he and Jessica were on their feet and darting up the staircase. They ran into the room to find Boston sitting up in her bed, her face illuminated by a small nightlight. She wasn't crying, but her breathing was rapid.

Jake sat on one side of the bed and Jessica sank down on the end. Jake reached up and wiped sweat from Boston's face.

"Another nightmare?" he said.

Boston nodded.

"I thought you weren't having those anymore," Jessica said.

Jake answered for her. "Not often, but every once in a while."

Jessica reached out and put a hand on Boston's knee.

"Are you okay, now?" Jake said.

"Mr. Wilson, I know you usually stay with me, but do you think Jessica can sit with me tonight until I fall back asleep?"

Jake shot a glance at Jess.

"Well, Ms. Jessica needs to get home," he said.

"It's fine," Jessica said. "I'd love to sit with you."

Boston smiled, contented. Jessica moved around the side of the bed and cradled Boston against her body as Jake rose.

"Do you want some water, baby?" he said to Boston.

Boston's eyes were closed, and she was already drifting back into sleep, worn out from staying up so late and the excitement of Jessica's arrival.

"No, thank you, Daddy," she mumbled.

Jake froze. He looked to Jessica and his chin trembled ever so slightly. After a moment, he leaned over and kissed them both, then left the room.

CHAPTER 21

Jessica awoke fully in an instant, her mind and body telling her something was off. Something was different than normal. Then she felt the lump next to her, noticed the unicorn decorations on the walls, and the sun shining through the second-floor window. Uh-oh.

As she realized her predicament, she carefully and quickly extricated herself from where Boston had placed an arm across her waist. Boston was sleeping soundly and didn't stir. She rose and tiptoed down the stairs, to the right, and into the living room where Jake was snoring like a tugboat on the couch. Peaches was lying beside him and raised her eyes at Jessica's entrance.

Jessica leaned over and gave Peaches a rushed pat on the head. The dog rolled over, wanting its belly rubbed, but Jessica turned to Jake instead.

She whispered. "Jake." She was still afraid to wake Boston if she was too loud. Jake stirred a little but didn't wake. Jessica said louder, "Jake." Still nothing. She rolled her eyes and reached out, took his shoulder, and shook it while calling his name again as loudly as she dared. "Jake."

He sat up, startled, their heads colliding painfully. He went back down, cradling his head as Jessica stood doing the same.

"Oh my gosh!" Jake said. He looked around, his eyes glazed, not quite awake yet. Slow realization dawned in his eyes as he realized Jessica was standing over him.

"Really?" she said.

He still didn't say anything. Acted as if his mind was full of mud. Finally, he smiled, then frowned, noticing the light.

"You're still here," he said.

She shrugged sheepishly. "I kinda fell asleep with Boston and now I'm late for work."

"It's Saturday."

She growled in frustration.

"Oh. Right."

They both sprang into action.

"What do you need?" Jake said.

"My keys are in my jacket," she said, running into the bathroom. "I think I left my jacket outside if you can get it for me."

As she entered the bathroom at full speed, her foot slipped on the bathmat. She crashed into the shower curtain, pulling it down along with the curtain rod.

Jake flew in a second later to find her huddled in the tub.

"Crap. Are you okay?"

She took his offered hand and he pulled her up.

"I'm fine." Her tone sounded anything but. As she came to a stand, they both paused, both looked at the ceiling, and when they heard nothing from Boston's room, continued on. She shoved past him with an embarrassed giggle and stationed herself in front of the mirror.

"Keys," Jake said.

"Keys," she agreed.

He took off, and a moment later she heard the back door open followed by the storm door. Heavy footfalls echoed across the deck as he ran to fetch her jacket from the gazebo.

She looked forlornly at her reflection. Her clothes were hopelessly disheveled. She tried to brush through her tangled hair with her hands only to succeed in yanking painfully on a knotted section. Oh, well. She had a brush in the car.

Jake returned. Surely he had broken some kind of Olympic record in his retrieval of her keys. She glanced at him in the mirror.

"Where's my jacket?"

Jake grimaced, scrunching his nose up hard. "Koi pond. Here."

He tossed the keys to her, but Jessica wasn't ready. They sailed through the air past her and landed squarely in the toilet. They both stopped and stared in horror.

"Nice catch," he said. They laughed.

Five minutes later – time spent mostly by Jake sticking his arm in the toilet to retrieve her keys and then washing them and himself with the meticulous paranoid attention of a man with OCD – Jessica climbed into her car and cranked it. She hit the down button for the window as she shut the door. The one-touch mechanism kept it going until it was fully down, and Jake leaned in to give her a quick kiss.

She backed down the driveway, running over a bed of flowers and nearly ramming the mailbox in the process.

She yelled out the open window. "Sorry."

As she pulled away, for the second time she failed to give any consideration to the dark sedan that was parked on the side of the street a block down from Jake's house. Nor did she notice the man sitting inside with a camera pointed at her.

DEWEY KNAPP STOOD IN his living room. He was still in his bathrobe – the one he'd hastily pulled on when Harley rang his doorbell and awakened him from a fitful sleep – as the morning sun glinted through the palatial floor-to-ceiling windows that stretched the length of his living room. All around him reposed the finest accoutrements money could buy. He spared no expense when it came to the luxuriousness of his home. Antique tomes populated the bookshelves to either side of the twelve-foot fireplace. Overhead, a massive chandelier of moose antlers hung from the central beam of the vaulted ceiling. Complimentary beams fashioned from full tree trunks ran north to south forming the requisite look of the chateau lodge that Dewey had constructed on a hill overlooking his fifty acres of property just outside of Perry.

He noticed none of it, his mind swirling with gleeful machinations. He stared unseeing into the lifeless fireplace, the remnants of last night's fire nothing more than a pile of ash. An introspective man may have seen a parallel. That's what his life had devolved to — a tepid pile of ash. At sixty-five years of age, he had every luxury money could buy, but none of it made him happy. Oh, he would say it did, but really, it was all superficial fluff.

He was the saddest example of a man. The kind of man that wasted his life on outward riches while his soul rotted inside. He attained success in business yet remained ignorantly unaware that true happiness was found not in what you had, but who. He was a social leper, oblivious to his own condition, so consumed by hate and power lust, that he could see nothing else. Unable to appreciate that he had no family or friends, only employees.

His throat burned from recurrent acid reflux, and he mindlessly pulled a pack of Tums from where they sat on the coffee table. He fiddled with it, hooking a fingernail in behind the tablets and pushing three to the forefront before popping them into his mouth. They were the fruity kind, so they tasted tolerable, but the chalky texture always threatened to gag him.

In his left hand, he held a large envelope, the one Harley Wright had just dropped off. The anonymous tip to DFCS had been a long shot. Dewey knew probably nothing would come of it, but at the very least it had caused Jake Wilson several days of inconvenience. That gave Dewey some small satisfaction. The PI, Harley, had turned up some useful information about the girl. Jessica Maracle had quite the past. Dewey waited for the opportune time to utilize it, and with the contents of this envelope, the time had come.

He raised it to his lips and kissed it like a dear friend. He smiled to himself, thinking of the look on Jake Wilson's face – that smug, know-it-all, self-righteous prig. He couldn't wait to bring him down.

He tossed the envelope on the coffee table, sat gingerly on the couch – his rebellious joints guaranteed he did nothing quickly– and gazed at it. It was not his most aggressive move, but hopefully it would render that other option moot. Because that option was not ideal. It had the likely effect of further impacting Dewey financially, and if that could be avoided, then all the better.

Either way, he would outlast Pastor Jake Wilson. He would win because he always did. He didn't read much of the Bible or study much about the God he claimed to admire, but he was sure of one thing – God made Dewey Knapp for success. It was his "gift" from God. It had to be because it was so obviously what he was good at. And that meant whoever stood in his way was standing against God. That included any pastor who thought himself better than Dewey. When examined under the proper light, it became apparent that his destiny was to bring about the downfall of Jake Wilson. He was God's instrument for that purpose, and he was a more than willing vessel.

For now, he would play the opportunity that had coalesced with surprising fortuity. As dad always said, "Timing is everything. If you're patient, even the best opportunities can get better." It was how Dewey had managed to amass a fortune in excess of his wildest dreams, and it was how he was about to cause Jake Wilson a lot of pain.

WILLIAM TYNDALE AND Jake Wilson squared off from either side of Tyndale's desk.

"For heaven's sake, Jake, what were you thinking?"

Jake blew an exasperated breath. "What was I thinking? Nothing. It was an accident, Bill. Plain and simple."

Tyndale had just shown Jake the set of photographs. They came from an envelope that had been taped to the door of the State Offices building that morning with nothing on the outside other than the scrawled words "For William Tyndale". It was a series of dated, time-stamped pictures of Jessica Maracle entering Jake's house, shots throughout the night of her car still parked outside, and a final set of photos of her leaving the next morning – Jake kissing her through the open window of her car. And a blackmail letter.

The letter was short and to the point. Dewey Knapp demanded Jake Wilson resign as pastor of Life Church the following Sunday, or Knapp would go public with the photos through social media along with the evidence he obtained of Jessica Maracle's prior divorce and the accusations of her ex-husband that she had been unfaithful to him during the proceedings.

"No, no, no. There's nothing plain and simple about any of this. You're a single pastor whose girlfriend just spent the night at his house."

Jake thrust a finger at Tyndale. "That's not how it was! I already told you. She fell asleep with my kid, Bill."

"I get it, Jake. But it doesn't matter if I believe you or not. You see what Knapp's implying."

Jake was nearing the peak of frustration. He knew everything Bill was saying was right, but he was at the point of being argumentative for argument's sake. "So what?" he said.

"So what? So what? So, you know how this goes. I went to bat for you to get you that church. Single men don't get put in churches that big. And given that you're single, you're scrutinized even more so than other pastors."

"I didn't ask for that," Jake said.

Bill gave a conceding not. "Doesn't matter, though. It goes with the job."

Jake flopped into a chair and put his face in his hands, then looked back up. With great effort, he struggled to calm himself.

"Okay, fine," Jake said, reeling back on his tone and volume. "Yes, I understand what you're saying. I don't like it, but it's true. Still, don't you think it's a problem that Dewey Knapp is spying on me?"

"Of course it is. It's a vile thing to do. We can kick him out of the church if you want, but it doesn't solve the problem of these." He pointed at the photographs and letter lying on his desk.

They both sat for a long time, mulling over the situation. Finally, Jake spoke again.

"I wish you would have told me it was him that filed that first complaint."

Bill hung his head. "I know. I do too, but the silly, cockamamie bologna he was upset about was so ridiculous…I just thought nothing would ever come of it. I'm sorry, Jake. You know I've always got your back. I didn't take it seriously enough. I mean, people love you, but you can't please everybody. You know the junk we deal with from members sometimes. Even the apostles made people mad. I figured he was just a crackpot."

Jake's eyebrows arched nearly to his hairline. "I think he's *proved* he's a crackpot."

Bill smirked. "Agreed."

When Jake spoke again, his tone was softer. Thoughtful. "You know, I think he's the one that told DFCS I was abusing Boston."

"He did what?"

"Few weeks ago," Jake said. "Somebody – anonymously – called DFCS and told them they had reason to believe I was abusing Boston. She had a couple of accidents, not even close together, just kid stuff. Dog knocked her over and busted her head, then she fell at the fair and fractured her arm. But they did an investigation."

Bill looked dumbfounded. "Are you serious?"

"Didn't come to much. They didn't really believe the tip off. Did character references and that kind of thing. Most of all, they asked Boston and of course she told them what really happened. But it was a pain in the butt having to deal with it."

"Makes sense considering this," Bill said. He leaned forward and rested his forearms on his desk, his fingers steepled together. "Let's say it was him. Making a complaint about your monetary teachings to the State Administrative Bishop is one thing but lying to DFCS is on a whole other level. Wouldn't that be a felony or something?"

"I don't know. Maybe not that bad. Still."

"Right. But I bet it's still bad enough to get him in real trouble if he got found out. You really ticked him off. Tell me about the loan he proposed again."

Jake recounted the details of his meeting with Dewey Knapp and his loan proposal, the way Dewey had been insulted, and how he threatened Jake. When he was done, Bill sat back, pulled a handkerchief out of his pants pocket, and swiped it across his forehead.

"It would take a long time to pay back, but he's what, early sixties? A twenty-year loan on 2.5 million dollars, once interest is applied...that's a lot of money when it's all said and done. I can see how a temperamental person could get upset about losing that prospect."

"Temperamental? He's acting like a vengeful member of the mob, Bill."

"I wasn't trying to underplay it," Bill said snidely. "Either way, the fact remains he wants your resignation on Sunday. He's expecting it or else he's going to go public to try and tarnish you."

"And Jess," Jake said.

Bill nodded with a frown.

"What do you suggest?" Jake said.

"There may be one thing you can do, but it's not totally up to you, Jake."

"What's that?"

Bill's response was marked by a sense of solemn dread and Jake understood why. It could seriously backfire.

CHAPTER 22

Sunday morning arrived like a rolling freight train. Despite spending the last several days in prayer, Jake awoke with no great feelings of peace. In fact, he couldn't remember ever feeling so distraught. A balloon of lead had settled into his stomach and every single step was like dragging his feet through thick mud.

He recalled the conversation the evening after he met with Tyndall. He left Boston with Amber again, the young lady from the youth group, and gone to Jessica's apartment. He told her everything – the photos, the threats, the ultimatum. Jessica sat glued to her couch, a look of abject disbelief on her face, her hands shaking from fear or adrenaline, or maybe both. When he finished, she spoke with trembling lips.

"And you think he'll actually do it?"

"I do," Jake said. "But if we get on top of it, make the first move, he won't be expecting that. He'll have nothing left to threaten us with."

"That you know of," Jessica said.

Jake shrugged, acknowledging the possibility.

Jessica's temples pulsed as her jaws worked feverishly as she ground her teeth together. She stood, crossed her arms, and stared out the glass door to her deck and the grounds below.

"This is exactly the kind of thing I was afraid of, Jake. The reason I told you we couldn't be together. I knew it would come back to haunt you. My life and all the terrible stuff I've done. You're having to pay for it."

Jake was up in a flash, his arms around her, pulling her close. "No," he said, kissing her tenderly. "You're seeing it through his eyes. That's how Dewey Knapp sees it. We're gonna take that away from him. Instead of being threatened by a hateful old man, we're going to put our trust in the Lord and in His people. If I've taught my congregation like I've tried, they'll give the same grace to you that I preach to them every week. If I need to, I'll tell them everything wrong I've ever done in my life so they'll know without a doubt that we are all the same at the cross. If they can't accept that, then that's their problem and we'll move on. But I'm not concerned about *my* reputation. And I'm sticking with you no matter what. I won't lose you, whatever it costs me." He paused until she looked into his eyes. "That's what I believe is right, Jess. But I can't ask you to do the same. That has to be your decision, and I won't take this approach without you."

Her smile didn't hide her fear, but it accentuated her resolve. "Okay," she said.

He had expected to hear trepidation in her voice, but instead there was quiet strength.

"It's time I stopped running from my past," she said. "I almost let it destroy what I have with you, and if there's anything I can do to keep it from destroying your ministry, I'm willing to do it. I think I'm ready to trust God to take care of what's behind me." She cradled her head against his shoulder. "After all, if you can forgive me, that's all that really matters. You're always preaching about the grace of God. Maybe it's time to ask the church if they really believe it or not."

To Jake, it was one of the single greatest moments of bravery and honesty he'd ever seen from anyone. And it made him love her even more than he thought possible.

All throughout the song service that Sunday, Jake was in another place in his mind, considering what was to come. Beside him, Jessica's body language reflected his own somber anticipation. She had chosen to be here with him today not only to lend her support, but to lend credence to his words. To show that she also was willing to face the truth. As the song service wound down, and one of the associates was taking the offering before the start of the sermon, Jake said one final prayer.

Jesus, let your will be done. Whatever happens to me, take care of your people, and take care of Jess.

DEWEY DROVE TO CHURCH that morning with a feeling of smug satisfaction that rivaled anything he'd ever felt. Today was the day that he would be rid of Pastor Jake Wilson. Dewey greeted everyone he passed that morning. "Good morning." "How do you do?" "So good to see you." The same greetings usually reserved for him, he now bestowed on others, so excited was he about the prospect of what lay ahead. *If you only knew,* he thought to himself, looking around at the people in the building.

He could hardly contain his excitement through the worship service. Though he usually never participated other than standing from time to time, this morning he clapped his hands and smiled. To anyone around him, they would have thought that he was excited in the Lord. And maybe he sort of was because he was finally getting the retribution he deserved. What was that verse? Touch not mine anointed and do my servant no harm? Wasn't that what Jake Wilson had done to him? Belittled him? Disrespected him? Treated him with contempt? And if Dewey was God's man of action, wasn't Jake Wilson doing him harm by coming against him in that way? He savored justification. All that was left was for the show.

JAKE TOOK THE STAGE with determined dignity. As he took the first step from his seat, he felt suddenly energized as he remembered who he served. He was a child of the Creator, the Author of Life. And Jake had the promise from the Word that God would work all things for his good. The peace that eluded him before, now came as he stepped onto the stage behind the pulpit. He was assured in his spirit that this was his place, the place he was supposed to be, the place God had called him to. And God would stand with him.

"Good morning," he said. "Thank you all for being here this morning. Today, is going to be a little different than our typical service," he said. "I have a special announcement to make at the end of my sermon, so I ask all who can to please stay until the end."

He preached about original sin, the failure of Adam and Eve to obey due to deception and a desire to be more like God as promised by the serpent. Jake spoke of how the entire Bible was the story of God's journey to reconcile fallen men to Himself, and that He did it by taking upon Himself the form of flesh, living the perfect life no man ever could, and dying and resurrecting so that all who believed in Him would not perish but have everlasting life. As Jake closed the sermon, the very atmosphere seemed charged with a mood of love and forgiveness. He said a final prayer and asked everyone to remain seated.

He began. "Today, I'm afraid I have to bring some bad news to you."

IN HIS SEAT, DEWEY sat a little straighter, unable to repress a grin of satisfaction.

"First of all," Jake said, "I want to introduce you to someone today." He motioned towards Jessica sitting in the front row and she stood. Jake could see the uncertainty on her face, but she smiled beautifully. He gave her an encouraging nod and she responded in kind, then sat back down. "This is Jessica Maracle," Jake said. "Many of you know her, though you may not see her very often because she is one of the hard-working teachers in our Sunday school and youth department. Over the past several months, I've had the privilege of getting to know this young woman, and I can say without a doubt that she is a woman of great character and a beautiful heart. I can also say that I have grown to deeply love her."

Across the church were noises of pleasure and affirmation. A couple of teen boys from the youth group whooped and catcalled. "Go Pastor Jake," they shouted. "You're the man." Jake was sure he turned several shades of red. As the laughter died down, Jake continued.

"Unfortunately, I have something negative to share with you as well." A few murmurs buzzed through the group. "In recent months, I've come under a personal attack. The first event came when I was reported to the Department of Family and Children's Services for abusing my goddaughter, Boston. This was a despicable lie, and something that DFCS verified was completely untrue. For reasons I will not go into, I believed this act to be retribution for turning down a business proposal from someone who will remain nameless. I admit this part is speculation and I could be wrong. However, I received a threat this week from this person in the form of a blackmail letter. He included his name to leave no doubt."

There was more murmuring, and several angry exclamations at Jake's revelation.

No, no, no! This was going all wrong. Dewey squirmed in his seat. He clenched his jaws painfully. His fingernails dug into the flesh of his hands from clenching his fists. He didn't know where Jake was going with this, but it was bad. Would the man dare to call him out? In front of all these people?

Jake gave a quick cough, clearing his throat. "The Friday night before last, Jessica came to see me and Boston at my home. We spent a long time talking that evening, and as the night was winding down and Jessica was preparing to go home, Boston had a nightmare. We both went upstairs to check on her, and Boston asked Jessica if she would sit with her until she fell asleep. Jessica agreed to do this even though it was very late. Unfortunately, she fell asleep with Boston, and I fell asleep downstairs watching television. Neither of us woke until the next morning. Let me say first and foremost that *nothing* improper happened. I do not want my little girl dragged into any of this, but she knows the truth because Jessica was with her all night. It was an accident. I understand and know that as a pastor and a man of God this perhaps doesn't look too good. But I'm asking you to believe me and to trust me today, to trust any reputation I've built with you over the past years. What we did not know, was that this person was spying on us. I don't know if he did it himself or if he had someone else do it, but Thursday of this week, the State Administrative Bishop of Georgia, William Tyndale, received a series of photographs and the blackmail letter at his office."

Jake explained the contents of the photos, then read the letter to the church, leaving out details of Jessica's past and Dewey's name. When he finished, there was nothing short of an uproar. Several people shouted demands for the instigator's name. A few of the women were weeping, and angry conversations and complaints created an animated din of noise in the large sanctuary.

Jake looked to where Jessica was seated, saw that her own cheeks were wet. She nodded again, encouraging him on. Jake raised his hands for silence. "Please, ladies and gentlemen. Please, if I may."

Slowly, the noise died down, not completely, but enough that Jake could continue. "Let me finish if I may. The things threatened to be revealed about this woman that I love," his voice broke, and he paused to gain composure. "These are things from her past that she does not deny. But they are mistakes covered by the blood of Jesus. Just as all of us have sinned and come short of the glory of God. And you all know that I teach that once something is covered by the blood, it's over and done in the eyes of the Lord. So, Jessica and I have made the decision that whether this person makes these things public or not, I will not resign from this church and neither of us will back down from our relationship. We love each other, and we're excited to see where the Lord takes our relationship. I only ask that you give her and me the same grace that Christ freely offers to us all."

There was a pregnant pause, then someone clapped, and it was quickly joined by several more, and so on and so on until the place rang with thunderous applause and many shouts of "Amen" as the crowd stood up in solidarity and support. Jake struggled for composure at the outpouring of love and marveled at the unity of the people, the way the Body of Christ was meant to be. He managed to nod through dripping eyes, something reflected in the countenances of many of the good men and women standing before him.

Dewey was beside himself with rage. He barely stayed in his seat throughout the tirade. When everyone else stood, he did so as well, only so he wouldn't stand out. A murderous hatred welled in him, his face red and blotchy. He muttered curses under his breath, his eyes stark and maddened.

After the applause subsided, Jake said, "I want all of you to know that Jessica and I have decided not to retaliate in any way against this man. It is our hope that he will repent and be blessed. Please pray for us as we do our best to move forward in the wisdom of God for ourselves and the church. We love you."

As he said these final words, Jake's eyes met Dewey's and held his gaze. Dewey glared in return, not even attempting to conceal his animosity. It was time to play that trump card. Dewey smiled with wicked glee. He was going to crush Jake Wilson, and this time, there would be nothing he could do about it.

A WEEK PASSED, THEN another. Dewey had stopped attending church. He had not released the photos and information on social media as threatened. Jake continued to grow closer to Jessica, and Boston thrived with her return. Jake began to think it might be over. After all, apart from making things up, what else could Knapp possibly have to lord over him? As the holidays approached, life began to seem normal again. Little did he know, that's exactly what Dewey Knapp wanted. For him to feel free, happy even, before the steel trap snapped shut with finality.

CHAPTER 23

Jake arrived at the church at nine-thirty a.m. on the Monday morning of Thanksgiving week. The weekend had been rainy and overcast, but the morning had dawned bright and clear. He was light-hearted as he pulled into his reserved parking space and put the vehicle in park. Everyone had been given the week off, and he intended to use the morning to get some work done since there would be no distractions. Jess had taken Boston for the morning since they were both off from school. The plan was for Boston to get a haircut, something which Jake had a surprising amount of trepidation about.

As he approached the front of the building, he climbed the front steps, considering how silly it was for him to be afraid that Boston would come back with a haircut he didn't prefer. Besides, Jess had great taste and she wouldn't...

Jake came to a sudden stop. Ahead, taped to one of the doors was a large manila envelope. It hung there ominously. Across the front, in large black letters, it said "Jake". He looked around, half-expecting to see Dewey Knapp in the parking lot hiding behind a light pole, but he was alone. It was Dewey. He knew it without even looking inside the envelope. It was left the same way as the photos were left for Bill.

He forced his feet to move, plodding with dread toward the letter as if it was a death sentence, no clue as to what might lie inside. He pulled it down in one swift motion, tucked it under his arm like a football, and unlocked the door. As he stepped inside and locked it behind him, he scanned the parking lot once more, unable to shake the creepy feeling that he was being watched. But again, there was nothing. No other cars. No one within sight.

He didn't bother to go to his office. Instead, he stepped up to the greeters' stand and slapped the envelope down on it. His keys still in hand, he inserted one into a small open space at the edge of the envelope where it sealed and used it to make a rough slit along the side. He pulled the contents out, a thick set of papers stapled together with an industrial strength staple, and laid them on the counter beside the now empty envelope. The top page glared at him with malice. In red ink – a macabre choice in Jake's estimation – was written the following:

Dear Jake. This is your last chance. Resign, or else. See page eight.

Below that was Dewey's signature, just in case there had been doubt. Jake rifled quickly through to page eight and found a section that had been highlighted in bright yellow. He read it, trying to make sense of some of the legal jargon. It fell into place, and he looked up, dread filling his stomach with thick unbelief. He hastily flipped to the last page of the document and there it was – First National Bank of West Georgia. Underneath were multiple signatures, but the two that stood out most prominently to Jake were those of Dewey Knapp and Ed Grogan, the previous pastor of Life Church.

Oh, God. This can't be happening. Please tell me this isn't happening.

Jake yanked his phone out of his pocket and dialed Bill Tyndale.

By noon, a three-way call was started between Jake, Bill Tyndale, and a gentleman named Arnold Hoffstetler.

"Jake. Can you hear us okay?" Bill asked after Arnold had dialed in.

"Yeah. I'm here," Jake said.

"Good. Arnold is the head of the New Creation in God denominational legal team. He's got about as much experience as you can get. Arnold, did you get the fax from Pastor Wilson?"

"I did." Arnold's voice was weathered, an older man with a lot of miles on him.

"And you've had time to look it over?" Bill asked.

Jake was impatient, fearing the worst, and every single second was like an eternity of having his head on the chopping block waiting on the axe to fall.

Hoffstetler sighed. *Not a good start,* thought Jake.

The old man spoke. "I ran through it with several members of the legal team. Everything is straightforward and simple enough considering the damage it could do."

Jake blinked, felt his throat tightening. He thought his nose might start running as his eyes burned. "I read it right, Mr. Hoffstetler?"

You could hear the sympathy when Hoffstetler said, "I'm afraid so, son. It's called a demand feature. It appears that this Knapp fellow played a big one on Pastor Grogan."

Jake tasted bile. "Why didn't the State catch it? With my new building project, they're going over everything with a fine-toothed comb."

This time, Bill answered. "It's only been within the last five years that the State has undertaken to oversee all details of building projects for local congregations. It was put in as a fail-safe." He gave a mirthless grunt. "Probably because of stuff like this. Anyway, when Grogan upgraded the sanctuary, the checks and balances on the state level weren't in place. I mean, we still had to give the go ahead on projects, but once that happened, it was the responsibility of the pastor to make sure he had legal representation if he thought it necessary. We advised ministers and the local councils to reach out to Arnold and his crew, but it wasn't a requirement. Apparently,

Grogan trusted Knapp implicitly. He didn't get snagged by the hook. He plum swallowed it."

Jake hung his head and wondered if he might vomit.

Hoffstetler cleared his throat. "I'm afraid gentleman, it gets worse."

JESSICA SAT IN HER apartment beside Boston, who was busy reading a pristine copy of *The Lion, The Witch, and The Wardrobe* that Jessica had purchased for her.

"It's beautiful," Boston exclaimed when Jessica had presented it to her earlier that week.

"Have you read it yet?" Jessica had asked.

Boston shook her head no, then embraced Jessica in a thankful hug.

"Good," Jess said. "I was afraid after I told you about it all those months ago that you had already picked it up at the library."

On the couch beside her now, Jessica recalled what Boston had said that day in the lunchroom about taking care of her books. So far, Boston was true to her word. The book on her lap was still immaculate, the spine unbroken, the cover clean and unwrinkled. Jessica marveled at her, and briefly wondered how great Mike and Ruby Evans must have been to have produced such a child.

A pounding rang through the door, startling them both, and Jessica leaped up, glancing out the peephole. "It's Jake," she called to Boston. She pulled the door open and spoke to him. "Hi. Are you done for the day? It's not even noon," Jessica said. She noticed his expression, and her smile faded. "What's wrong?"

At these words, Boston looked up from the book on her lap. Jake pushed past Jessica into the room, his movements stilted and charged. "Mr. Wilson?" Boston said, startled at his pained expression.

Jake pleaded with his eyes. Jessica had never seen him look so burdened. Before she could even say anything, Jake's legs buckled, and he fell on his knees.

Boston leapt from the couch and ran to him, kneeling beside him, her face a mask of fear. Jake noticed her for the first time and pulled her into an embrace, cradling her like a life preserver in a hurricane addled sea. He looked up. His words were cracked and dry.

"Oh, Jess. We're in trouble."

CHAPTER 24

When Dewey Knapp left his office to go home late Tuesday evening, he was in a funk. He put his Land Rover – he'd felt like driving a big vehicle that morning – in gear and pulled from the parking lot of A Taste of Italy.

By his own reasoning, he should be happy. Ecstatic, even. He had closed the noose around Jake Wilson's neck. He acknowledged the possibility that Jake might refuse to step down as pastor, in which case Dewey would demand full payment of the loan and most likely foreclose on the church building. That could cost him financially because he might never recover the loss of the initial loan, but then again, he also might be able to sell the building and property to another interested party, in which case, he might get even more for it in the long run.

The deal had been a masterstroke. One that he did not know would work out so fortuitously at the time. Pastor Ed Grogan, who Dewey liked, was not a businessman. Dewey saw it as his sole responsibility to guarantee Life Church was under the control of a professional. Namely, himself. When it came time for the sanctuary upgrade, Pastor Grogan was only too happy when Dewey offered to procure the loan and handle the paperwork and business dealings associated with it. Dewey had provided the necessary attorneys – his own, of course – and prepped the paperwork, issuing the loan from his own bank. All Pastor Grogan had to do was sign.

What the poor old man didn't know was that Dewey had drawn up the paperwork so that the current property and all the structures thereon were used as collateral for the loan. And given the current market value, unless the church could pay a lump sum of $924,817 dollars, the entire property would become the property of Dewey Knapp via his ownership of the First National Bank of West Georgia.

Despite all of this, he was glum as he drove, and it irked him that he couldn't figure out why. He rolled down the window to allow a bit of fresh air in, hoping it would clear the headache that was forming behind his left eye. He drove mindlessly, letting his thoughts drift.

Dad would have told him to knock it off. Stop letting his emotions play with him. And if he failed to do so, Dad would have beat it out of him. Horace Knapp was a steadfast adherent to pain as a motivator. Dewey tried it now, to will his emotions into check. He forced a grizzly smile onto his face. Fake it till you make it. But it didn't work. He just felt like a fraud.

Emotions. Yeah, maybe that's what had him in such a foul mood. Not his own emotions. No, it was the emotional response of the congregation on Sunday. Dewey kept playing it over in his mind ever since that morning. On the surface, he was angered by the undaunted support of the people for Jake, and yet...something...what? Did he respect them for it? Was he jealous of it?

He turned onto Lake Joy. His headache was worsening. Maybe it was related to Jake Wilson too.

Something else had been eating at him. Jake incessantly talked about the grace of God, which seemed to Dewey like not requiring people to pay for their mistakes. Dad had always made him pay for his mistakes. Failure was not allowed. Screw ups were not allowed. Mercy was not allowed. But the last couple of days, he kept finding himself wondering what his life would have been like had his mom lived. Would she have allowed his father to rule with an iron fist?

Or would she have demanded he go easy on Dewey? Surely, Dewey would not be the success he was today, but would that have been such a bad trade-off for love from a parent? After all, most of the science he'd ever heard on the subject suggested kids responded better to parental affirmation. Horace would have said they were all drinking the Kool-Aid.

Jake Wilson had doting parents. He'd used them as sermon examples many times. They were in every way different from Horace, and Dewey might have been willing to write it off as insignificant if not for one thing. Jake Wilson smiled. Dewey didn't. Jake Wilson laughed. Dewey didn't.

He guffawed. Fools were slaves to mirth.

You're a slave to bitterness and greed.

Where had *that* thought come from? It was so out of character for Dewey, that it caught him off guard. That was rubbish. No, he wasn't a slave to anything. Being successful wasn't being greedy and defending yourself wasn't being bitter.

What about deceiving yourself?

Dewey shook his head to clear away the intrusive thought. It only succeeded in making his head hurt worse. He was losing it. This mess with Jake Wilson was causing him to question himself. He couldn't allow that. Dewey knew who he was, and he was proud of it. Nevertheless, he was unnerved. *Rest. I just need rest. I've been pushing too hard lately.*

As he approached the intersection of Lake Joy and Russell Parkway, he felt the first twinge of heartburn. He looked over to see if his Tums were in the cupholder. It was at that moment the crippling pain began.

JAKE WOKE UP EARLY Friday morning, the day after Thanksgiving, to the ringing of his cell phone. He had been up late worrying about the church, trying to figure out what move, if any, to make. Thanksgiving had felt like anything but. Jessica had come over and they'd prepared a lovely meal. They spent the day with Boston, doing their best to deal with the fear and grief threatening to consume them. So far, Jake had not heard back from Knapp, but he knew it was inevitable. He didn't know if the man planned to give him an ultimatum date, or if he was just waiting to see if Jake would go ahead and resign. Now, as he attempted to rouse himself, his eyes burned and blurred as he cast a sidelong glance at the digital readout of the alarm clock beside his bed. The hazy-looking red numbers said six thirty a.m.

The phone stopped ringing. He had waited too long. How long had it rung before he stirred? He reached out from under the blanket to check the caller ID when it began ringing again. This time, he forced himself to sit up as he grabbed it and pulled it close, turning it over to see the number. Someone was apparently intent on reaching him and not willing to leave a message.

He eyed the number, pulling it back from his face a little to clear his vision. Jessica.

He quickly swiped upward on the phone to answer and stuck it to his ear.

"Hey, baby. Is everything okay?" he said.

"What are you doing?" She sounded anxious.

"I was still sleeping. Are you okay?" he said again.

"You haven't seen the paper?"

Jake was at a loss, his mind still befuddled. "What paper?"

"The newspaper," Jessica said. "You haven't seen the newspaper?"

Jake thought maybe he should slap himself. He was still half asleep. "I don't get a newspaper. Do *you* get a newspaper?" He paused. "Do people still do that?"

She barked a harsh chuckle. "Okay, love. I'm going to need you to wake up. This is important."

"Okay, okay," he said. He threw back the blanket and stood up beside the bed. "Sorry, I was up late last night. Alright, I'm better now." But he doubted his own clarity of mind. He still felt a little fuzzy. Coffee. He needed coffee. He started walking out of his bedroom to go downstairs to the kitchen.

"He's in the hospital!"

Her words stopped him at the top step.

"What? Who's in the hospital?'

There was a dramatic pause. "Dewey Knapp."

His mind cleared instantly, but his legs felt funny, and he sat down on the top step. It took him a minute to find his voice.

"He's...why? What happened?"

"It was on the front page this morning. It showed a picture of his Land Rover wrapped around a telephone pole."

"Lord, Jesus," Jake whispered.

Jessica continued. "The title says, 'Local Businessman and Entrepreneur Comatose After One-Car Accident Late Tuesday Night.' It goes on. 'Dewey Knapp, local businessman and owner of the popular Warner Robins restaurant, A Taste of Italy, was found unresponsive a little after 10:00 pm on Monday night after his car crashed into a telephone pole at the junction of Lake Joy and Russell Parkway. Spokesman for the Warner Robins Police Department said witnesses reported that Knapp's car was moving normally toward the junction when it veered off the road suddenly and hit the telephone pole head on. Knapp was admitted to Houston Medical Center. A spokesperson from the hospital would not reveal any details due to patient confidentiality, but an anonymous source has indicated that the accident was the result of a heart attack. Knapp remains in a coma at this time.'" Jessica paused. "Can you believe that?"

Jake was dumbfounded. He didn't know what to say. There was no love lost between Jake and Dewey Knapp, but he never wanted the man to end up in a coma. And yet, he had a twinge of satisfaction, a dark spot, well-hidden and deep. It began to climb to the surface, so subtly Jake didn't even notice it. It was fleeting, tiny, and dangerous in its outward insignificance.

"I wonder why nobody called me," Jake said. After all, the man was a member of his church and on the church council, though that admittedly would have been short lived given Knapp's recent behavior.

"The article said he has no family. There was nothing to indicate who to contact. I think we both know he probably didn't have many friends."

"If any. He never even let anyone on the council get close to him."

Jess was still off work for Thanksgiving break and had planned to come over that morning. Boston was asleep with her faithful guard dog.

"Are you still coming?" Jake said.

"Let me throw on some jeans and I'll be right over." She paused. "Jake, this could change everything."

Jake nodded to himself. She was absolutely right.

LATER THAT DAY, BOSTON sat at the small table that occupied what passed for a breakfast nook at Jake's house. She chomped into the bologna sandwich that Jake had made for her, made a face, and spit it back onto her plate. Jake and Jessica were standing at the kitchen island hunched over Jake's phone on the counter, so they didn't see her spit the food out.

She eased back from the table ever so slightly, careful not to move too fast so she wouldn't draw attention, then she lowered her left hand, sandwich still in it, beside her hip and let it drop to the floor. As hoped, Peaches, always attentive when Boston had food, sprang up and trotted nonchalantly under the kitchen table. Boston peeked to her left and watched in satisfaction as the sandwich disappeared in a few large gulps. Peaches seemed to like bologna.

Boston pulled the bag of barbeque Lay's potato chips closer to her plate and dumped out a large pile. She crunched a chip happily. That was more like it. She giggled to herself, satisfied that Jake and Jessica still had not noticed her deception. They were too busy listening to Jake's secretary, Nancy, talk about someone that had been hurt and was in the hospital. Boston wasn't trying to listen, but the phone was on speaker, and she overheard most of it anyway.

"...SO THEY CALLED THE church," Nancy said through the speaker.

"They don't normally do that, do they?" As a pastor, Jake had chaplain privileges at Houston Medical Center, so he was familiar with the strict laws that governed patient confidentiality. He'd had to sign certain agreements regarding privacy when he'd signed up. Ever since Jake had received Jessica's call this morning, he'd been in a state of bewilderment. What were the chances that the very man who was intent on wrecking his career would end up hospitalized and comatose?

"I don't think so," Nancy said. "But you know him, Jake. He has nobody. The man is a lifelong loner. They had the church's name on file from a previous admission and no other contacts, so they reached out to us to see if we knew of any family. Even the police haven't located any relatives for him."

Jessica cut her eyes up at Jake who shrugged.

"Did they tell you a prognosis?" Jessica asked.

Nancy said, "They don't know. Could wake up any day or maybe never."

"Okay," Jake said.

They exchanged a bit more information and small talk then Jake hung up the phone.

"Wow," Jessica said.

Jake nodded.

At the table behind them, Boston stopped chewing long enough to ask a muffled question through a mouthful of potato chips. The words were unintelligible.

Jess cocked an eyebrow and shrugged when Jake looked to her for a translation.

"I'm sorry, what?" Jake said.

Boston swallowed hugely then repeated her question. "Who got hurt?"

Jake kicked himself. He still had not gotten used to having a child around all the time, and it had not occurred to him that she was overhearing a conversation about a car accident. Judging from the look on Jessica's face, she was the same.

"A member of the church, honey. He was..." he trailed off, unsure again how much she heard and what he should say.

Jessica made the decision for him. "He was in a car accident, Boston."

Boston stopped chewing and looked at them both with a serious expression. "Is he going to die?"

"No," Jake said quickly, then, "I don't know. He's in a coma right now."

"Do I know him?" Boston said.

Jake thought back. "You met him once at the council meeting you went to with me. His name is Dewey Knapp. Older guy. Kinda heavyset."

She nodded. "I remember him. He's the man that wants your job."

"That's right."

Boston stared out the window. Jake wondered if that would be the end of it. Though they had explained the situation with Knapp and Jake, she had said little about it. That was fine with both Jake and Jessica. She didn't seem worried, and they didn't want her to be. But she turned and looked him directly in the eyes.

"I want to go see him. Can I go see him?"

Jessica walked over to the table and took the chair across from Boston. "I don't know if that's a good idea. Besides, you don't really know him. Why do you want to go there?"

Boston didn't hesitate. "He was in a car crash. I was in a car crash. He doesn't have anybody. He's like me."

Jake turned away to the fridge and pulled a Mr. Pibb from the door shelf, mostly so Boston wouldn't see the expression on his face. The thought of that miserable man being anything like his sweet little angel made him want to laugh. He was nothing like her, and in no way deserving of her sympathy.

He turned back after he steeled his emotions. "I don't even think kids can get into the ICU," he said. "Plus, I don't think I want you seeing him in that state."

Boston looked slowly from Jake to Jessica and back again. She sat with her hands in her lap, her napkin folded neatly between her fingers.

Jake realized she seemed so mature in that instant, and why shouldn't she be? She had experienced more tragedy than many adults did in their lifetimes.

"I've seen worse," she said matter-of-factly.

She was right, and both Jake and Jessica knew it. Jessica gave Jake an inquiring glance.

Jake struggled inside himself. He knew all the right scriptures, the ones about forgiveness and mercy and loving your enemy, but right now he felt none of that. All he felt was bitter, and he realized, as wrong as it was, he wasn't ready to let that go. Dewey Knapp had attacked him, attacked the woman he loved, and lied about Boston. There was a terrible part of him that was glad that Knapp had been injured. He hated himself for it, but it didn't make it any less true.

Boston watched him, waiting for an answer. She wasn't going to let this go.

"Are you sure, kid?"

She gave him a gentle smile. "He needs us."

Jessica leaned forward and reached across the table for Boston's hand. Boston put her hand in Jessica's, and they shared a smile. Jake wondered if Jessica was feeling the same conflict that he was.

"Okay," he said finally. "If they'll let us in, I'll take you."

CHAPTER 25

It didn't happen right away. Jake was right about the hospital not allowing children into the ICU except in cases when the patient was an immediate relative such as a parent, grandparent, or sibling. Dewey remained critical for several days, and each day Boston would ask Jake if she could go see the man yet.

Her tenacity surprised Jake. The last year had taught him one thing about Boston – her attention span was brief. However, with this, she stayed on him day and night about seeing Dewey Knapp.

Jake had no desire to visit the man. As the pastor of the church Dewey attended, he knew he should, if only for appearances sake, but he couldn't bring himself to do it. Jessica was actually advocating for Jake to go. She'd made it clear last night when they talked on the phone.

"It's your job, for one. But more than that, Jake, you of all people know we should extend grace to the people that hurt us. You certainly extended it to me."

"Yeah. Because you're actually a good person." The words came out sharper than he intended, and regret filled him. Whatever his issue with Dewey Knapp, Jessica was innocent and didn't deserve his short fuse.

"Didn't Jesus say something about nobody being good except the Father?"

It was a rhetorical question and Jake treated it as such, stubbornly refusing to acknowledge the passage of scripture.

"Look, I just don't see the point. I've already said I'd take Boston when she can go. Why do I need to go before that? The man is a beanstalk away from being a vegetable."

There was a sharp intake of breath from the other end of the line. "Jake."

She said his name softly, little more than a whisper, but it carried enough of a rebuke that Jake felt as if he'd been slapped.

She spoke again. "I get it. He came after me, too. There was a time in my life when I would have been happy to see him flat on his back, but that was before Jesus. That was before He forgave me of so much. How can I receive forgiveness for the awful things I did, then not give it to somebody else?"

Jake heard the implied, *and how can you?* People always made jokes about preachers stepping on toes from the pulpit. Jessica had just plowed over his with a Jesus steamroller.

"I'll think about it," he said. That was the best he could do. The wound was still too fresh.

She said goodnight, and Jake rolled onto his back. He stared up at the ceiling fan over his bed, his thoughts a jumble of tiredness and frustration. He watched the fan spin round and round. Much like his brain. Sleep eluded him.

He rolled back over and clicked on the lamp beside his bed. On his nightstand was his dad's old preaching bible. Jake usually used electronic versions, but seeing it lying there, he reached out and picked it up. He turned to the book of John and began to read the verses he could quote by heart.

In the beginning was the Word, and the Word was with God, and the Word was God...

He read for maybe five minutes before he realized the words were barely making it past his eyes and certainly not into his brain or heart. All it did was make him feel more guilty and unworthy. He slapped the Bible shut and chunked it back on the nightstand.

With a growl of frustration, he flopped his head onto his pillow. It felt uncomfortable, misshapen, and he raised up and smacked it a couple of times to work out the kinks. Then, he slapped it again. Then, again, and again, and before long he was taking his pent-up annoyance with Dewey Knapp out on his pillow.

After a while, he stopped, breathing hard, feeling like a fool, but at least a little better.

An odd sensation that he was being watched washed over him and he turned quickly. Peaches, who always slept with Boston now, was standing in his doorway. What she really was thinking, he could never know. She probably just wanted to know what all the ruckus was about. But what it *looked* like she was thinking, was that Jake was the biggest moron on the face of the planet with the temper control of a two-year-old. He gave the dog a sheepish grin. She stared at him a moment more, gave a snorting huff, then turned and walked back to Boston's bedroom.

Well, there you go. You've even lost the respect of your dog, Jake old boy. Just think of what kind of example you'd have set if it'd been Boston standing there.

He clicked the lamp off again, and laid back, gently this time, pulling the blanket up over his arms and chest. Underneath, he tried to think only of the weight of the blanket and the surrounding warmth. After a while, he closed his eyes. The last thing he *felt* like doing was praying, but it came as a habit, the thing he always did before sleep took him. So, as was his custom, he just talked, trusting the Lord to hear, and to respond when and how He was ready.

DEWEY WAS IN HELL. Sometimes he felt pain, although he was unaware of his body. But the worst part was the darkness. The darkness was persistent. His cognizance was also limited. There were stretches of time when he was aware of himself, of his existence, but nothing beyond that. Only the ever-imposing darkness. Crippling fear possessed him. He tried to cry out, to scream for God, for anybody, but he was alone. Utterly, completely alone.

He tried to remember something, anything, but his past crowded in on him in disjointed fragments of overlapping nonsense, no point to any of it, nothing he could grab to anchor himself. Just swirling, swirling, swirling, then the darkness again.

He became slowly aware. The pain was back with a vengeance. His chest hurt so much. And his head. Oh God, his head felt like it would explode. So much darkness! *God, if you're there, please save me! Please don't let it be too late!* Then nothing.

He didn't know how long this pattern continued. Time meant nothing in the darkness. Days could have passed. Months. Years. He was losing his mind. He couldn't deal with an eternity of this isolation and misery. *Please, Jesus!* He pushed back against the dark and the suffocating nothingness. *Jesus. Jesus.* It became his all-dominating thought. That one word. That one person. Jesus.

JAKE ENTERED THE ROOM, followed by Boston and Jessica in the rear. The place smelled of antiseptic and some industrial odor that Jake recognized from previous hospital visits but couldn't identify. The first thing that met his eyes was Dewey lying on the hospital bed, his body surrounded by machines. A tube ran down his throat, the ventilator breathing for him. Intravenous lines and wires extended out from him like external veins.

He turned to see how Boston was handling the sight, afraid it might be traumatizing. But she stood by him, Jessica now on her far side, gazing at the motionless man. She reached up and took Jake's hand, her eyes rising to meet his.

He smiled down at her, her elfin face sad and beautiful at the same time. Jess crossed her arms and shivered, perhaps from the sight more than the cold, although the room was chilled.

"What should I do?" Boston said.

"Whatever you want, love. Maybe just talk to him. Sometimes, even though he can't move, he might be able to hear you. It's hard for the doctors to know, so we just have to do it anyway and pray that he can." That was probably an oversimplification, like something actors said in movies to make sense of a much more complicated condition, but Jake knew it to be possible. This wasn't the first unresponsive member he'd been to visit in these halls.

Boston broke from them and walked with tentative steps towards the bed. Jake and Jess watched as she approached the end, then made her way around to the side. She appeared so tiny next to the beefy man on the bed. She placed her hands on the side rail, cast a backwards glance at him and Jessica, then started talking in a soft voice. Jake and Jess moved closer to hear her words.

"Hi, Mr. Knapp. My name is Boston. Do you remember me?" She looked back again, and Jessica nodded encouragingly. Boston was nervous but turned back to the old man. "I'm nine and Mr. Wilson is my new dad. I turned ten in September, and I had a cake with blue frosting that was a Barbie dress, and there was a doll in the middle. When she came out, her legs were blue, so I had to lick them. I heard you had an accident in your car. I did too. So, I wanted to come. I think God wanted me to come. Cause I kind of get it."

She paused. Raising a finger, she stretched out her arm and poked Dewey on the back of his right hand, then pulled away with a jerk. Maybe she had expected him to move, or just wanted him too, but nothing happened, and she took hold of the rail again after a minute. Jake smiled to himself.

She began to talk about everything and anything, her face attentive, her voice timid at first, but eventually taking on her normal tones of animation. At some point, Jake and Jessica made their way to seats, Jess in the only chair, and Jake sitting partially on the windowsill, which was not high, but was rough on his rear. They stayed that way for thirty minutes, Jake shifting from time to time to decrease the pain in his backside, all the while listening as Boston talked about school and friends and her favorite Gatorade, to the way Mr. Knapp sort of looked like an anteater with that tube coming out of his face.

Finally, Jake heard her say, "Well, I guess I'm going to go now. But I promise to come back and see you, so you don't have to be lonely or afraid." Beside him, Jessica placed a hand on his leg as they shared watching Boston's empathy and kindness at work. When Boston walked up and asked if they were ready to leave, Jake felt the prompting of the Spirit. Although his flesh didn't want it, he walked to the bed with Boston and beckoned Jess over. As they all stood there, he said a prayer that God would raise Dewey up and breathe new life into him.

A short while later, they walked through the parking lot, their breath misting in the cold air. Boston said, "I'm gonna have to think of something else to do. I ran out of things to say."

Jake snorted. "*You* ran out of things to say? You've got to be joking. You *never* run out of things to say."

Jessica laughed, but Boston threw him an exaggerated pouty face and playfully kicked him in the shin. Playful? Yes. Painful? Also, yes. Jake nearly went down to one knee from the stinging blow, and rubbed his shin while he half-moaned, half-laughed. Jessica went into a fit of cackling, and even Boston got the giggles seeing the damage she'd done.

"I think we need to sign her up for soccer," Jessica said.

Once Jake recovered, he limped to the car. Boston slid into her booster seat behind Jessica.

Jessica said, "You know, you don't always have to be saying something to him, Boston. You can just be there."

Boston chewed on that for a second. "Maybe, but I think he wants to hear me."

Jake's heart flooded with adoration for the child. His child. Her optimism buoyed his spirit, and despite his previous frustrations with Dewey Knapp, it was hard not to catch the contagious love Boston was exemplifying.

Something occurred to him. "You know what, B? I think I may have an idea of something you can do for him."

And so it began. Over and over, they went. Sometimes they would stay for thirty minutes. Sometimes an hour. Other days, they could only squeeze in a few minutes to their schedule, but they were consistent, because Boston was consistent. She had a stubborn, dogged determination to be someone the old man could rely on. She took it as her personal responsibility to be the family he never had. Every day, the visits chiseled a tiny sliver from Jake's bitterness, because he saw firsthand the love of Christ exemplified through the prettiest little angel ever to have walked on the earth, until all that remained in Jake for the man who wanted to destroy him, was love.

DEWEY DIDN'T KNOW WHEN he became aware of it, only that it was there. A voice. *Lord?* But no, that couldn't be right. It was wrong. *That's not how God sounds.* How do you know what God sounds like? He's not a child, and this is, could be...he listened hard. It was so far away, the words unintelligible, but the voice was a lilting soprano. Definitely like a child. An angel perhaps? But the voice faded, its chiming tones receding. Leaving. *No! Please don't go. Please don't leave me!*

The black void returned, always the demonic, oppressive blackness. Infinite days passed. Did they? Maybe it was only seconds.

TAKING BOSTON

He no longer had a grip on time. But, was there...? Yes. Yes! It had returned. The tiny, chiming, tinkling, melodious voice. What were those words? Some of them cleared, formed broken thoughts. "'You come of the Lord Adam and the Lady Eve...honor enough...poorest beggar, and shame enough to bow the shoulders...Be content.'" Lord Adam? Lady Eve? What did that mean? The voice was gone he knew not how long, but it came again. A little stronger now. Still distant, but clearer. "'Good,' said Aslan. 'If you had felt yourself sufficient, it would have been proof that you were not.'"

Aslan? He knew that name. Where did he know that name from? He strained against his addled brain, desperate for understanding. Something about a zoo. No, not a zoo. But a place with animals. A place where animals talked. Yes! And the king of that land...he was...Aslan. Aslan was a lion. Aslan was from a fairy tale. He felt the tiniest sensation, but after so long, it was as refreshing as a drop of water on the parched tongue of a man condemned to unending fire. His hand. He felt his hand. But...no. Not his hand. Someone else's hand. It was small and soft, a child's hand, wrapped around his own. The voice continued. It was the story. The voice was reading the story of the lion. Reading to him.

In an agonizing flash, something came back to him. Anger, uncertainty, hatred, isolation, something in his hands...the steering wheel of a car. It was not a car. It was an SUV. Pain. Pain crushed down on his chest, and he let go of the wheel. There was a horrendous screeching as the vehicle veered off the road, then an explosion of sound that made his ears ring. And again, the vile blackness.

The next time awareness came there was no voice, and Dewey felt more alone than any time before. He wanted to hear the voice so badly. Hear the words. Feel the tiny hand on his. He wanted to weep, but there was no weeping here. *Jesus, let the voice come back. It's all I have in this place. In this Hell.*

But the voice did return. Over and over again. Sometimes he could understand the words, but mostly they were distant jumbles. It didn't matter. It wasn't the words keeping him going. It was the voice. It came time after time for so long that he grew to depend on it. If he was ever awake – did you wake and sleep in Hell? – and the voice wasn't there, he was devastated. There were many of those times too, and he would pray for the voice's return. Long for it. And so, the pattern went.

Darkness.

Nothingness.

Loneliness.

The voice.

Pain.

Fear.

Darkness again.

"It's time to go."

Consciousness suddenly blazed in Dewey like a gasoline fire. That voice. It was a man's voice. But...?

"Okay, Knappy." It was the child again. "I have to go now. But next time, we'll be done with Prince Caspian, and we can start something else." The tiny hand touched his, squeezed gently. Dewey felt blood pulsing in his arm. Blood and pulsing. Life? Life. He was alive. "Do you want to stick with Narnia, or something else?" No one answered. Was she talking to him? Knappy? Was he Knappy? "Okay, Narnia it is. The next one's called *The Horse and His Boy*."

The male voice again. "Okay, Boston. Pack up your stuff and we'll pray alright?"

"Okay Mr. Wilson."

Boston. The child was Boston, and that made the man Jake Wilson. Dewey struggled to process this information. Why were they here to see him? Clarity inched back into his mind, an unhurried crawl. Pieces of remembrance slid into place, forming a picture. An imperfect one, but a picture nonetheless. Aslan. Prince Caspian. Boston had been reading the Narnia books to him. For how long? He didn't know how long he had been here, in and out of consciousness, but he knew she had been there many times. And they planned to come back. She said so. But *where* was he?

There was a commotion of rustling, presumably Boston gathering her things as Jake had told her to do, and the next thing Dewey knew, the tiny hand was on his again. But from the other side, someone grabbed his other hand. It was large, powerful yet gentle. Jake Wilson's hand.

"Father, we ask you again for healing for Mr. Knapp. The doctors don't know if he'll ever come out of this, but You're a miracle worker and we know You can do it. Raise him up, Lord. In the name of Jesus."

"Amen," Boston said. Something touched his cheek, light like a feather. Lips. She had kissed him. It was in that instant that Dewey had an epiphany. Everything he had ever experienced seemed to congeal into a pinpoint moment of clarity. The dreadful realization threatened to suffocate him. Lack of love had taken a terrible toll on him, and he had become a wretched shell of something that had once been human. He was alone. He was empty.

Their hands pulled away, and Dewey heard soft footfalls, then nothing except periodic beeping and a hissing sound. He was jolted by the realization that he could hear other things beside the voices. His mind refused to cooperate. This was the most lucid he'd been in – how long? – but reasoning was a chore.

He understood. The beeping and hissing had to be machines. Medical equipment. He noticed his chest was rising and falling, but he wasn't making it happen. He was on a ventilator. It was breathing for him. The memory of the accident came again, this time more clearly. He remembered driving, coming home from work when his chest had seized with pain. He remembered the car going off the road – then blackness.

God, I'm alive. You let me live. You brought me out of my own Hell. If you'll just wake me up, give me another chance at life, I think I can be better.

Something – Someone - shone a light on his soul, and without knowing how, he clearly saw his own deprivation. He was sickened by it, dirtied, and ashamed. Words began coming to him in his head. They were the words of Jake Wilson. Scriptures and sermons wove through his brain as he remembered things Jake had said. Things he never realized he was paying attention to. But even though they were Jake's words, Dewey also knew something else. It was God that was speaking, giving him truth through the very man Dewey had been convinced was his mortal enemy. For years, Jake Wilson had been offering him seeds of truth, and with the watering of the Spirit, they had come alive.

CHAPTER 26

Jessica was in autopilot mode, giving no conscious thought to her driving as she battled rush-hour traffic on Watson Boulevard at 5:15 pm on the first day of Christmas Break. On the passenger side floorboard were the remains of a half-dozen gift boxes and bags from Christmas presents she had received from students the day before. The gifts themselves had been lovingly removed and placed on her desk or brought home to her apartment, but the bags, boxes, and wrapping paper she left in the car with the intent of dropping it in the dumpster at some point. The air in the car was imbued with the bitter-with-a-hint-of-mint aroma of the stale coffee from Starbucks still sitting in her cup holder from that morning's breakfast run.

She made a quick detour through Chick-Fil-A to pick up a number one combo with cheese and Dr. Pepper for her and a three-piece chicken strips combo with a Coke and plenty of Polynesian sauce for Boston.

It was her night to take Boston to see Dewey Knapp, or "Knappy", as Boston had taken to calling him. The little girl had been adamant about keeping up her regular visits to the hospital, and Jake and Jess were switching off doing visitation duty. Boston would have gone every day if she could, but Jake insisted it be every other day just so they had time to get other things done.

Pulling back out onto Watson, she turned right at the first break in the steady stream of cars, something she had to wait two minutes for, then slipped into the turn lane. When another break came, this time in the opposite direction, she gunned the engine and the R's three hundred horsepower launched the hatchback like a small jet giving her plenty of head start over the approaching semi that was just passing Dunkin Donuts roughly a hundred yards from the turnaround.

She took a quick right on Margie, crossed through the four-way stop at Osigian, and took a left onto Smithfield Church Road. Ten minutes later, she pulled into Jake's driveway and hit the remote to the garage – Jake had insisted on giving her one considering the time she spent there – and pulled her car into the left-side door, easing to a stop beside Jake's Santa Fe. She shut off the car and pressed the remote button again to close the garage. Before the garage door could descend fully, Boston bounded out of the door from the kitchen, as full of life and as beautiful as always.

Boston angled behind the car – the clutter in front of it made it difficult to squeeze through if you pulled in too far – and approached the door as Jessica pushed it open, careful not to let it hit the wall since the garage was sufficient for two cars but by no means wide.

"You have a job," Jessica said, handing the two sodas to Boston to carry inside.

"You got Chick-fil-a?" Boston said, leaning over and giving Jess an armless hug while taking the drinks. She took a step back. "Can we eat in the car?"

"Absolutely not," Jess said with a smirk. "Mr. Knapp's not going anywhere. Let's take our time eating dinner, then we'll go like we always do."

Boston gave a pouty face but made her way back inside to the kitchen. Jess grabbed the rest of the meal and followed. As she entered the kitchen, Jake wrapped her in a huge hug and made a move to kiss her neck but blew an enormous raspberry on it at the last second. She tried to pull away, but not before he darted in and placed a real kiss on her lips. Peaches looked up from her spot on the couch, then put her head back down, perfectly disinterested.

"Thanks for picking up dinner for the munchkin," Jake said, pulling a frosted twenty-ounce bottle of Sprite out of the fridge.

Jessica eyed him hard until he noticed, then made a point of looking at the drink.

He rolled his eyes. "I'm trying," he said. She'd been working to get him to change some of his consumption habits, one of which was way too much soda. "Why did I start dating you again?" he said with a smirk.

"Because I'm not going to let you turn into a buffalo by the time you're forty."

"Buffalo?" Jake made exaggerated stomping motions around the kitchen and put his index fingers up to his head mimicking horns. Boston laughed as she dipped her chicken finger into a pack of Polynesian sauce then raised it to her lips. More of the sauce dripped onto the table than what made it to her mouth.

"Hey," Jake said. "Prayers." He crossed to the table, took Jess and Boston by the hands and said, "Lord, thank You for this food and for my heathen family that doesn't bother to give You thanks before chowing down."

This earned him a good bit of guffawing and ribbing from both girls.

Jessica sat across from Boston and pulled her own food from one of the bags. As she arranged the items in front of her, she couldn't stop smiling at the way Jake was rushing about getting ready to leave for a special meeting tonight with the council. It was supposed to be the night he told them about the loan and Dewey Knapp, but against all reason, he seemed happier than Jess had seen him in weeks. She knew that beneath the surface, in Jake's deepest parts, God was working healing.

He shoved the soda bottle into a mesh holder on the side of his backpack, grabbed some papers from the counter, and shoved them into the bag as well. He zipped it up, careful to make both ends of the double zipper meet in the middle, then kissed the girls and sprang out the door promising to be back no later than 9:30. A few seconds later, there was the sound of his car starting followed by the garage door opening. A few squelching sounds from the tires on the concrete as he backed out, the garage door closing, and he was gone.

They finished eating and cleared away the trash. Jessica did most of the clearing while Boston hunted for her shoes. She finally found one in the dining room and the other in the bathroom. While she slid them on, tied them, untied them because they didn't "feel right", and tied them again, Jessica opened the back door and tried to get Peaches to go out to potty before they left. Peaches must not have been feeling it, because no matter the amount of Jessica's cajoling, she refused to move from her warm spot on the couch.

"Okay," Jess said. "It's your bladder."

Boston returned and lifted her green and white-striped tote from where it hung on the doorknob of the pantry and slung it over her right shoulder. She turned to Jessica. "I'm ready."

JESS AND BOSTON STRODE through the main entrance to Houston Medical Center out of the evening chill. As the automatic doors slid in opposing directions to permit access, a bracing whoosh of warm air greeted them as it ballooned out of the interior lobby. They turned left towards the bank of elevators.

"Hi, Ms. Liz," Boston called across the lobby to an elderly woman sitting behind the welcome desk. Liz was a volunteer in her mid-seventies, married for forty plus years, and an avid crafter. Jessica knew all this because in two weeks of visits Boston had befriended every regular face she'd come across and obtained, and remembered, their life stories with uncanny recall.

Liz waved at them. "Hi, Boston. Hi, Jessica," she said, her smile warm and friendly. "Back to see your friend?"

"Yep. And today I have a new book." Boston paused, retrieved *The Horse and His Boy* from her bag, and held it up proudly for Liz to see. The embossed cover of the C.S. Lewis classic glimmered in the atrium lighting, the corners new and crisp, and the spine perfect.

"You're all done with *Prince Caspian*?"

Boston beamed. "It was amazing. We gotta go now, Ms. Liz. I'll say hi on the way out."

Boston spun and swept towards the elevator as Liz and Jessica traded nods.

Jessica was, as always, mystified by the lack of shyness in the little girl and the way she made easy conversation with anyone and everyone she chose. Jessica's parents had often remarked that Jessica was the shyest child they had ever known, something she thankfully had outgrown.

They approached an elevator that opened at the perfect time to spill out a woman being pushed in a wheelchair by a nurse in teal scrubs. Boston and Jess stood to the side to let them pass, then entered the lift. The elevator deposited them on the third floor, and they ambled down the left hallway – Boston stopped no less than three times to speak to someone on staff or another patient in the hallway – to room 307 where Dewey was being kept.

Boston beat Jessica to the door and entered the room a second before her.

"Mr. Knapp!" Boston said.

Jessica rounded the corner to find Boston standing transfixed, staring at Dewey Knapp sitting up in bed, an irrepressible smile burrowing from his craggy face like a ray of sunshine penetrating through the cleft of a rock. The effect was disconcerting. The face she had only ever known to be locked in frowning disapproval, now shown with a strange vigor, transforming him despite his disheveled state into a handsome older gentleman.

"You're awake," Boston said.

Jessica could feel the excited energy rolling off the girl; and then, the most unexpected thing happened. Something that Jessica would never forget no matter how long she lived; something that would be sealed forever in her heart as the first true miracle she'd ever seen. Tears sprang like a flood into Dewey's eyes, and he opened his arms wide, welcoming Boston into an embrace.

Boston leapt forward, crossing the distance, and fell into the old man's arms.

Dewey hugged her tightly for a long time, his face now streaked with weeping. When he finally looked up, Boston still held in his arms, he looked directly at Jessica and said one simple thing.

"I need to see Jake Wilson."

JAKE WALKED INTO THE room nervous and not a little bewildered. According to Jessica's call, Dewey Knapp was a completely different man now that he was out of his coma, and for all Jake's desire to believe it, he was having a hard time picturing it as real. But as soon as Jake stepped into the door, he could see the difference in Knapp and feel the change in the atmosphere. His mouth fell open as he took in the scene before him.

Boston was sitting on the bed beside Dewey, an over-bed table pulled across it. On top of the table was one of a few coloring books that Boston kept in her bag along with her books for reading and her tablet. They were laughing – laughing! – as Boston colored on one side of the book and Dewey colored the adjoining page.

Jake came to a complete stop mid-stride, bemused. Out of the corner of his eye, he saw Jessica sitting in the chair, scrolling on her phone. She looked up and their eyes joined. She saw the unasked question on his face and shrugged with an "I'm as shocked as you are" air.

By now, Dewey noticed Jake's arrival, and he turned in the bed, grimacing as he did so.

"What's wrong, Knappy?" Boston said with a concerned look as Dewey groaned.

The old man smiled down at her. "Oh, don't you worry. Just some aches and pains. I've still got a lot of healing to do." He motioned to Jake, waving him over. "Pastor Wilson, please, please," he said, beckoning with both hands. Jake noticed Dewey's voice was weak and raspy, the aftereffects of the intubation, but apart from that, the man acted surprisingly healthy considering what he'd been through.

Jake approached and stood next to the bed. He still couldn't bring himself to say anything, so drastic was the change in Dewey's countenance. As cliché as it sounded, there was a glow about him.

"Hi, Daddy," Boston said. "Knappy is a lot better. The doctor said it was like a miracle. He should have damage on his brain, but there's not. Can you believe that?"

"I guess I can," he said, feeling the corners of his mouth begin to turn upward. Dewey's eyes met Jake's, and Jake saw them welling, threatening to spill over. "Mr. Knapp..." he started, but the older man cut him off.

"Dewey. It's just Dewey. Or Knappy," he laughed. "I'm getting used to Ms. Boston's nickname."

Boston nodded her head with pride and Jake couldn't stop himself from laughing along with Dewey.

"Boston," Dewey said, "I'd like to talk with Pastor...with your..." He stopped, uncertain.

"Daddy. It's okay. I call him Daddy now."

"Your daddy," Dewey finished. "You think you can go see Jessica for a minute while we talk?"

Boston slid off the side of the bed. "Okay, but you keep the coloring book."

Dewey nodded consent.

As Boston walked away, Dewey waited until she was with Jessica and engaged in conversation, then lowered his voice and spoke to Jake. "Pastor Wilson, I owe you an apology. I've been terrible to you. There's no excuse. I want to make it right."

Jake didn't want to sound condescending, but the words came out before he could evaluate how they might come across. "What happened to you? I mean…I'm sorry…it's just…"

"No, I get it," Dewey said. "Let's just say while I was in that coma, I had a road to Damascus experience. I met Jesus." He paused and stared across the room. When he spoke again, his voice was choked with emotion. "Except, when He appeared to me, He came in the form of a little blonde girl that read to me and kept me company while I was trapped and afraid in my own personal Hell."

Jake looked at Boston with new appreciation. He knew her insistence to visit Dewey all the time was an act of great compassion, but he was starting to see how divine her actions had been.

Dewey continued. "I know you might not believe me. I wouldn't blame you. But you have my word, Pastor Wilson, you have nothing to fear from me ever again. I could never hurt that little girl or anyone connected with her." He placed a hand on Jake's arm. "I've been in contact with my attorney today. He'll be calling you tomorrow. Once he finishes the business I've instructed him to do, the loan for the sanctuary will be paid in full. I'm paying it off. You don't need to be concerned about it or the fact that the existing property was used as collateral. You'll be debt free."

The statement knocked the wind out of Jake, and he stood there, unbelieving. Dewey gave him time to process the information. "Mr.

Knapp," Jake said. "That's incredibly generous, but if you feel you have to do that to earn my forgiveness, I'm afraid I can't accept. It flies in the face of everything I believe about the grace of God. You don't owe me anything."

Dewey shook his head. "It's not that. I assure you. I'm glad I can help you and the church, but I'm doing this because it's my way of saying goodbye to the old Dewey. The bitter, selfish, unloving, unloved man I used to be. I don't want to be that guy anymore. If it's okay with you, I'm ready to start over."

Boston had trudged back to the bed. "Are you done talking yet?"

Dewey looked to Jake and extended a hand. "What do you say, Pastor?"

Jake shook his hand. Dewey turned his face away from Boston and mouthed the words "thank you" to Jake, then he glanced at Boston. Dewey patted the bed beside him, and she climbed back up. She picked up a red crayon and began to meticulously fill in the rose petals on the picture.

Jake watched her with the old man, and he began to see her as Dewey did.

The profundity of it came to Jake like a revelation. So much of the church in the United States put a premium on pastors and evangelists, but the real heroes were the ones who were in the trenches every day working as nurses, or trash men, or architects, or little league coaches. It was those believers who never stood on a stage, never had a huge platform or television ministry, and who were known by few save for their small circle of friends and co-workers that were making the biggest difference. Because they walked the Gospel every day. They allowed their lives to show forth the wonders of His marvelous grace. They taught by example what it meant to know Jesus; to love Him and be loved by Him. It was Boston, who lost her parents in an unspeakable tragedy, who got up and went to school morning after morning, facing the day with a strength beyond her years, smiling at those around her, brightening their lives with her smile; she was the light. In a very real way, she was Jesus to them.

CHAPTER 27

July rolled around with sweltering vengeance upon Warner Robins, as if angry for the atypically cold winter they'd experienced. Not to be outdone, Old Man Summer made a spectacle of his prowess, turning roads into ovens and lush lawns into scorched wastelands.

Despite the miserable heat, a group of people sat outside a stately home on the fourth of July, their smiles unfazed by the thick, humid air. To an outsider, they would have appeared to be the perfect all-American family, burgers and hot dogs smoking on a stainless-steel Weber grill, an ice chest filled with Cokes and Country Time Lemonade bottles placed against the wall of the house under the shade of the eaves. Around the table, laughter rang out often, smiles abundant.

Dewey Knapp shifted in his chair, his attention rapt on the blonde-haired child executing a picture-perfect cartwheel across the deck. He laughed and clapped as she rounded it off and took a bow.

"Excellent, excellent!" he exclaimed. Boston ran over to him and gave him a solid high five.

At the grill, Jake Wilson, sweat pouring from his forehead, stepped back from the heat long enough to poke Dewey on the shoulder with a finger. "We'll have you doing that before long."

Dewey scoffed. "That'll be the day. I couldn't do that *before* the accident." He laughed, something that not long ago would have seemed as out of place as a shooting star at noon. But of late, Dewey found it was his go-to disposition. And who could blame him? He had reason to be happy; indeed, he felt genuinely happy for the first time in his life.

It had been a grueling six-month battle with physical therapy as he learned to walk again. But he had no brain damage, which the doctors said was a miracle in and of itself. If he had some physical issues because of the crash, he wouldn't complain. There had been a bit of impairment to his heart from the heart attack, but not bad considering. Boston, Jake, and Jessica had supported him throughout the journey, often going with him to his therapy sessions. Boston called every week, usually multiple times, to check on him and say hi.

Dewey had come out of the coma with a new lease on life, and one thing he knew for certain, was that he wanted Boston to be a part of it. She had been, and continued to be, Dewey's lifeline. Her love and acceptance had worked a change in him he would not have thought possible. He also knew it wasn't just her. She had been the vessel. But God had met Dewey in that coma; something for which he would be forever grateful. The Holy Spirit had opened his eyes.

When it came time to begin work on the family life complex, Dewey had paid for that as well. He only had one stipulation – that it be named for the person he loved more than any other in the world. Hence, the complex would be called The Boston Evans Family Life Building. They had yet to break ground but would do so in the next few months.

But this day, he basked in the joy of new friends, of life restored, and second chances. He smiled as Jake strode over and kissed Jessica, their eyes shining with love as they watched Boston's continued gymnastics show. Dewey thanked God they had accepted him, taken him in as a member of the family. And he reflected that God had worked all this good because Jake Wilson kept a promise he never expected to have to keep – taking Boston.

End

Thank you for reading *Taking Boston*. If you enjoyed the book, please consider leaving a brief review and/or rating. It helps get the novel out to more potential readers. Also, I would love to hear from you. You can email me at jsbword@gmail.com. You, the reader, are the hero to my story!

Printed in the USA
CPSIA information can be obtained
at www.ICGtesting.com
LVHW051934221124
797366LV00004B/14